LETHAL LIAISON: THE LACY LANGFORD CHRONICLES

JOEY JAYMES

PIVOTAL PUBLISHING
turning pages, shaping lives

THE PATH THROUGH THE PAGES

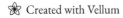

Thank you so much for choosing Lethal Liaison: The Lacy Langford Chronicles. I'm thrilled to have you join me on this thrilling journey with Lacy, where love, danger, and secrets collide. Your support means the world, and I hope you enjoy every twist and turn of this story as much as I enjoyed writing it.

*If you'd like to stay up to date on Lacy's adventures, discover upcoming series, and receive exclusive free content, I invite you to visit **JoeyJaymes.com** and sign up for updates.*

In addition to writing romantic thrillers, I also have a children's fiction line called Maddie's Adventures—perfect for young readers looking for heartwarming tales. And for anyone who love to jot down their thoughts, I've created a line of notebook journals designed with you in mind.

Thank you again for your time, your enthusiasm, and your love of stories. I'm excited to share even more adventures with you.

CONTENT WARNING

Trigger warning: This novel contains scenes of violence and sexually explicit content that may be upsetting for some readers.

PROLOGUE: THE WITNESS

NATHAN

I become aware of my own misery and discomfort, not all at once, but in little bits and pieces as my focus shifts between what I can't remember and what is happening to me now.

First, there's the sense that my eyes are open. As I blink, I realize that the blackness clouding my vision is not total. Instead, I can see points of light filtering through the blackness. As I blink furiously, trying to clear my vision, I realize that my face is covered with something. Now that I'm aware of it, the material of the mask, or whatever it is, feels rough in texture, scratching at the skin of my sweating face.

I open my mouth to scream, but the sound that escapes me is muffled, almost inaudible. Now I realize there's a gag stuffed into my mouth as well, and with the mask covering my face, I can't spit it out. This induces a feeling of claustrophobia so intense that I thrash around, trying to free myself. All the while, disjointed thoughts are tumbling through my mind. *Where am I? How did I get here? What the hell is going on? Who's doing this to me? Why are they doing this?*

My hands and feet are bound, and I'm tied to a chair of some kind.

The bindings eat painfully into my skin as I try to pull my hands free, and I have to stop. The chair feels hard and uncomfortable underneath me, and I suspect I must have been unconscious, perhaps for hours. My feet are both asleep. As I move them, the pain of pins and needles shoots up my legs, effectively drawing me away from the mindless panic and back to the reality of the predicament I'm in.

I can't free myself. Since stopping to think is my only option, I find myself doing exactly that. For a moment I have no idea how I got here. The last thing I can recall is... having breakfast with my family. It was a regular Tuesday morning. Is it still Tuesday? Melody, my wife, was telling our daughter Phoebe about a dress she saw on sale for prom. They were chatting about going to get it after school. I was only half listening, drinking my coffee and contemplating the day ahead.

Then the gunmen came. They burst through the back kitchen door, popping it off its hinges. Men in black clothing, wearing black masks. They broke into our house with guns raised, screaming at us to get down on the ground. Phoebe and Melody were screaming... I recall that I tried to protect them, but there was nothing I could do. It all happened so fast, there was barely time to react. I wouldn't have been able to fight off four men with guns. I work at the Helen Bentley Shipping Port. My arms and upper body are strong from years of physical labor, so I can hold my own, but I'm not a trained fighter or soldier. And these men were. The more I think about it, the more it seems to me that what felt like chaos and my little family was actually a perfectly orchestrated operation. That makes me feel cold inside.

I remember how the gunmen pushed all three of us to the ground and searched the house for other people. All the time we were lying with our faces on the cold kitchen tiles, I saw Phoebe crying softly. Looking at her, seeing her terrified, broke my heart. I found myself reassuring her again and again that things were going to be okay, though I had no idea if I really believed it or if I was just trying to placate her. I couldn't see Melody. She was lying at my other side, and my face was being pushed down to the floor by a gunman standing over me, one booted foot on my head.

When the gunmen were satisfied that it was just the three of us, they pulled me up off the ground. I tried asking them what was going on, but

LETHAL LIAISON: THE LACY LANGFORD CHRONICLES

it was hopeless. They never bothered to answer any of my questions. They took me away, and the last I saw of Melody and Phoebe was them being warned by one of the masked men to keep quiet, to keep still, to count to two thousand before getting up.

The gunmen walked me outside to the back alley, where there was a van waiting. Just before we reached the van, my hands were tied with cable ties, a piece of cloth was stuffed into my mouth, and a hood was put over my head. The last thing I remember thinking before being hit over the head and losing consciousness was that I had gone to sleep the night before in Baltimore, Washington in 2024 and had woken up in Nazi Germany in 1938. Then I felt the explosive pain at the back of my head, and the feeling of drowning in darkness, being pulled down and down until there was nothing.

With the memories all sorted, I feel the ache at the back of my skull and wonder if I have a concussion. Given the situation, it's a silly thought. Right now, a concussion is the very least of my problems.

A quietness comes over me, and I'm just listening to my own ragged breathing, my own heart beating loudly in my ears. Slick sweat is running down my back. I'm a 40-year-old dockworker, so I'm not exactly in prime physical condition. I smoke too much, drink too much beer, and eat too much junk food, so my gut has gotten a bit out of hand these last few years. I can feel slick sweat rolling over my belly as well, and it tickles horribly. Not being able to do anything about it is frustrating, but my assessment of myself brings up another important question: What in the world could I have possibly done to provoke these people, whoever they are, into kidnapping me from my house?

Is it because of the crates? I realize with dawning horror that it must be. Last night Tony and I came across a broken crate. The contents of the crate were suspicious, so we were left with no other option but to phone it in. Derek, our supervisor, assured us that it was nothing to be worried about, probably props for a movie or something. But it sure as hell hadn't looked like props. That must be it, then! Whoever that shipping crate belongs to is probably worried that I'm going to spill the beans. If that's the case, then I can just explain that I know how to keep my mouth shut. I didn't tell anybody, and I'm not planning on telling anybody else about it! Not even Melody.

I wonder if poor Tony got the same treatment—if he was kidnapped this morning as well, and is sitting in a chair all tied up like I am. My concern for Tony, who has a young wife and two small boys, is interrupted by the sound of footsteps slowly approaching.

I try to call out, but of course the gag is still in my mouth. I end up only making soft mewling noises that sound so pathetic to my own ears that I stop. The hood is pulled off my head in one fluid motion. Cold air hits my face, and I gasp. It's an enormous relief, even as I'm squinting into the bright light, my eyes watering.

When I can finally see, I look around at the large warehouse I'm sitting in. Steel roof high above, dusty cement floor underneath my feet, and crates lining the walls. The familiarity of it makes me feel for a moment like I'm dreaming. I recognize this place, just as I should. I've been working at these docks for the last 15 years, and I know this warehouse inside and out.

Looking at the man who is sitting across from me on a metal table, his legs dangling off the edge, I feel another stab of fear in my gut. He is looking at me with cold, dark eyes. Everything else about him is almost disturbingly ordinary. He must be in his mid-30s, judging by the strands of gray in his dark brown wavy hair. His hair is neatly trimmed. A sharp Roman nose contrasts with his wide jawline, and his smoothly shaved chin protrudes arrogantly from his face. Despite his well-tailored suit and clean-cut appearance, I get the impression that this man is tough, that he's seen some things. He has the distinct air of military about him.

He breaks eye contact with me to nod to someone standing at my right. Hands appear, and then the gag is removed from my mouth. I swallow at the dryness of my tongue, the awful taste of the gag still lingering in my mouth. The person who removed the gag walks over to stand next to the cold-eyed stranger, and as I recognize his face, relief floods through me. It's Derek Phillips, my boss!

"Derek, thank God! What is this? Listen, man, if it's about the crates, you guys don't have to worry, I—"

"Shut up!" The cold-eyed guy barks this at me with so much vehemence that I hear my mouth snap shut of its own accord. Never in my life have I been told to shut up like that!

"Now, Mister Shepard... Nathan... please listen to me. You saw something last night that you shouldn't have. While I appreciate your need to clear all this up very quickly, there's a specific way we're going to do this."

The cold-eyed guy stands up from the table and starts pacing in front of me. He's not a very tall man, but I can see he's athletic, his movements sure and graceful as he walks. While he's speaking, he's rubbing his hands together, and I notice that they are covered by a pair of thick black gloves. It doesn't bode well. Neither do the instruments lying on the table that he was sitting on a moment before.

"We want information. We want the truth from you. And I know you're going to give it to us, Nathan. Because of that pretty wife and pretty daughter who are waiting for you back home."

"You bastard! Don't you dare touch my family! You hear?" At the mention of my family, all the fear and rage suddenly bubble up and over, spilling from my mouth.

The cold-eyed man shakes his head. "We can go and fetch them right now. And I will, if you don't shut up!"

I look at him helplessly, knowing that I can't do anything. I've never felt this powerless, this impotent.

"That's better. Now, where was I? Oh, yes. We're going to ask you questions and you're going to answer them. It's really simple. Lie to us, and we'll make you suffer. And if you die before we've gotten all the information we want, we'll take it out on your family."

He falls quiet and looks at me. He seems to be waiting for an answer. I don't trust myself to be able to speak past the lump in my throat. This is a mess, and I'm scared. No, I'm terrified. I feel like crying. I just nod, and he seems satisfied with my answer.

"Tell me why you and Tony opened up the crates. Who are you working for? Did someone put you up to it, ask you to take pictures on your cellphones of the contents?"

My mouth falls open. I can't believe it! Who exactly does this guy think I am? Jason Bourne?

"Listen, you guys have got it all wrong! I'm not some... some spy! I have no idea what dirty little operation you guys are running, and I don't care! I'm just a damn dockworker!" I look over at Derek, who seems uncomfortable with this whole situation. "Come on, Derek! You know me! I'm just Joe Average! We've been working together for four years, man! I'm not involved in this!"

"So what you're saying is the crate was already open? That you and Tony just came across it by accident?"

I nod, glad they're finally understanding. "Yes! That's right! We didn't know. I swear!"

The guy with the cold eyes walks over to the table. He slowly picks up one of the knives off the gleaming metal surface. My stomach turns seeing that the blade of the knife, now being lazily played with by the psycho in the suit, is covered with blood.

"That's really funny," the guy says. "Because that's not at all what Tony told us." He points the knife to the left, and I look over to what he's pointing at. On the floor of the warehouse, I now see for the first time a crumpled and bloody heap lying there. My stomach plummets to my feet as the implication hits me. It must be Tony, and if it is him, then he's dead.

"Tony over there, with much persuasion, told us the two of you have been stealing little bits of product for months now. Only little bits, for yourself. Thought you'd try it, because you were curious. Then you started selling the samples you stole. The crate the two of you deliberately damaged didn't contain the usual product though, did it, Mister Shepard?"

He starts pacing again as I swallow once more at the dryness in my mouth. Nervous sweat is springing from every pore on my body. I suddenly feel the sick twinge of deep regret in the pit of my stomach. Because I know that if something happens to my family, then I'm to blame. I wish I could explain to this guy about a house mortgage, about a teenage girl who has her heart set on the perfect dress for prom, even though the economy has dropped out of the bottom these last few years. I already know this man won't understand, won't listen to reason.

With a feeling that's indescribable, I realize that I'm already dead. The best I can hope for is that this man with the murderous, sharklike eyes will be satisfied with my death. That he'll leave my family, who never did anything to him or the people he works for, out of it.

ACCIDENTAL ACTIVATION

LACY

"*C*ome now, Lacy!" I tell myself as the big, flashy Mercedes cuts me off. "Using road rage as an excuse to commit murder will not hold up in court."

Talking to myself when I'm alone is one of many nervous habits I have that I'm sure other people find annoying more than endearing. The sound of my own voice, not to mention the practical, if somewhat dark-humored, advice has the effect of calming me, and I'm able to take a deep breath instead of leaning on my car horn, as the jerk in front of me surely deserves.

It's been a long and chaotic day, not least of all because I had three meetings with new clients today. Great news for business, but it did mean extra pressure for me since Jamie, my usually stellar assistant, has been preoccupied with some personal issues she's had to deal with. I feel sorry for the troubles that Jamie has had to face since her husband abruptly walked out on their little family a few months ago. I've suggested that Jamie take some personal time off, but she's insisted she's fine and would rather save her paid leave for when one of her little children get sick.

Seeing Jamie's suffering, I'm reminded of why I've elected not to get married and have kids. I'm only 35, so despite my mother's gentle pestering that it's time to settle down, I know I can still have both the career and the family, if that's what I want. Many women have kids at a later stage these days, so I'd be in no way unique. The only problem is I don't really know if having a family will ever appeal to me. So far it hasn't, and being this reluctant of commitment is ironic, considering the line of work I'm in.

I'm a relationship advisor. Often people think that means I'm the expert on relationships. What it really means is that I help couples or individuals who have difficulties in their relationships figure out a healthy way to deal with the underlying issues. It's not only people facing difficulties in their marriage that come to me for help. I've had clients who wish to foster better relationships with their coworkers or bosses, and families who have become estranged and want to reconcile. I do know a lot about other people's relationships. You know how it's not a good idea for a doctor to treat themselves because they won't be objective about their own symptoms or illness? Well, my situation is kind of like that.

My degree in psychology from Penn State University, as well as my Master of Arts in Mental Health Counseling from George Washington University, may make me the ideal person to help other people navigate the difficulties of a relationship, but it certainly doesn't make me infallible when it comes to my own.

I arrive at the outskirts of Dupont Circle, the neighborhood I've called home for the last eight years or so. It always lifts my spirits. If ever there was a sign that a girl from a lower-income neighborhood like Mount Union in Huntington County can make it out and make it okay, it's ending up in a historic and culturally rich neighborhood like Dupont Circle in Washington D.C. The first step was getting a field hockey scholarship to Penn State. I did that and then went further. If it was up to me, I'd never set foot in Mount Union again. Unfortunately my mom, a retired school teacher, still lives there. Despite my urgings for her to move closer to me, she'd never leave the small town where I grew up and where she has happy memories of marrying my father. He was a detective, and died from heart disease due to diabetic complications. He was always my rock, came to every hockey game, and I miss him a lot.

My mom is about a two and a half hours' drive from me, so I do go to see her as often as I can. During the time in between, I miss her a lot. We've always been close. I remind myself to call her as soon as I'm settled in with a glass of wine, before Evan comes over.

The reminder that my boyfriend of the last two years, Evan Steele, is coming over later makes me smile, and my heart goes all aflutter. That's a good sign, isn't it? Usually, I'd be looking for the exit sign long before now, but Evan is so laid-back. As a hockey player for the Washington Revolution's team, he's in peak physical condition. We met at a party of one of my friends. Charlotte's husband, Gary, is the physical therapist for the hockey team, and he and Evan are good friends.

I was taken with Evan from the moment I first saw him. With his striking good looks and his killer body, there's few women whose heads wouldn't have been turned. I was pleasantly surprised to find that he was more than just tall, dark, and handsome. Now, two years later, I'm still as attracted to him as I was the first time I saw him. Only problem is, I've noticed a shift in our relationship that I don't know that I'm ready for. I love spending time with Evan, but lately it's been feeling more and more as if there's a restless quality to our relationship, like he's searching for more. Maybe I'm just reading too much into it—he hasn't voiced any dissatisfaction with how things are going between us.

As I unlock the door to my apartment, deposit my handbag onto the counter of the large, open-plan kitchen, and walk through to my bedroom to kick off my shoes, I push the worries about where my relationship is headed aside. Today was just too stressful to worry about that.

I pour myself the glass of wine that I've been craving since three this afternoon, take my handbag into the living room, and sit on the couch. My plan to call my mom for a nice long chat is momentarily suspended as I frown. I place my glass of wine on the coffee table to free up another hand so I can properly rummage in my handbag for my cellphone. After a few minutes of this, I give a frustrated growl and tip my handbag out onto the coffee table.

Lip gloss, some loose change, a pack of Kleenex, gum, tampons—all of it spills out onto the table. Some of the change rolls off onto the floor. No cellphone, though. "Hic!" Oh no! As another nervous tic, a serious case of the hiccups, firmly takes hold of me, I try to remember when I last had my phone. "Hic!" I giggle nervously. This is just perfect, isn't it? The shit cherry on top of a generally shit day. "Hic!"

I decide that sitting on the couch, hiccupping like an idiot while feeling sorry for myself, won't solve the problem of my missing phone. I probably took it out and then left it in the car. Just because I can't —"Hic!"—remember doing that doesn't—"Hic!"—mean I didn't. Oh my gosh, how I despise this nervous hiccupping tic I have! It's ridiculous! I sound like some kid's squeaky toy. It's hardly conducive to maintaining the image of a serious, grown, professional woman!

Walking outside on my bare feet, I unlock the car again and give the interior a thorough search. My frustrated cursing is underlined by hiccups while I'm searching in vain for my missing phone. Finally, with my hands on my hips, I stand upright and try to stretch my diaphragm to try and ease the hiccups. "Hic!" Great, it's not working.

I look at the car roof for a moment, wondering if I was stupid enough to place my phone there before driving off. I remember doing it only once in my life with a Styrofoam cup of coffee. My reward was having to clean my car, because of course the coffee spilled all over the back window. It seems unlikely that I did that with my phone, because it's not a mistake I'm in the habit of making. My thinking is punctuated with hiccups, and finally one frustrated growl as I throw my hands in the air and lock the car again.

My stomach starting to hurt because of the hiccups, I walk back inside and close the front door, feeling dejected. I look around at my spacious, tastefully decorated apartment. *Now what?* It's sad that we've become so dependent on our phones, like they're extensions of ourselves, but it's a fact of modern life. Bemoaning it is not going to change the fact that losing mine will certainly derail my plans for my evening. I hate it when plans change unexpectedly! It makes me feel like I'm spinning out of control.

My eyes wander over to the blinking box beside the kitchen cupboards. It's a new feature that I've had installed a few months ago: a smart home assistant. I haven't really had time to learn all the features just yet, and I've only really learned how to set the alarm, the automatic temperature control function, and reminders of people's birthdays, that sort of thing. Vaguely, I remember now some of the features that the tech who installed it for me babbled on about while we were standing in this very room. The guy took both my phone and my laptop to install the app for the home assistant on them. I distinctly remember him joking, "The great thing about it is, if your phone or your laptop is ever lost, you can use the home assistant to help locate them now with GPS tracking!"

Breathing a sigh of relief, I walk over to the kitchen drawer where I keep manuals and other stuff I don't use every day. Between packets of unused batteries, light bulbs, screws, thumbtacks, tape, and other useful junk, I find the user manual for the home assistant. The first thing it advises me to do is to set my laptop up so I can see the location of my missing phone on the laptop screen. A few minutes later, with my laptop set up on the kitchen counter and the home assistant app open, I return to the box and open the white panel in front.

What I see is another computer screen, with a touch pad and buttons like a computer keyboard. I browse the manual carefully, but I've never been the best at using technology, and I already feel a tension headache forming between my eyes. The good news is I've been so distracted by actually doing something that my hiccups have disappeared. It's a relief, but short-lived, as I sense too much fiddling with the damn home assistant will bring them on again.

There's a little bell icon in the right-hand corner of the screen. On the black touch pad that acts as a mouse, I navigate the little arrow there and double click on it. Instead of showing me the notification, a message pops up with a progress bar: File Transfer Activated.

Behind me, a notification sounds on my laptop. *God dammit! What is this nonsense now?* Frustrated, I walk over to my laptop. I go to the recent downloads section and see a new file there. What if it's a virus? I mean, if the home assistant uses GPS tracking, then surely it must be connected to the internet, and that means that it can be hacked, doesn't it? I have no idea if this is true. My limited knowledge of this kind of stuff doesn't extend to what is possible in terms of virus transfers, but everyone knows it's a bad idea to open files that you don't know the source of.

The question is, is the file important for locating my phone? I realize that it's not, and that should be my main concern now. Deciding to leave the file alone for now, I go over to the home assistant box again. I type in the code for the home assistant to search for my phone. Soon, another notification sounds behind me from my laptop.

I walk over and see that the address the GPS pinpointed is, in fact, my office building. My dear phone is probably still sitting under the pile of paperwork that I was busy with this afternoon. The relief that washes over me feels great, and I take a sip of my wine. My tummy rumbles, and now that I'm not panicking about my phone, I realize that I'm starving.

Hmmm... that leaves me with the other problem—plans that need to change because I don't have my phone with me to order pizza, like I had planned. I still don't feel like cooking, and everything decent I have is frozen solid in the freezer. Can I order food through the home assistant? I glance at the mysterious file. Would it even be a good idea to do that? Ordering food would necessitate me putting in my credit card info, and if my home assistant's system has been hacked, whoever is behind it will have all my info, won't they?

My goodness, it's all starting to sound like the kind of stuff you see in an action movie! That's exactly the source I'm basing these fears on, since I don't have any real-world knowledge to draw from.

I navigate the cursor over to the offending file. What is it, anyway? Curiosity is like a siren's call, and the more I stare at the file, the more difficult I find it to resist. What if it's something normal and harmless? If I get the same tech guy to come out to look at it, and it turns out to be a perfectly normal update or something, then I'll feel like a complete ass for being so paranoid. On the other hand, if I activate a destructive virus by opening a file I shouldn't have, the tech guy will give me the most condescending of looks as he warns me that I shouldn't do that, ever. Damned if I do, damned if I don't. If I open the file, at least the curiosity nibbling at me right now will be satisfied.

I'm just about to double click on the file after all when a booming knock at my front door startles me into snapping my laptop shut.

KNIGHT IN SHINING ARMOR

EVAN

*W*hen she opens the door, Lacy only peeks at me from behind it for a moment. I feel my smile falter as a fleeting thought flits across my mind—*Who were you expecting?*—but it's gone before I can register its existence. Then it's just Lacy, smiling up at me, her eyes twinkling with good humor.

As she holds the door open for me, she notices the bags of food I'm carrying from our favorite restaurant, Hank's Oyster Bar, and her smile widens. "Well, if it isn't my knight in shining armor!"

As I walk past her and she catches a whiff of the seafood, garlic, and fried onions—a combination that's irresistible—her stomach growls loudly. "More like saving you from imminent starvation, by the sound of it," I quip back. "You skipped lunch again, didn't you?"

I know I'm right when she doesn't answer me, and treats it instead like a rhetorical question. I resist the urge to roll my eyes and bite my tongue before I can say what I'm thinking: that I've never met a woman less interested in her own self-preservation. It's not true—it's just that often in her life, Lacy's clients take priority, even above simple things like stopping for a few minutes to have lunch.

Her dedication to her job and to the people she's helping is admirable, and one of the many reasons I'm infatuated with her. It does make me worry about her, though, and I wish she'd take better care of herself.

I put the bags on the kitchen counter and get plates out for us as Lacy pours each of us a glass of Merlot. It's not a wine that you're supposed to have with seafood, but neither of us really care about propriety when it comes to that sort of thing, and drink the wine because we enjoy the taste. I've been in Lacy's kitchen often enough to know where everything is by now, and soon we're able to take the food, a variety of specialty tacos, into the dining room.

"You wouldn't believe the day I've had!" Lacy says, and tells me about her missing phone. She managed to track its location to her office.

"Well, at least you'll be able to pick it up tomorrow. Despite the inconvenience of having to be without your phone for the night, I'm glad you won't have to suffer through the irritation of having to get a new one." I grin, knowing that she and tech have never been best friends. I'm much better with it than she's ever been. "I'm impressed you managed to figure out the home assistant function that allowed you to track it without any trouble. It seems complicated to me, and I probably would have messed something up."

She smiles drily at this, and takes another sip of her wine to indicate that it wasn't as uncomplicated as all that. All's well that ends well, though, and she changes the subject.

The conversation flows easily to other things, and as I'm watching her talk between mouthfuls of food, I marvel again that I've been able to be with this woman for the last two years. Sure, she's beautiful. With her olive-toned skin and Mediterranean looks that contrast with her light blue eyes, she is breathtaking. She's on the short side of average height for a woman, with a curvy, athletic body. It's not her looks, though. As a star hockey player, I can have my pick of beautiful women, but Lacy is different. She's hands down the most sophisticated woman I've ever been in a relationship with, and I know that if things don't work out between us, I'll never again be able to settle for the vapid, empty-souled women I knew before her. She's set the bar pretty high, and I've done my best to make sure I don't screw things up between us.

The trick with Lacy is to give her all the space she needs, to respect her boundaries, and not to push her, but let her set the pace for the relationship. The only problem is, I've been head over heels in love with her since first meeting her at Charlotte and Gary's annual Halloween house party. Neither Lacy nor I had gotten the memo that it was supposed to be a dress-up party. Sticking out like two equally awkward sore thumbs, we naturally gravitated toward each other. The evening had ended a lot better than it had started, and we've been together ever since.

I've kept to the unspoken rules, haven't pushed her into giving more than she can faster than she can. Only in the last few months or so I've come to the realization that at some point, I will need more from her than she'll be willing to give. And then what? This realization came shortly after one of my teammates, Rob Maloney, suffered a serious knee injury that forced him to quit the hockey team. It's happened before, and it truly sucks. What opened my eyes, though, was the fact that Rob is my age.

I went over to his house to knock back a few beers, and he told me he's scared about what the future holds, but not as scared as he would have been. Turns out Rob, a smarter man than I am, saw the writing on the wall and started saving for exactly this eventuality. He told me he'll be opening his own restaurant, and seemed excited about it. "It's not as if I expected to play hockey forever. When that big four-oh hits, you have to have a solid backup plan. I would have had maybe six or seven great years of hockey left, tops."

That really scared me. Not because I'm bad with money. Growing up in a small town in Minnesota with a local hockey coach for a dad and a nurse for a mom, if there's one thing I learned that I carried with me straight to the NHL and beyond, it's how to live frugally, how to take care of your blessings, because the rain doesn't last forever. I have a large nest-egg of my own stashed away, so starting my own business will not be a problem. It's not really the *how*, but the *what*. Besides hockey, no other career path has ever appealed to me.

I'm the only son in a family of six, and I'm the youngest. Having three older sisters taught me a lot about respecting strong independent women. My sisters are all married and have kids and careers of their own. To my core, I'm a family man. I just never found the woman who made me want to get married and have kids... until Lacy.

When I imagine my future, as I have been doing more and more over the last few months, it's always with her by my side. We've talked about it before at the very start of our relationship, and she told me for her, having a family is not something that she wants in the immediate future, and it may not be something that she'll ever want. She was completely honest with me.

That was two years ago, and I was willing to wait, to see where the two of us were headed. I was willing to make the unanswered questions in our relationship the problem of our future selves to deal with. Now, here we are. We are our future selves, and I don't regret a damn thing. I just wish I knew how to continue from here, because I don't want to lose Lacy.

I'm interrupted from these depressing thoughts when Lacy gets up to do the few dishes. I help her so it goes faster, and we discuss what movie we want to watch. She agrees to watch the first few episodes of *The Fall of the House of Usher* with me. It's been on Netflix since forever, and neither of us has had time to watch it. That's another surprising thing about Lacy; she loves horror movies and TV series. When you look at her, you'd think she's into cozy mystery novels or period dramas. Instead, her guilty pleasures always seem to turn to the macabre, just like mine do.

The series we picked is fantastic. It's riveting, based on the works of Edgar Allen Poe. We're snuggled up on the couch with the lights turned low. The third episode is about to start when Lacy leans over and presses pause on the remote.

She turns to me, and the dark look in her eyes isn't just from the lights being set low. I know that look, I love that look. Her eyes going from their normal light blue to a few shades darker is the look of lust, of need, and there's nothing more sexy.

Taking her face in both my hands, I bend down toward her, kiss her hungrily. Her lips touch mine. When her tongue slips into my mouth, slick and wet, I feel the flush of need wash over me.

She pulls away and stands up, holding her hand out to me. I take it and let her lead the way to the bedroom. The excited anticipation is coursing through my veins. God, how I want her!

Much later, we are lying between the covers. Lacy is lying with her head on my chest, and I can tell she's ready to fall asleep. Holding her close, I realize that if being with her means giving up my dream of having a family, then I would be willing to sacrifice some of it, if she at least agrees to be all mine.

I close my eyes, not willing to spoil this perfect moment with fears and doubts.

I'M FALLING DOWN, DOWN, INTO SOME DARK ABYSS. THERE'S nothing to hold onto, and I can't stop myself from falling. I grope for something, anything, to stop this helpless, blind decent into this lightless crevasse, but there's nothing around me but open air.

I come awake with a start, and for a few moments the darkness makes me wonder if I'm still in the grips of the nightmare. The same nightmare has been plaguing me for months now, and it doesn't take a degree in psychology to know the dreams are really about my uncertainty regarding my future. The soft pillow underneath my head lets me know where I am, and I breathe a sigh of relief. By her floral perfume lingering in the air, I know that I'm with Lacy, in her bed still. I don't usually sleep over. It's one of her unspoken rules that I should leave after our lovemaking because she needs her privacy and routine in the mornings.

Before, it suited me just fine, because I always want my own space in the mornings too. Now, I'm wondering if she'll start letting me sleep over once in a while. I turn over and reach for her, wanting to ask her how she'd feel about it.

My hand finds the other side of the bed cold and empty. I frown, bothered by the fact that she's not lying next to me.

I get up and switch on the bedroom lamp. While I dress, I'm listening for the sound of the TV from the living room, but all is quiet. I already know what that means, and my irritation turns up another notch.

As I suspected, I find Lacy in her study, sitting behind her desk and poring over her laptop. The light from the screen is illuminating her face, and I can see she's looking tense. "Hey, why don't you come back to bed? It's way too early to be up, doing whatever it is you're doing."

I'm crossing the room to stand behind her, and as I do, she surprises me by slamming her laptop shut and turning to me angrily. *What the hell is going on?* It's almost as if she's feeling guilty about whatever it is she was looking at, and didn't want me to see.

The anger drains from her as she looks up at my face, but there's still an awkward atmosphere hanging over us.

"Yeah, I think I may be done sleeping for tonight. Are you heading home?"

She says this with too much sweetness in her voice, and it answers my question about spending the night. I nod, dragging my fingers through my hair. I guess I've been dismissed. She walks with me through her place and outside to my car. She even leans in through the window to kiss me goodbye, maybe to show me that there's not supposed to be any hard feelings.

As I drive away, my insides feeling uncomfortable despite her subtle reassurances, I can't help but wonder what she was looking at on her laptop that she was so desperate to keep from me.

UNSEEN SIGNALS

LACY

*a*fter I watch Evan drive away, I go back inside my apartment and make sure the door is locked and the security system is activated before I return to the study.

I feel guilty for rousting Evan from my apartment so ungraciously. I had planned to ask him to spend the night, which would have been a first for us, an important milestone in our relationship to see what it would have been like in each other's company. Since neither of us are morning people, it would have been an interesting test.

I had woken up an hour and a half after we had gone to sleep, and the mysterious file had popped up in my head like a demented Jack-in-the-box. I wouldn't have been able to go back to sleep without seeing what the file contained. I didn't want to show Evan the file just yet, mainly because I knew he would call me crazy for even opening it. I desperately had to know—I couldn't just ignore it or delete it, hoping my curiosity would go away. That's just not how I'm built.

At dinner the night before, I had told Evan about my missing phone, but not about the file I had inadvertently downloaded to my laptop. It's not that I don't trust Evan, it's that his reaction would have spoken to a more cautious part of me, a more logical part, and I didn't want to listen to that just now. I wanted to see what the file contained, plain and simple, and nothing was going to convince me otherwise.

Unfortunately, opening the file hadn't been immediately enlightening, either.

As I scooch in behind my laptop once more, I open it again and let my eyes travel over the mess of random data... or what appears to be random data. Besides the jumbled sequence of letters, symbols, and numbers, there appears to be emails of some sort referencing different locations and events.

Whatever this is, it doesn't seem dangerous in the sense that it's a virus that's going to destroy my computer's files, at least, but it is troubling. It appears that the file is encrypted. That would explain the randomness of the data I'm looking at. But why in the world was this file sent to the system of my home assistant? It feels like it's important, that just deleting the file would be a mistake.

It was sent to me, but I can't figure out why. Maybe someone wanted to hide this file because the information it contains is dangerous in some way? Someone who knows me very well would know it was a safe bet to hide the file on my home assistant's system until it could be safely retrieved. Maybe I'm jumping to wild conclusions here, but it feels like I'm at least in the right ballpark. I wouldn't have known about the file if not for stupidly leaving my phone at the office. Anyone who knows me very well would know I wouldn't bother with the home assistant's more intricate features. That means that someone I know very well may be involved in something at least marginally shady, enough to want to hide it. But what? And more importantly, who?

Each time I go through the catalog of people that are close enough to me to know my personal quirks, the next candidate seems even more unlikely than the one before. Evan, Jamie, Charlotte, Gary, Rebecca... none of them seem like the type to get involved in anything dangerous or illegal. Imagining any of them using me to hide information obtained illegally is just unthinkable.

Trying to make sense of it, I get a notepad out from the top drawer of my desk, along with a pencil. I guess the best way to answer the question of *who* is to figure out what this is. The only way to make sense of the bits of actual information is to find some sort of pattern among the chaos. Certain coordinates that are repeated stand out, so I write them down. By cross-referencing them to locations, I discover that all of them are of addresses in and around Washington D.C. They all seem to be industrial areas, the locations of warehouses, factories, or docks.

The seemingly random content of the file isn't really random at all, and the fact that it's related to places in my own backyard, so to speak, gives me an uneasy feeling of foreboding.

There's nothing left to do about the file at the moment, and I'm feeling drained. I have a busy day ahead of me, and know I'd better get some sleep if I want to be at my best for my clients.

As I lie here in the dark, the mysterious file and all the possible meanings of it keeps tumbling around in my mind. At this point my tired, overused mind's defenses are way down, and my imagination is running wild, coming up with theories that only get more outlandish. It's like a dog chasing its own tail—not helpful at all.

It's a long time before I manage to fall asleep.

~

BEEP! BEEP! BEEP!
My eyes fly open. I must have carried my worries into the dreamworld with me, because instead of just getting up and silencing the alarm from the home assistant, I jump out of bed and try to make a run for it. My feet get tangled up in the sheet, and I fall to the floor.

At least I'm wide awake now, but this is a less than ideal start to the day. Standing up grumpily, I give a big yawn and stretch, trying to force some semblance of good feeling into my tired body. It doesn't feel like I slept at all. I groan, knowing that it's going to be a *long* day.

After a hot shower, two cups of coffee, eggs, and toast, I feel more energized and able to face my first meeting with a client at her office in downtown Washington. I make a quick stop at work, greeting Jamie and grabbing my phone before heading out to my meeting with Alice Bradshaw, an executive at a leading multinational audit, tax, and legal consulting company. She's young to hold such an esteemed position and, as a result, suffers from near-crippling impostor syndrome. I've been working with Alice for the better part of a year, helping her to foster a better, more realistic self-perception.

As I sit across from Alice, I try to listen carefully to an incident that happened earlier this week where she had to give a warning to another woman, one of Alice's subordinates, who has been working for the company for longer. It's clear that this woman resents the fact that she has to work for Alice, and Alice told me before about this lady's bad attitude and general lack of respect. I suspect that she may have applied for the position that Alice now holds as well, adding salt to the wound when she was unsuccessful and someone from outside was employed instead.

"Alice, we've gone over this before—the fact that this job comes with the task of handing out warnings to employees, sometimes even having to fire them if they do something to warrant it. It sounds to me like you've been giving this woman enough of a chance to change her attitude. Her continued disregard for company rules is what forced your hand. It wasn't personal."

Now I sit back as Alice explains about this woman's little clique within the company. I try to keep my mind on Alice and her worries about the woman, Judy, infecting the other staff members with negativity. Soon, though, my mind wanders back to the file on my laptop and how it got there. I already know that if I want to know more about the file, I'm going to have to ask someone with a hell of a lot more knowledge of computers than I possess, but who? It's not like I can just google a person and trust them with a file containing information of possibly illegal stuff. I may have to, though. Much as I hate the idea of bringing someone else in on this without knowing what it's all about, I need help, and I can't do this alone.

I realize that Alice has been staring at me, waiting for a response, and I have no idea what she just said. I flush, feeling my cheeks burn. "I'm sorry, I didn't get much sleep last night, and I guess my mind slipped away for a moment. Would you mind repeating what you just said?" It's mortifying, because my clients pay me to listen, so I was caught not doing my job. I'm usually much better at this.

Alice, a real sweetheart of a woman, smiles and waves it away.

"That's okay. I know all about being distracted. But are you okay? You do seem very pale. I hope you're not coming down with something."

I don't want to focus on my own problems, and me confiding in a client is out of the question, so I move the conversation on to positive things in Alice's life, areas where she feels fulfilled. It's good to remind oneself of one's blessings. It tends to put things into perspective.

Later, when I say goodbye to Alice, she is looking more at ease with herself and with the tough decisions she has to make at her job. I'm glad that my lack of focus wasn't a big deal, but I'm wondering how I'll possibly see the rest of the day through, feeling this on edge.

There's a huge traffic jam a few blocks from my office, cars standing gridlocked and unmoving. By the time I reach the office, it's already way past noon, and I'm starting to feel the effects of the late night and next to no sleep I had.

Stepping into my office, I've just placed my handbag on my desk and am unbuttoning my suit jacket when Jamie, my assistant, appears in front of my desk. I hardly look at her, but see she has my appointment book in her hands.

"Oh, please tell me I have some time before my next appointment? I'd like you to order me a giant cup of coffee and something to eat. Maybe chicken salad from that place..."

The words in my mouth turn to ash and trail off as I get my first good look at Jamie's face today. Her eyes are red and puffy from crying, and she is shaking, visibly upset. This is not the first time I've seen Jamie upset since her husband Tony walked out on her and the kids. This is not like the other times, though. Before, she was angry, hurt, scared about the future, frustrated, and sad... all understandable, considering they've been married for eight years and have two beautiful small boys.

I met Tony a few times, and I liked him very much. He struck me as an intelligent, devoted, and loving husband, a great father. My opinion of him changed drastically when he disappeared and the police told Jamie all the evidence suggested he went back to Turkey without his family. Jamie and Tony Kaplan used to be Jamilya and Tolga. They came to the states as a married couple with Jamie's older sister and her family six years ago and chose names that were more common here. Their two boys were born here. Both of them wanted a better life. Back in Turkey, they had friends and family. Here, they had to start over with little to no money, barely able to speak English.

I have yards of respect and admiration for people able to do that. It takes courage beyond anything that I can even begin to understand to leave everything you know behind in search of a better life for you and the family you plan on having. It baffled me that Tony could go through all of that and then leave his family high and dry like he did.

Now, as I look at Jamie, I'm shocked. This is not her normal range of very understandable emotions. This is terror and hopelessness. I walk over to Jamie and put my arm over her shoulder. "What happened? What's wrong?"

She bursts into tears again, and I hand her a box of Kleenex I keep on my desk. She puts my appointment book down and takes it gratefully as I take her by her shoulders and sit her down in the chair. Going around my desk again, I get my phone out and order my own coffee, and get one for Jamie too. My idea of having lunch completely forgotten, it gives Jamie a chance to get her emotions under control.

After she's wiped her face and I can see she's able to speak coherently, I fold my hands on my desk. "Jamie, what happened?" I repeat my question from earlier. "And please don't say it's nothing. You're still shaking like a twig, and I've never seen you like this."

"I messed up! Oh God, I messed up so badly. I... I had this file that I stored somewhere for safekeeping. It was my only hope of finding out what really happened to Tony! And now it's gone! I risked my life to get it, maybe even the lives of my children, and now..."

My mouth falls open as I stare at Jamie in utter disbelief. It's... It's just too much of a coincidence that I downloaded that creepy file from my home assistant, and now here Jamie is, talking about a file, her husband's disappearance, and saying that she risked her life to get it. It must be the same file!

"That was you?!" I can't keep the confusion and accusation out of my voice. "You downloaded the file to my home assistant?"

RED FLAGS

LACY

*a*s Jamie and I stare at each other, she opens and closes her mouth a few times, like a fish out of water. Obviously her plan hadn't involved me discovering the file.

The sudden ringing of my cellphone makes both of us nearly jump out of our skin. I answer my phone, intent on getting rid of the person on the other end quickly so I can continue my conversation with Jamie. I motion for her to stay where she is—we're not even close to done with this yet.

"Hey Lace, where are you? Did you just stand us up?" I hear someone else laughing in the background and realize it's my friend Rebecca, and that I completely forgot I was supposed to meet her and Charlotte for lunch today.

"Oh my goodness, I'm so sorry. I'm a jerk!" Now what do I do? It would be the worst time to leave right now. I can't just leave Jamie here with all these unanswered questions between us. How am I supposed to concentrate on having a good time with my two best friends with all of this hanging over my head like the sword of Damocles?

"Having a bit of a rough day?" Rebecca asks. *Girl, you have no idea,* I think with an internal smirk. "Don't worry, we can have the lunch date tomorrow. But don't stand us up again! Since Charlotte's wonderful husband is selfishly taking just her away for the kind of weekend I only read about in my favorite smut novels—" she laughs, and I can imagine Charlotte elbowing her, "this is the last chance we have to celebrate her birthday!"

By how giggly they sound, I guess that there was more than a glass of wine had over lunch, and I smile, wishing I was there. With a promise to meet them tomorrow afternoon for lunch instead, I end the call.

Placing my phone back on my desk, I turn to look at Jamie, who is regarding me with a careful look that I don't care for. "You're going to tell me the truth now. It's the least you can do, seeing as you dragged me into God knows what!"

"I didn't mean to! Look, I have no idea what the file contains. I downloaded it hoping to get some answers about Tony, that's all!" She seems sincere, but it still doesn't answer any of my questions.

"Downloaded it from whom?"

"From Derek Phillips, Tony's boss." When I give her a perplexed look, she goes into more detail. "Derek was the one who first pitched the idea to the police that Tony isn't missing, but went back to Turkey. None of the people who Tony or I knew back there has seen him or even heard from him. The police think he's trying to avoid me, that we were on the brink of getting a divorce and now he's avoiding paying child support. I know that also came from Derek, but I've never met him. How would he possibly know anything about our marriage? We weren't having problems! We were in a good place. Things were even starting to look up for us financially. None of it makes sense."

I try to keep the look of pity from my face, because I've obviously heard it all before. It's amazing the extent a person's level of denial will go when the other person brings up the idea of divorce, but often the signs are all there long before the actual blow falls.

Jamie sees the look, so I guess I wasn't successful in hiding it after all.

"Look, I know how this sounds. And I swear, I'm not imagining this! Something happened to Tony. He didn't leave us! Not by choice, anyway!"

27

When I still don't answer, Jamie throws her hands up in exaspera-tion. "What about Tony's friend, Nathan Shepard? They worked at the docks together. They were really good buddies, but didn't socialize outside of work. Nathan disappeared as well. They found his wife and daughter murdered, and the police think that Nathan is responsible. It happened at the same time as Tony's disappearance."

Nathan Shepard... I remember reading about the case. It was one of those stories you read online that you shake your head over before clicking to the next story. A senseless, brutal act of violence that you feel depressed about but try to forget because it's just too terrible to have any personal feelings over. I had no idea the case was connected to Jamie and her missing husband.

Two men who knew each other went missing the same night and the police just shrugged and didn't think it was weird? That in itself makes me feel squirmy inside. It's too much of a coincidence.

I can only imagine how terrified Jamie must have been to realize that the murder of Nathan's family may be connected to her own husband's disappearance. This certainly changes things for me. It explains Jamie's erratic behavior over the last few weeks. It actually amazes me that she was still able to get up in the morning, to make herself look presentable and do her job.

"How did you get the file, anyway? Surely you didn't just waltz into Tony's boss's office and download it from his computer?"

For the first time, Jamie laughs. "No, it was a little more complicated than that. I found out that the shipping yard Tony works for uses a cleaning service. So I've been moonlighting, working as a maid after hours for the same company, knowing it was only a matter of time before I was placed on the detail that goes out to the offices of the ship-ping yard bosses."

That would explain why Jamie has been so distracted and looking so exhausted all the time lately. Working two jobs while playing amateur sleuth... all while still caring for two busy little boys. My admiration for this woman only grows.

"I caused a distraction so I would be left alone, hacked into Derek's computer, and retrieved the file. I haven't even looked at it yet. I have no idea what's on it, but it was all I could grab in the short amount of time I had."

I look at Jamie, feeling the need to reevaluate everything I thought I knew about her. She's talking about hacking into a person's computer as if it's the easiest thing in the world. "How did you know how to..."

Jamie shrugs. "Back in Turkey, I worked for a software company. I was a software developer over there. When we first got to the states, I looked for a job in the same field. Unfortunately, your country doesn't recognize my university degree."

She says this without any bitterness or resentment, but I can't help but feel sorry for it, even though it's not my fault the system is like that. She must have sensed how I feel, because she shakes her head.

"We came here for a better life, and that's what we got, so don't sweat it, boss."

I can't help but give a self-conscious laugh knowing that if things had been different, I might have been the one to call her boss. The strength of this woman, the balls-to-the-wall sheer guts of her, makes me think that if circumstances were different, she would have been a force to be reckoned with; a successful businesswoman or an executive of a software company, maybe even CTO.

"What did Tony do over there in Turkey before he came here?" I'm curious, and feel silly that I never thought to ask before. Successful, well-educated people tend to gravitate toward each other. Now that I realize that there are things I never even suspected about Jamie, I feel the same may be true of her husband, Tony.

"He was a mechanical engineer."

I whistle, thinking about the comment she made about how things had been starting to look up financially for them. "And he wasn't... uhm... dissatisfied by what he was forced to do in terms of work here?"

Jamie nods. "Of course he was, but he was also a realist. He always hoped to find some means to be a better provider for me and the boys. We even dreamed about getting degrees over here. We talked about it all the time. There just wasn't enough money to actually do it. It came down to a choice between putting our funds toward our own studies or saving up so perhaps the boys can go to college. Of course, the boys' education took priority."

"If things were that tight, how did it start to get better the last few months before he disappeared?"

Jamie bites her lip and shakes her head. "I don't know! Tony didn't want to tell me. He said he was getting more shifts at work, and it looked that way, because he was working longer hours. He had more money. As in... cash. I don't know what my husband was involved in, but I think it got him killed!"

As Jamie wipes away the tears running down her cheeks, I drum my fingers on my desk, thinking. If it's true, and Tony and Nathan had indeed gotten themselves involved with dangerous people, it stands to reason that those people were the ones who killed Nathan's family. Why didn't they kill Jamie and her kids too? Was it because two family murders committed by the husband who then up and vanished would have looked too suspicious? Maybe Tony's boss, Derek, knew what had happened to Nathan's family and didn't want the same thing to happen to Tony's family. If that was the case, him telling police that Tony and Jamie were on the brink of getting a divorce was him being kind.

Maybe I'm too naive. Maybe it has nothing to do with kindness, and Jamie and the boys are still in danger. Maybe the people involved in this are biding their time, patiently waiting to finish the family off when it won't look so suspicious.

It's a creepy thought, but makes me determined to help Jamie, even though the idea of confronting those people is frightening.

"The file is encrypted. But I'm guessing you can do something about that?"

Jamie nods, and I stand up. "See if you can clear the rest of my day. Move my appointments around to the rest of the week."

Jamie stands up too and takes my appointment book from my desk. "That's what I wanted to discuss with you when I came in here. It seems you don't have any appointments for the rest of the day."

"Well, that's fantastic!" I just remember that I forgot to tell Jamie that I cleared my schedule last week to have lunch with the girls. *I guess I forgot to share the information with myself as well,* I smirk as this thought runs through my mind. *It's time for apology number 1,238 this month.* "Jamie, I forgot I cleared today last week. We can lock the office and go to my house. I want you to see what information you can extract from the file, but I don't want to do it here. I'll feel much better if we do it at my house."

We decide to leave Jamie's car at the office. It will be safe here until we return. She gets into my car with me instead, and soon we are driving back to my place. Luckily, there's not another traffic jam, and we reach my apartment in next to no time.

I get Jamie settled behind my laptop in my study. By now I'm starving, and I make us a quick meal we can have behind my desk. I've placed another chair next to my usual office chair so I can watch Jamie as she types furiously away at the keyboard. I have no idea what she's doing, so I keep quiet and let her work. I feel mesmerized by the way she expertly handles the decryption of the files.

After a while, Jamie has a eureka moment and turns to me excitedly. "Look at this! These emails mention a person called Thomas Albright. Does the name mean anything to you?"

The name tickles something at the back of my mind—a memory of reading that name before. I can't quite put my finger on it, though, so I shake my head.

Jamie opens an internet search tab and types the name into the search bar. We are rewarded with a flurry of information. Jamie sucks in a breath, mirroring my own feeling of surprise. She opens the Wikipedia page for Thomas Albright, but it's hardly necessary. Now that the photo of Thomas Albright is on the screen in front of our eyes, I remember where I heard the name. By the grim look on Jamie's face as she scans the page, it's clear she heard about the allegations connected to the senator as well.

Months ago, Senator Albright was connected to an arms deal scandal. Criminal organizations within both China and Russia were mentioned in connection with Albright. The news articles we scan now highlight a suspicion of illegal transactions not sanctioned by the Minister of Defense. Because of the scandal, the senator's political influence was compromised. What saved the senator from arrest and prosecution was the fact that no one could prove the validity of these claims one hundred percent, as the merchandise—the illegal weapons that Albright and whoever was part of the organization were supposed to have been transporting overseas—was never found.

"These locations around Washington, do you think they're..." Jamie asks, wide-eyed, pointing to the list of coordinates in the file that I had written down and cross-referenced with locations scattered in and around Washington D.C.

I know what Jamie is asking. "The locations where the illegal weapons were stored that they never found? Places where there's physical evidence of Albright's involvement in illegal weapons trading? Yes, I think that's exactly what it is. My God, Jamie, what the hell did you get us involved in?!"

As if on cue, my front doorbell rings. The sound of it has never been so ominous.

I get up from my chair on legs that feel shaky. When I get to the front door, I curse myself for the fact that I never figured out how to use the outside camera function of the home assistant. If I did, I could have checked who my unexpected visitor is before opening the door. As things stand, I have to do it the old-school way, as if the technology to help in situations like this one wasn't invented yet.

"Hello? Who's there?" I ask through the door. There's no answer, and I can't hear anything from the other side. With a hand that feels shaky, I open the door and peek into the hallway just outside my apartment. There's no one there. I undo the chain of the door and stand just outside my apartment. Looking up and down the hallway, I don't see anyone, not even people living in the other apartments. It's still reasonably early, and most of my neighbors are either stuck in afternoon traffic or still at work.

As I step back inside my apartment, something crackles under my shoe. I look down and see that I've stepped on an envelope. Frowning, I pick it up. It's some cheap, generic stationary that anyone can buy at a discount store. Obviously, it was hand-delivered and slipped under the door.

Feeling uneasy and creeped out, I tear the envelope open. This note is written on a humble little yellow Post-it. I read the short message:

Stay out of matters that don't concern you.

SAFEHOUSE

LACY

*J*amie immediately sees something is wrong by the look on my face as soon as I step into the office again. "What happened? You look like you've seen a ghost."

I don't feel able to answer her at first, so I just hand her the note. She reads it and turns it over, then does the same with the envelope.

Unsticking my tongue from the roof of my mouth, I say, "Someone hand-delivered that here. To my apartment."

The implication of the note and the way I received it crashes down on Jamie, and she looks at me with wide eyes. "They know we're on to them? But how could they possibly know?"

I shake my head. Jamie grabs her handbag and abruptly stands up from behind my desk. I stop her from leaving my home office in a state of panic by grabbing her arm. "You came here in my car. Remember? Where are you going?"

"I... I have to go get the boys, take them to a motel or something. I have to get them away immediately, before those people decide to kill all three of us!"

I think I understand her need to get her children away from all this as quickly as possible. Poor Jamie is now realizing that by downloading that file, she opened up Pandora's box. Booking herself and her kids into a seedy motel is the worst idea, though. She'll scare the boys, and they've already been traumatized enough by their father's disappearance. If he's dead, as I suspect he must be, then there's a world of hurt still waiting for her and her children down the line dealing with the reality of loss and grief when the hope that Tony will be back is taken from them.

Also, in a motel, they'll be exposed, stand out like a sore thumb. A mom with her two boys in tow checking into a place like that... people will immediately assume it's because of a custody battle between the mom and the kids' father, or something like that. If the people connected to Senator Albright are really after them, then a motel is the worst possible place they can go. It's too anonymous, too full of people who can be paid or threatened to look the other way.

"Come on," I say to Jamie. I lead her outside to my car in case the place is really bugged. "I have a better idea, but we'll need to go to your place, get clothes for the three of you for a few days, and then go and pick the boys up."

On the way to go get Jamie's car, I give her a rundown of my plan. I've already sent Evan a message asking him to meet us at a little diner I know that's just outside of the city. Evan agrees immediately, no questions asked, and I feel a burst of affection for him so strong that it makes me giddy.

We get Jamie's car, and I drive behind her as she drives to her place. We park her car, and then I help her pack for a few days. Clothes and other essentials are thrown into bags and a suitcase that we load into my car. We'll leave Jamie's car here at her house. On our way out, I scan the parking lot and the street in front of her building for people watching us. I can't see anyone suspicious, but that doesn't mean they're not there. I'm all too aware that I'm not an expert at this.

Then we make our way to the boys' nursery school. Waiting outside while Jamie picks them up, I get the feeling that I'm being watched. I scan the faces of the few people sitting in the parking lot in their own cars, waiting for their spouses or parents. Everyone seems aboveboard, and I can't pinpoint anyone suspicious that looks like they don't belong here. Still, the feeling of being watched by hostile eyes persists.

I watch as Jamie buckles her two boys into their car seats. They are still very small. Sam is four years old, and Billy is two and a half. They are cute kids, and it's clear from this interaction and from previous ones I was a spectator to that Jamie absolutely adores her sons, and there's nothing that she wouldn't do for them. In my book, that means that she deserves all the help from me she can get.

We drive for half an hour and reach the diner. By now, it's just after four in the afternoon. The boys are hungry, so I offer to buy them dinner. They're excited and very chatty. Normally the little family would have been at home, eating dinner in their condo in Takoma Park.

Evan finds us in the diner just after we've finished and I've paid the bill. Jamie's met Evan before, and gives him a shy smile before taking the boys to the restroom. When we leave here, we'll have a three-hour journey ahead of us.

"Lacy, what the hell is going on?" Evan asks, sitting across from me and grabbing my hand. "Are you in trouble?" I look at his face, so handsome and sincere, and I know sooner or later I'm going to have to tell him everything. There's just not enough time right now.

"Please trust me, baby. I'll tell you everything tomorrow night. Thanks for doing this. I know it seems crazy, but just know I appreciate your help with this."

Evan leans back and regards me for a moment. I wonder what he thinks this is all about. Probably that Jamie's husband is abusive and she's trying to get away from him, or something along those lines. I can't recall if I even mentioned Tony's disappearance to him. Finally, he sighs and takes his car keys from his pocket, handing them to me. I hand him my car keys in return.

"I filled the gas tank, and bought some supplies for them that should last a few days."

I smile and thank Evan, squeezing his hand. When Jamie and the boys return, Evan helps to load them into his car, along with their luggage and the car seats for the boys. Every now and then I find myself scanning the parking lot, looking for people watching us, people who seem too interested in what we're doing. I don't see anyone like that, and hope that by exchanging cars with Evan, I can get Jamie and the boys away to a safe place until this matter has been resolved.

Before we leave, Evan kisses me in a way that leaves me breathless, flushed, and a little self-conscious, knowing that Jamie and the boys are watching this spectacle. But I'd be lying if I said I'm not pleased by it, too. "Take care of yourself. Drive safe, and let me know once you're home again. I hate the idea of you driving back alone."

I shake my head. "I know the roads very well, and it won't be the first time I drive it at night." We break apart then, and I promise to call Evan as soon as I'm back home later tonight. He watches as we drive off in his car. I watch Evan in the rearview mirror. A tall, very good-looking, athletic guy leaning against my car, he seems strangely lonely.

The three-hour drive to Deep Creek Lake is a cheerful one, considering the reason for the trip. Jamie and the kids play games and sing songs to pass the time. She's managed to push her own worry and fear aside and to make it seem like an exciting adventure. The effort isn't wasted, and soon even infects me. We may as well have been friends going on a vacation together.

As the city gives way to the natural beauty of Maryland, I feel in my gut that this is the right thing to do. The sunset is spectacular.

Much later, we pull up in front of the three-bedroom cabin, and it's already past eight. I can see the kids are tired. They've become progressively subdued, and now look rather starry-eyed. It's bedtime for them. Luckily the beds are made, and Jamie can just give them a bath and tuck them in. I just linger long enough to help her move their luggage inside.

It's a spacious cabin that I bought for my mom three years ago. We come here every year for a few weeks to just unwind, get out of the city, and spend time together. It was one of the best investments I ever made, and I know it's the perfect place for Jamie and the boys to hide out in until I can think of a more permanent way to make it safe for them.

While the boys are exploring the bedrooms, I show Jamie where the passwords for the security system is, and the one for the Wi-Fi. "You guys won't have a car, I'm afraid, but I think it's better that you stay here for now. The place is under my mom's name, so if they do a bit of digging, they'll be able to discover it. It's the best solution I could think of, though."

Jamie nods, and then surprises me by hugging me tightly. "Thank you so much! I'm so sorry I dragged you into this. It was never my intention."

"It's okay," I say, and give her shoulder a squeeze.

"Are you sure you don't want to spend the night and drive back in the morning? It's so late already, and you look exhausted, too."

I do feel tired, and knowing I still have the three-hour drive back home ahead of me makes me feel wrung-out. I manage to paste a smile on my face and repeat to Jamie what I told Evan before—that I'm used to driving at night. It's not exactly true; I've only done it a few times, but I don't want Jamie to worry about me.

I don't want to tell her the real reason why I have to go back home tonight: because tomorrow morning I'll have to face the task of letting my clients know that I'll be closing my office for a while, and thus won't be available. Jamie has enough to deal with without feeling guilty for leaving me high and dry regarding my business. But the fact of it is, I can't run the office, see clients, and figure out a way to resolve this issue all at the same time. By closing my office for a while, I'll at least be able to give myself some breathing room to figure out where to go from here.

I haven't even begun to consider how I'm going to get us all out of this mess. The obvious solution—to just go to the police with all of the information—is tempting, but in my gut I feel that it wouldn't be the right call. Their less-than-thorough investigation of Tony's disappearance leads me to believe that some of the detectives assigned to the case may have been paid off to bury the leads. They were so quick to take Derek Phillips at his word that Tony ran off back to Turkey rather than the word of Tony's wife of eight years.

The fact that a state senator is involved in all of this makes the police's attitude toward the case make sense, if one is to be cynical and believe there's some sort of conspiracy afoot. The note left at my door, the realization that I'm being watched and that my place is possibly bugged, gives credibility to the idea that Jamie and I inadvertently stumbled onto a deep and dark conspiracy involving the senator and illegal distribution of firearms to criminal organizations overseas. It is, after all, what the senator was accused of before.

I'm too tired to think straight. All I know is that I'm hopelessly out of my depth on this thing. I'm not some super spy able to infiltrate places more secure than Fort Knox, roundhouse kick bad guys, and save the world, all while looking fabulous doing it. That's for women like the hundreds of female superheroes portrayed in popular movies, video games, and TV shows. The problem with getting involved in this thing is that I know nothing of government conspiracies, and the limited knowledge I have of these kinds of things is based on watching too many action movies.

As I say goodbye to Jamie, I feel a tug at my heart, because my short and petite assistant seems very vulnerable in this moment. She's pretty in an understated, girl-next-door way, with long, thick dark hair. She has olive-toned skin, a bit darker than my own, and her best feature by far is her eyes. They are large and dark, framed by thick eyelashes. It's easy to mistake the softness in them for weakness. What it is is kindness and compassion. I say goodbye to Sam and little Billy, too.

Then I brave the long journey back home. By the time I reach my apartment, it's already past 12. I am dead on my feet as I park Evan's car. The thought of having to exchange cars with him again in just a few hours to sort out the mess of the office, make excuses to my clients, and try to figure out where to go from here... it's all weighing down on me like I'm carrying the whole world and its problems on my own two shoulders.

I step into my apartment and close the door behind me. Before, this place was my sanctuary, the place where I could escape from the outside world and feel safe when I needed to. Now, it's taken on a sinister air, like it's been corrupted. I suppose it has been, by the thought that the people who may have murdered Jamie's husband bugged it and are listening to my every word.

I don't have the time or the energy to turn the place upside down in search of recording devices. Honestly, I wouldn't even know what to look for. A vague idea of perhaps using the fact that they're listening to my advantage flickers across my overworked mind and is gone.

What I need most in the world right now is sleep. Despite being grateful for Evan's help today, I can't face having a long conversation with him over the phone. I send him a quick message to let him know I'm home and everything went well. Lying in bed waiting for his reply, I feel my eyes starting to close. They're so heavy, as if my eyelids have been dipped in cement. I can't force them open, and I feel myself drifting away, succumbing to sweet, blessed sleep.

BIRTHDAY LUNCH

LACY

*E*ngrossed in research to try and piece together some more of the information in the file, it takes a while for the chime of the doorbell to pull me out of my own thoughts. Irritated by this interruption, I walk over to the front door and then stand there, undecided.

I know it's not Evan, because I already spoke to him this morning and arranged to meet him at my place later so we can exchange cars. I don't really mind driving around in his gunmetal gray Jeep for the day, though it's not really my style. I prefer sleek cars that go fast, like my cherry red Subaru. It's a minor inconvenience, and one I bear gladly, considering how much Evan helped me out yesterday with Jamie and the kids.

Standing at my front door, I have visions of dangerous men with guns just waiting for me to open the door. I know I'm letting my imagination run away with me, but knowing that I'm at the very least being watched... well, who could blame me for being paranoid?

I finally open the door, and there's a UPS delivery guy standing there holding a package that I know I didn't order. I sign for it without argument, mainly to get rid of the delivery guy. He's around 60 years old, if I had to guess, so it's not that I feel nervous about him for any reason but that he's a stranger and he's at my door.

Carrying the package inside as if it contains an explosive device, I place it down on the kitchen counter. The only address on the package and delivery note is mine. There's the name of the person who supposedly sent the package, but since it says it was sent by Mr. S. Anta, I know it's an alias. I roll my eyes. *Santa? Seriously?* As if it wasn't bad enough to be caught up in this thing, now I also have to deal with some faceless smart aleck making bad jokes. *No, please*, I think sarcastically, *anything but this. Just come and shoot me now.*

Trying to open the package with a knife, I accidentally cut my thumb. Bleeding over the kitchen floor, I place my hand under the tap to wash the blood away. It's not too serious, just a cut on the side of my thumb, but it dampens my mood even further.

After applying a Band-Aid on the cut and cleaning the mess up, I manage to open the package. Inside is a cream-colored envelope. The stationary is expensive, the kind that is most commonly used for wedding invitations or other very important black tie events. My name is etched on the front in gold lettering. No address, and no return address either.

I open the envelope and pull out a note. Also in gold lettering, there's a single, cryptic message: "The walls have ears." *No shit.* At least now I know it as a certainty, whereas before I only suspected it. But it's interesting. Obviously the person or people who sent me this are not the same ones who sent me the threatening note yesterday. Why would they tip me off about their own listening devices? There's something else in the package: a black device with a handle on one side and lights at the top. The lights are dead as a doornail. Maybe there's some way to switch it on? Holding the device in my hand, I wonder what it is. I'm guessing it's either a listening device to illustrate the point that there's someone listening, or a device to detect listening devices. Hmmm...

Obviously "Santa" doesn't know me very well. Otherwise, they would have placed detailed instructions inside the box along with the gift. I have no idea how to use this. I angrily place it back in the box and check my watch. It's time to leave for my first appointment of the day.

I've emailed most of my clients explaining that I need to take some time off from work. Mrs. Yulanda Summers didn't want to reschedule her appointment, though. It's a marriage counseling session, and she's been using it to complain about her husband's many shortcomings while he is sitting right there next to her.

I suspect Mrs. Summers wants a divorce, but due to the prenuptial agreement they signed, the one who initiates a divorce without just cause and without proving that they did everything in their power to make the marriage work will be penalized when the assets are to be divided.

I've been contemplating dropping them as clients because of this, but every time I come close, I remember the look on Mr. Summers's face, sitting there all gloomily while his wife reiterates what exactly she finds so dissatisfying in their marriage. If it was at all within my power, I would have urged Mr. Summers to get a divorce, penalties on the shared estate be damned. But it's not my job to make people's minds up for them, and I can't just drop clients because I don't like them. That would be the epitome of unprofessionalism. The best I can do, and what I've tried to focus on, is steering the conversation into a more positive direction, where both of them, God willing, will be able to benefit from the counseling.

I fight my way through traffic, and then sit down with Mr. and Mrs. Summers in their luxury condo in Columbia Heights.

"So how has your week been?" I start by asking politely, with a chirpy note in my voice that I hope will set the tone for the appointment. Unfortunately, my Disney princess singing-to-woodland-animals tone cuts zero ice with the formidable Mrs. Summers.

She frowns at me and rolls her eyes. How anyone can do both things at the same time, I have no idea, but she does. "It would have been a fabulous week, perfectly dandy, if Daniel hadn't forgotten to pay the gardening services. I had my annual summer barbecue, the one that we do every year, and the garden was an absolute mess."

The meeting goes just as badly as I anticipated, and when I leave to head to the office an hour later, I feel emotionally drained.

I have some important filing to do before my lunch with Charlotte and Rebecca. With Jamie out of commission, I spend a few hours catching up on important correspondence, sending some invoices to my accountant, and fielding a few phone calls from colleagues and potential new clients.

Feeling frazzled and out of sorts, I force myself to take a moment to catch my breath. My cellphone is not in my handbag. Oh no! Did I lose the damn thing *again*? Before the inevitable meltdown can occur, I find the little bugger under a heap of paperwork, and smile sheepishly at myself. "Sorry, self," I say loudly. Should I be apologizing to myself for stressing needlessly, or to the phone for blaming it for getting lost? I'm pretty sure I'm at apology number 1,229. I take my cellphone and head out the door.

There's a little courtyard next to my office building with a bench under a Sycamore tree. It's a bright and sunny day; beautiful, really. As I sit down to give Jamie a call to check in, I realize that I haven't had time to do any more digging on the information that Jamie was able to extract from the file. I've been too busy putting out fires all day to prevent my business, that I've worked very hard to build over the last eight years, from going up in flames.

At least by doing that, I've bought myself a few days of grace.

Jamie answers on the second ring. She sounds breathless, and for a moment I feel a stab of worry in my gut. I brought my cellphone out here because I didn't trust that whoever bugged my house didn't do the same in my office. It's a terrible thing to realize that you have no privacy anywhere. It also makes me nervous, feeling that perhaps I'm just fooling myself to think that Jamie and her family are really safe from the people involved in whatever illegal activities the file she obtained is evidence of.

Hearing Jamie laugh on the other end of the call, I feel myself relaxing. "You just caught us dripping water all over your place! I took the kids for a swim. The water was freezing, but they had a blast. I'll clean it all up, of course."

Hearing the boys chattering excitedly in the background warms my heart. I assure Jamie again that they should make themselves at home.

We talk for a few more minutes; I don't mention the file or the fact that I'll have to bring it through to her at some point so she can decode the rest of it. She does ask me how it's going, and how I'm coping with not having her there. Here I tell a white lie, saying that I haven't had too much trouble navigating everything around the office, but I do assure her that I'll be glad when all this is over and I have her back here, helping me.

By the time we say our goodbyes, it's just after one in the afternoon, and it's time for me to head to the restaurant for Charlotte's celebratory lunch. Despite all the worries and the pressure weighing on me, I feel excited about seeing my two best friends.

On the rare occasion people find out that Rebecca and I briefly dated in university, they are surprised that we've been able to remain friends. "Isn't it weird being friends with your ex?" is always the most common question they'll ask.

Even Charlotte was politely confused by this until I introduced her to Rebecca. They instantly clicked, and it was then obvious to her how we are still friends. Rebecca is one of the most vivacious, outgoing, and fun people you'll ever meet. She always brings the party to every occasion. Her friendship meant more to me than any residual awkwardness as a result of our brief, stormy, and very passionate affair. The issue was that she's not the kind to settle down with one person, and I always valued monogamy. We parted amicably, and over the years, the fact that we already tried being in a relationship once showed us we are better off as just friends, and it's never like an unanswered question hanging between us.

We played field hockey together in university, and with her long, supple legs and fearless attitude, she could have been a star, but hockey was always just a hobby to her, something fun to pass the time. These days her sport of choice is kickboxing. She's very good at it, and I guess it helps her with some of her anger issues. If I had to sum Rebecca Adams up in three words, it would be fierce, sarcastic, and loyal.

At the kickboxing club where she spends most of her Saturdays, a lot of the guys are hopelessly in love with her. Even the ones that are much younger. With her long, strawberry-blonde hair tied in a braid hanging to her waist, her porcelain-white, flawless skin, green eyes, high cheekbones, and sharp, elven-like chin, she looks like she could have stepped out of a fashion magazine, even when she's sweaty and flushed from physical exertion. The fact that she's off-limits and completely unavailable often adds to the intrigue. Then there's her body language and the way she has of talking: chic and high-class. In both appearance and attitude, she reminds one of the iconic actress Nicole Kidman.

The fact that she's a successful and very wealthy public relations specialist makes her a formidable woman, one who other women are either in awe of or hate on general principle.

Charlotte Robinson is a lot more shy. She's the friend I hang out with when my social battery is way down and I need to do something quiet that doesn't drain me even further. I met her through Gary seven years ago, after my business had been open for a year. Gary came to see me because he needed advice on one of the guys on the team who, following a serious injury that required physical therapy, seemed to be dealing with a lot more than just physical recovery. Gary and I instantly hit it off, and he introduced me to his wife.

Charlotte is half Korean. Her father moved to the states with his parents and older siblings when he was 11 years old. There was some family drama when her dad married an Irish-American woman instead of the traditional Korean bride that his parents had all picked out for him. The result was that Charlotte and her twin sister Charmaine have very little to do with their paternal grandparents.

Her Korean heritage is obvious in her long, thick dark hair and almond-shaped eyes. I once saw her in a Hanbok, the traditional dress of Korean women, with her hair in an updo, showcasing her slender neck. She looked breathtaking. Of our group of friends, she is the shortest. It's this, along with her delicate features, that makes her seem vulnerable, but Charlotte is self-assured and self-contained. She has a quiet strength about her that appeals to people, especially to ones like Rebecca, who are the opposite.

Charlotte and Gary are a child-free couple who decided early on in their marriage to focus on their careers and each other. She's a financial analyst for a leading international financial company. She loves her job, and is obviously excellent at it. To me and to everyone who knows them, Gary and Charlotte are the perfect couple. I'm sure that's part of the reason why I'm so unsure if I want children. I've had them as a prime example of what a successful marriage should look like all these years.

I'm pulled from my thoughts about my two friends as I park at the back of Opaline Bar and Brasserie, one of the best restaurants in Washington D.C. that offers French cuisine. Besides the delicious food, they also have a range of refreshing cocktails. As my stomach gives a loud rumble, indicating that I'm starving, I look forward to having a nice meal underneath the blue umbrellas at our usual patio table. Walking around the building, I see Charlotte and Rebecca already seated.

Rebecca spots me first. She gets up and starts waving like a lunatic. I laugh, because her flapping arms remind me of some exotic bird trying to take flight. Charlotte smiles at her, looks over at me, and shakes her head. This *Rebecca will be Rebecca* look from Charlotte makes me grin even wider, and I realize how much I've missed them both since our last lunch almost two weeks ago.

I reach the table and am enveloped by a big, enthusiastic hug from Rebecca and a smaller but no less warm one from Charlotte. As I take a seat and the two of them fill me in on what they were discussing before I arrived—Charlotte's upcoming romantic weekend with Gary—I feel that warm, fuzzy feeling in my heart, and I'm glad that I didn't miss out on this moment with them.

For a few minutes there's more good-natured, naughty teasing about Charlotte's weekend plans, and she takes it in her stride, only blushing a little bit. I tease about Rebecca and I corrupting her delicate sensibilities. There's much giggling from all three of us about this, until the waitress arrives with our cocktails. I thank the other two for ordering my favorite, a mango martini. Charlotte waves it away, but Rebecca is distracted, obviously enamored by our waitress, who is in her late 20s, blonde, and beautiful.

The waitress, whose name tag says she's called Mandi, takes our food orders, and when it's Rebecca's turn, she manages to make everything sound like it's tinged with sexual innuendo, a trick I have yet to learn.

"My God, Becks," Charlotte remarks drily when the waitress is gone after giving Rebecca a long, lingering look. "Can't you keep it in your pants for one lunch? Aren't you supposed to have a girlfriend?" Charlotte is only teasing, though, giving me a meaningful look that I should play along. Rebecca is unfazed.

"Shush, you! You'll blow my chances if she hears you. Besides, Alyssa and I are not exclusive." Rebecca is referring to the woman she's been seeing for the last few months, Alyssa Ramirez, who happens to be a daytime soap star.

"That's a shame. I like Alyssa," I say a little sadly.

"Well, she also sees other people, and we're both happy with this arrangement. There's no need to regard her as the orphan Annie."

Charlotte and I laugh at this analogy. It's an inside joke because Alyssa is drop-dead gorgeous, has money in spades, and lives a life of glitz and glamor most people can only dream of. She also lives in California, meaning the simple logistics of it makes it understandable why there can't be anything more serious between her and our beloved Becks. It's probably why she appealed so much to Rebecca to begin with.

Then Rebecca skillfully turns the tables on me by asking about Evan. "That guy is so in love with you. It wouldn't surprise me if he proposes to you soon."

I can feel myself turn an alarming shade of red. "Uhm, well..."

Charlotte distracts both of us by choking a little on her drink. I look over at her and notice that she's blushing, too. I frown, suspicious now. "He is?! You know something that you don't want to tell!"

"Well..." Charlotte shifts uncomfortably.

"Come on, Robinson... spill!" Rebecca says, as if she's a detective interrogating a witness. Both of us are leaning forward now.

"He mentioned to Gary that he's been thinking about it, but doesn't know if you'd say yes."

CHASED AND CORNERED

LACY

I sit back, feeling like I'm in free fall. The world is rushing past, and I have nothing to grab on to. Yes, I suspected Evan was contemplating our future together, but to hear that it was weighing so heavily on him that he confided in Gary... that really came as a shock.

With one shaky hand, I take my martini glass and finish my drink in one gulp. Charlotte, seeing this, calls the waitress over for a refill.

"What... what are you going to say if he does ask you?" Rebecca is looking at me worriedly. Despite her teasing, I know she really has a soft spot for Evan. He's the first guy I've been in a relationship with where I don't feel like I have to have an exit strategy in place all the time just in case. He's the only one who I've ever really let my guard down with, up to a point. Both of my friends know this, and they've been quietly rooting for me and Evan to make it work.

Rebecca doesn't have to say it in so many words, but if Evan asks me to marry him and I reject his proposal, that could be the end of us. Just because I may not be ready to take the next step with him doesn't mean I won't be devastated if we break up.

"Please don't tell him you know he and Gary spoke!" Charlotte says. "It's not often that guys even talk about that stuff to each other, and he'll never forgive Gary for telling me!"

"Don't worry, it's fine." I lean over and squeeze Charlotte's hand. "It just came as a bit of a surprise, that's all."

Rebecca bursts out laughing. "Yeah, I'll say! You looked like you saw a ghost."

Our food arrives, and I'm saved from answering Rebecca's earlier question about what I'd say to Evan if he proposed to me. The truth is, I don't know what I'd say.

The food is delicious, but the mood has been dampened a bit by Charlotte's revelation. To try and bring it back, I tell them about Jamie having to take personal time off and how swamped I've been at the office this morning. Big mistake! Both Rebecca and Charlotte remember me telling them how Jamie's husband just up and left a few months ago, so naturally they're concerned for her and the kids. This leads me to try and think up a valid excuse for Jamie's extended absence that doesn't involve the file and Thomas Albright, the messages I've received that seem to be coming from two opposing groups of people, and setting Jamie and the kids up at my mom's holiday home.

Part of me is dying to confide in my two best friends. I think that's the reason why I mentioned Jamie. But I know I can't tell them everything that's been happening to me. I have no idea how much danger I'm in, and the last thing I want is to drag Charlotte and Rebecca down with me.

I give them some feeble excuse about Jamie having to be out of town for a family emergency, and then try to steer the conversation in a different direction. Charlotte and Rebecca let me, but both of them are giving me suspicious looks, and I don't think I've fooled them. They've known me for too long. I'm guessing they've decided, by an unspoken agreement, to wait until I'm ready to tell them what's really bothering me. I'm glad I parked on the other side of the building, because if they saw that I'm driving Evan's car, they'd want to know why, and I can't think of a good excuse.

Now that I mentioned Jamie and thought of all the reasons why I've been so stressed lately, I feel the paranoia return. I shift uncomfortably, and the food I was enjoying a moment ago suddenly loses its appeal. I don't want to alarm the others, so I force the rest down, all the while feeling more and more as if I'm being watched. My skin is crawling, and I feel like a pair of menacing eyes is watching me, burning two holes into my back.

By the time the waitress comes to take our plates away, Charlotte and Rebecca are looking over their menus and trying to decide what to have for dessert. All the while, I'm getting more and more nervous. I know it's only a matter of time before the hiccups start. When that happens, both of my friends will realize something's wrong.

I mumble something about having the cheesecake and excuse myself to go to the restroom. I have to walk through the restaurant to use the facilities, and while I do, it feels like everyone, all the other patrons sitting in their own little clusters at their own tables, can see I'm in distress and are wondering what's wrong with me. Here and there I catch a glimpse of faces staring back at me, and they've taken on a threatening quality, eyes filled with loathing, staring at me as I hurry past. I'm fully aware that I'm losing it, imagining things, but I can't seem to help myself.

I push open the door of the restroom, and luckily it's empty. Leaning over the basin, I try to steady my breathing, trying to get my heart to stop thumping so loudly. I splash some cold water on my face, cup some in my hand and sip it. It seems to work to stave off the hiccups that were threatening me a moment ago. Looking at my damp face in the mirror, I barely recognize my reflection. I'm way too pale, and my eyes are staring back at me, large and frightened.

I take a few moments to just calm my nerves, knowing if I go back to the table in this state Charlotte and Rebecca will force me to admit what's been eating at me, and I can't bear the thought of dragging them into this. It's my problem to fix, not theirs. Sure, I didn't ask for it either, but like it or not, I'm involved. Finding out what Jamie suspected happened to Tony, there really wasn't ever a choice. I was going to help Jamie, regardless of what it cost me.

I walk back to the table, and the other two women look up questioningly as I arrive. "I think I'm coming down with something. Don't think I can eat that."

Rebecca nods. "You do look a little unwell. Don't go back to the office. Go home and take it easy. I'll swing by your place later to check in on you."

After that, Charlotte and Rebecca realize that we should wrap the lunch date up. We give Charlotte our gifts, and she's delighted. Rebecca got her a silk Gucci scarf, and I got her two of Freida McFadden's latest mystery novels. Charlotte is thrilled, and I'm glad she likes her gift. I know how much she loves a good suspense novel, and by the ratings and reviews on Amazon, the two I gave her are supposed to be some of the best new releases in the genre.

We say our goodbyes just outside the restaurant. While I hug each of them, the feeling of being watched persists. I scan the street, looking for someone sitting in their car, watching my exchange with my friends. I don't see anyone like that or notice anyone paying more attention to us than is strictly necessary. Both Charlotte and Rebecca parked in front of the restaurant. I wave to them as they pull out of the parking spaces and melt easily into the traffic.

With my carefully wrapped-up box of cheesecake in hand, I start walking along the front of the building toward Evan's parked car. A dark-haired man coming from the opposite direction catches my eye. He's just sauntering up the road casually with his hands in his pockets. Our eyes meet, and I feel a weird sense of déjà vu that I dismiss almost as soon as it comes. We walk past each other, and the moment is gone.

As soon as I reach the side alley, the feeling of nervousness gears up a notch. The alley is deserted, and I'm supposed to walk through it to get to the other side. I look, and from the shadows a little bit down the alley, a strange man appears. He was leaning against one of the closed door-ways of the building, so I didn't notice him at first. Now, when he sees me, he steps forward a few steps. He doesn't say anything, just keeps on moving forward. It's his sudden appearance coupled with his silence that's freaking me out. There's no way I'm getting anywhere near that guy. Was he waiting for me, or is that just my imagination running wild again?

I turn around and head out of the alley, walking down the street so that I can stay visible to pedestrians and people walking past. Now I'll have to turn the corner way down the street and walk down that alleyway and all the way around to get to Evan's car.

I glance behind me, expecting the guy from the alley to be gone so I can feel like an idiot for being freaked out by him. What I see instead makes my blood freeze. The guy is approaching, walking fast. He's wearing jeans and a t-shirt. His face is nondescript—brown hair, brown eyes, no beard. What stands out most about him is his size. He's easily a head and a half taller than I am. From shoulder to shoulder, he is easily one and a half times wider than I am. The muscles of his enormous arms are flexing as he walks. He has this cold, determined expression on his face that reminds me eerily of The Terminator.

He's not running, but walking with purpose in my direction. I turn back around and walk even faster. I suppose I should be grabbing someone, telling them that the guy is following me, and asking for help. Or I should be calling the police myself. I don't want to do that for the very reasons why I haven't called the police sooner. What if whoever is behind this has some of the police officers in their pocket? What if this guy is just a normal guy, and not at all interested in me and my affairs? If I make a scene here on the street, it would be mortifying if it turned out to be nothing.

When I reach the end of the street, I have a choice: either continue running along this busier sidewalk, farther away from where I parked the car, or turn here down another alleyway and hope I can get to the car before the guy catches up with me. I already know that there's not much of a choice. I regret now being too busy these last few months to hit the gym as often as I should have. I'm not really unfit, but I've definitely let it slide for far too long, and I know I can't keep going like this indefinitely.

Just before I go down the alley, I look behind me again. The man with the cold eyes is still there, and he seems to have gained on me. It makes sense; his stride is much longer, and he seems to be in top physical condition. As I glance at him, our eyes lock, and he smiles. It's a shark-like grin, one of a predator enjoying the hunt. My stomach clenches in a painful knot. There's no doubt that he is really chasing me. He's determined to catch me, and when he does, there's no telling what he's going to do to me. All I know is it's sure to be unpleasant, and maybe even painful.

I see him picking up speed, and that urges my own feet that for a moment had felt like they were frozen to the sidewalk. I turn the corner and run down the alley. I almost knock into another pedestrian as I do, bumping rudely into a teenager with earphones on. I don't even stop to apologize, and I hear the teenager shout angrily behind me. "Jeez, lady! Where's the fire, huh?!"

Now I'm passing overflowing and smelly dumpsters. I feel my feet slipping in something questionable, but I don't look down, and manage to keep my balance. I'm full-on running now, vaguely aware that the cheesecake, still in the box I'm carrying, has probably already turned to mush.

I almost reach the end of the alley. Just before I do, another person turns the corner. I see it's another man. He's African-American, tall and lanky. He holds his arms out and grabs me, my box of cheesecake flattening between us. For a second or two, I think this man may be my salvation. For one, he doesn't have the same cold, dead expression as the other one. Secondly, he seems to be comforting me.

"There now, what's all this then?" He pats me on the back, and doesn't seem to care about the cheesecake paste oozing out the box and onto his shirt.

"There's this guy. He was chasing me, and..." I stammer between gasps of air.

"That's okay. You're going to be okay, Lacy. Just tell us what we want to know, and you won't be hurt."

I look up at him, horrified to hear that this stranger knows my name. The realization hits that the two men are working together to corner me. Before I can say anything or react in any way, I'm grabbed from behind, roughly turned around, and pushed against the wall. I stare straight up into the face of the first guy. His face is flushed, either from chasing me or from anger. It's difficult to tell, but I'm guessing it's a combination of both.

I feel something cold press up against my flushed skin, and think I know what it is. He's holding a knife to my throat.

"The file. Where is it? Did you send it to anyone?"

I bite the inside of my cheek to keep myself from giving him a sarcastic reply. This is not the time for clever comebacks.

"We know you know what we're talking about, so don't insult our intelligence by lying about it." This from the other guy, who may be the scarier one because of the fact that he sounds so reasonable, calm, and collected.

I glance at him and see that he has a gun in his hand. He's not pointing it at anything, but the intent is clear. He wants me to see it.

"It's sort of difficult not to insult the intelligence of you two goons," I hear another voice speak, just before I see a third man appearing from the alleyway right behind the tall and lanky guy. Before he can react, there's a blur of movement as he grabs the guy's clothing and throws him sideways. The guy with the gun hits his head hard against the wall and goes down in a crumpled heap, unconscious.

I see that the third man who appeared seemingly from nowhere has short dark hair and is wearing a dark blue shirt. I feel a strange feeling wash over me as I realize it's the guy I casually passed before all this started. He retrieves the gun and then turns to me and the other guy, who are watching this development with our mouths hanging open.

I know this guy! I walked past him and almost recognized him, but dismissed it as part of the paranoia I was experiencing. Now that I'm seeing him again, I suddenly realize where I know him from.

"Marcus?" I ask, flabbergasted at seeing my ex-boyfriend again for the first time in years, and under such strange circumstances.

"Hey, Lacy." He grins. "Okay if we catch up later? I still need to kick hunk-of-stupid over there's ass."

The guy with the knife at my throat pushes away from me with a growl, angered by the insult. "What did you call me?"

Marcus points the gun at him. "I called you stupid. Now, step away from the lady and put the knife down on the ground. Easy does it."

I'm amazed when the guy does as he's told. He looks at Marcus furiously. He's clenching his teeth, a little vein pulsing in the side of his temple. "You have no idea who you're messing with. The guy who sent us is not the sort of guy you want to get angry."

"Yeah, yeah," Marcus says, sounding bored by the whole exchange already. "Go pick up your friend, and the two of you get out of here!"

He points the gun at the guy until he does as he's told. Marcus and I look on as guy number one picks up guy number two, who gives a groan, holding his bloody head in his hands as he leans on his friend for assistance.

Only when they've disappeared around the corner does Marcus turn back to me. He gives a shaky little laugh. "Thank God I was in the right place at the right time, huh?"

THE PAST SLEEPS UNEASILY

MARCUS

*G*rin at Lacy, noting the look of bewilderment etched in every line of her beautiful face. Can't say I blame her for looking this surprised. It's been years since we've seen each other. I'll bet the last thing she expected when she woke up this morning was to be saved by her ex-boyfriend from two thugs chasing her down the street.

I feel my smile fade from my face and my eyes widen when I look down and see her white silk blouse covered with a splotch of red. *God, if those idiots hurt her...*

She sees my gaze turn to worry, and shakes her head with a laugh. "It's only raspberry sauce. I was carrying cheesecake when that... that jerk pressed me against the wall."

I hardly pay attention to this as I step forward to give her a once-over. Wiping away cheesecake from her throat, I see she's not completely unharmed after all. There's a shallow cut on her throat from where the knife broke through the skin. Probably when I surprised the bigger of the two guys by appearing the way I did. Still, there's no excuse, and for

LETHAL LIAISON: THE LACY LANGFORD CHRONICLES

a second or two I want to chase them both down and make them suffer for hurting her.

As my fingertips brush over the cut, Lacy sucks in a sharp breath through her teeth. "Ow!" she says, and looks up at me accusingly.

"Not unharmed after all," I remark drily. "You'll have to get that cleaned up as soon as possible."

As I say this and she looks up at me with those remarkable blue eyes of hers, the moment between us seems to screech to a sudden halt as memories, bittersweet and vivid, wash over me.

I'm transported back in time to a little coffee shop in downtown Washington, where a waitress puts a hot chocolate down in front of me.

"I didn't order this," I tell the tired-looking, frazzled older lady. I'm already anticipating an argument from her, insisting that I'm mistaken.

"That's mine," a pleasant, friendly female voice pipes up from another table to my right. I glance over and see two eyes peeking out from underneath a lumpy blue knit beanie. The eyes belong to a very pretty woman, and for a moment I'm speechless, taken aback by the contrast between her olive skin, chestnut brown hair, still dusted with melting snowflakes, and arresting blue eyes. They shine with intelligence and good humor. Sure enough, the black coffee I ordered was placed in front of the young woman instead. As we exchange drinks, our fingers brush, and I feel something pass between us, an undercurrent of attraction that I've never felt this strongly before. I look into her eyes again, and by the "O" of surprise her perfect full lips are forming, I know she felt it too. Talk about a serendipitous meeting—I thought these kinds of things only happen in movies.

The waitress apologizes, and I wave it away. I'm secretly wishing she'll leave so I can find my voice and talk to the pretty young woman. The waitress obliges, and the young woman turns to me.

She introduces herself as Lacy Langford, and before long, we are chatting up a storm. I ask her about the thick textbook she seems to be reading at her table, and I'm pleasantly surprised when she shows me the title. It's a psychology textbook, and she tells me she finished her Master of Arts in Mental Health Counseling at George Washington University only a few months before. She's planning on opening her own business soon, and as the minutes rush by, I'm more and more taken with Miss Langford.

Psychology is something I myself have always been very interested in, both in a personal capacity and because understanding how the human mind works can help me in my chosen career.

As undeniably beautiful as Lacy is, I soon find out that I can listen to her talk for hours. She's endlessly fascinating, self-confident, direct, and endearingly straightforward. There doesn't seem to be the slightest trace of duplicitousness about her, and I find that... refreshing.

I move my stuff over to her table, and we talk the afternoon away. We end up having lunch there and agree that it's surprisingly good, especially considering the establishment isn't one of the best or most well-known in D.C.

That's how I met Lacy. Our coffee dates became a regular occurrence, even though I knew it couldn't go anywhere. Not in the long run. I kept that front and foremost in my mind, or tried to. We ended up dating for eight glorious months. The sex was spectacular, but it was more than that. Lacy had a way of getting under my skin, of making me lower my defenses and letting her get closer than anyone has before or since.

She confided in me about how losing her father when she was young still hurts. He was a detective. Lacy and her mom became much closer after his death, since she was a daddy's girl and her mother was one of those teachers who took their job to mean taking care of the whole community.

In turn, I confided in her about how being raised by a career Army Officer for a father and a nurse for a mother meant that discipline and service was engrained into me from a very young age. I told her how moving around so much for my father's job made me resilient and adaptable, but also detached, since forming lasting friendships was never really a realistic option.

Looking at her, I remember afternoons at the coffee shop, and spending lazy days in bed talking about everything: philosophy, morality, what a successful life looks like to each of us. It was a relationship that was both passionate and meaningful. I know I broke her heart when I ended it abruptly and left town soon after. I couldn't even confide in her that I had been assigned overseas, and made it sound instead like it was just a regular job opportunity that was necessitating the move.

At the time, Lacy thought I had moved to London. In reality, I spent the next two years in Afghanistan. Then it was parts of Europe, the Middle East, India, and Africa. I only moved back to the states a year ago. I still remember the look of hurt in Lacy's eyes when I told her we needed to break up since I wasn't going to put us through the grueling emotional turmoil of trying a long-distance relationship that would only end up failing anyway. It didn't feel good lying to her or breaking her heart back then, and it doesn't feel good now either as I see her regarding me warily, like I'm a stranger.

"Come, I'll walk you to your car." I let go of Lacy then. She accepts my offer without argument, which shows me more than anything else that she's still freaked out by the attack.

We walk to her car in silence, and I wonder what she's thinking about, if she's also struggling not to relive the past like I am. Being near her, I find myself longing to draw her closer. It's a temptation I resist all the way back to where she parked her car behind the restaurant. Looking at the Jeep, it hardly seems like Lacy's style, but I remind myself that I haven't known her for many years, and in that time she could have changed drastically.

When she tries to unlock the car, her hand shakes so much that she drops the keys. I bend down to pick them up. When I stand up, Lacy has her hand to her forehead and is swaying dangerously on her feet. I reach out and grab her, steadying her on the side of the car while I unlock the passenger door.

"Looks like I'm driving you home. I think you're in shock." She nods, and again I'm struck by how easily she agrees. This is not the stubbornly independent Lacy I remember. I open the door and help her into the passenger seat. Then I walk around the car and open the door on the driver's side.

I glance over at her once I've started the car and we're ready to go. "Don't pass out, okay? I've got no idea where you live these days."

She gives a shaky laugh, and then says, "Dupont Circle."

I give a low whistle. "Business must be good."

"Yeah, how about you?" she asks carefully. I know she's wondering why I'm here, how I just showed up out of the blue, in the right place at the right time to save her.

"No, I don't live in Dupont Circle." She rolls her eyes at my bad joke, but doesn't smile. Then she opens her handbag in her lap. Taking out her cellphone, she starts typing a message to someone. I can't see the name at the top of the screen without leaning over and making it obvious that I'm trying to snoop. Hmm, boyfriend or girlfriend maybe? That would complicate this situation unnecessarily. It could be her mom. I remember Lacy and her mom being very close. I assume that's still the case.

While we were dating, Lacy took me to visit her mom in Mount Union once. That's when I knew that things were becoming too serious between us. She wasn't the kind of person to take just any old boyfriend to meet mom. I knew then that I should break up with her. I just couldn't find the words to do it. I was the one who actually asked to be assigned somewhere far away. I remember telling my supervisor that I didn't care where, as long as the assignment was overseas. Only then did I find the courage to break her heart.

Now here I am, back in the lion's den, it seems. It would be interesting to see this time around if I can resist Lacy's unique charms. Every minute in her company is proving to be a slow, drawn-out torture. She's always been uniquely dangerous for someone like me.

Lacy's never really known her own power. Her uncanny insight into human nature, to sense a person's motivations... No, she's always been a very interesting woman, and by being in her company now, I think the years have done nothing to dull those instincts. Instead, they only sharpened them.

As soon as she puts her cellphone away, I lay on the charm, playing the part of the worried ex-boyfriend. It's not all an act. I really am worried about her. She's clearly been through a lot. I can tell by the sickly pallor of her usually vibrant skin and how drawn she's looking that she's probably been skipping way too many meals, been getting way too little sleep.

We chat a bit about trivialities, and she tells me about her work as a relationship advisor, about the sort of clients she sees. It's very interesting, and good seeing her talk about something that she's so passionate about. She's always been good at reading people.

When we step into her apartment for the first time, I feel like I'm in more familiar territory. Her personality is littered around the very chic and stylishly decorated place. Obviously she hasn't changed that much, and I'm glad.

She excuses herself to change out of her dirty clothes and tells me to make myself at home. I take her up on the offer, pouring each of us a stiff drink. "Where's your first aid kit?" I call to Lacy. I hear her say something about the kitchen drawer, and I find it in a cluttered space underneath the kitchen sink just as she reappears, now cleanly dressed in a t-shirt and shorts.

I hand her her drink and make her sit across from me in the living room as I investigate the contents of the first aid kit. I find Band-Aids, cotton swabs, and an antiseptic ointment. After getting a bowl of warm water from the kitchen, I gently clean up the wound on her neck. As my hands are working, I can't help but be fully aware of her closeness. Her floral scent, achingly familiar, brings up a whole slew of memories from the past.

She tries making some small talk, and I can see by her pulse beating in a little flutter at her throat that my close proximity is making her nervous.

"What do you do for a living these days?" she asks. I've just placed a Band-Aid on her wound and move to adjust her head so I can apply another one. I grab her chin in my fingers and look into her eyes. We are suddenly frozen in place as I stare into the blue depths that have always made me feel like I'm looking at an ocean outside of reality or time.

I have no idea what would have happened next, but the front door of her apartment bursts open, and a man comes walking into the living room. "Lacy? Lace? Are you okay? I got your message and—"

He stops short when he sees us sitting across from each other. Lacy turned her head as soon as she heard the front door open, but my hand is still on her throat. She stares at this tall, broad-shouldered guy with shock, and then stands up abruptly.

"Evan! Thank God you're here."

I watch as she steps into this guy's—*Evan's*—arms. He folds her into a hug and looks at me over the top of Lacy's head. We give each other a knowing look, and in his expression I can see the typical hostility of a self-assured man when the woman he loves is being hit on by someone who may be a threat.

Lacy pulls away from him and gestures to me. "Marcus was there to fight off the guys that attacked me. He drove me home because I was in such a state."

Evan looks over at the two glasses of whiskey and ice, reliving the moment he entered the room and the intimate situation he found us in. "Lucky," he remarks, and the single word is tinged with sarcasm. Looking at Lacy, he asks, "Do the two of you know each other?"

"Well, yes... we—" Lacy starts stammering a reply, but I interject before she can downplay our history to make her boyfriend feel less threatened by this situation.

"Yeah, we dated for a year. We're good friends, and Lacy knows I'll always take care of her."

Lacy frowns at what I said, and I enjoy how uncomfortable this revelation is obviously making Evan.

"We dated for eight months years ago, and I haven't seen him in years. He was just at the right place at the right time today."

I know then it's time to make my exit. I tell Lacy that I'm going to get a cab and that I'll see her real soon. I make a point of kissing her on the cheek, and enjoy the look of fury on her boyfriend's face, knowing if he said anything he'd come off as a jerk.

I hold my hand out to him, and we shake, sizing each other up. The tension in the room is so thick it can be cut with a knife. Just before I step out of the apartment, I look back at them. Lacy's boyfriend is once more holding her close. It's an intimate moment, and I feel a stab of jealousy watching them.

Just before getting into the cab, I glance up at where I suspect Lacy's apartment is. Giving a longing sigh, I tear my eyes away and tell the cab driver where I want to go.

KILL ON SIGHT

LACY

"Stupid damn machine!" I try to yank the paper out from the gaping maw of the printer, and my impatience is rewarded with the piece of paper tearing off in my hand, giving me a stinging paper cut.

Cursing loudly, I slap the top of the printer in frustration, and now my hand is aching even more. I sit down in my office chair and want to take a sip of coffee, but realize I've left it sitting on my desk for too long, and it's now ice cold.

Grimacing, I go to the kitchen to make myself a fresh cup, only for the red top I'm wearing to get stuck on the handle of my office door as I pass it. I feel it tear as I yank it, and then the cold coffee spills over my skirt and shoes. Dammit! I should have just stayed in bed this morning! It's just one of those days where nothing seems to be going my way.

A few minutes later, as I'm standing in the kitchen scrubbing at the coffee stain on my skirt and voicing a few colorful curse words, I hear someone clear their throat behind me, and I nearly jump a foot into the air.

It's only Evan, though, standing in the kitchen doorway. "Am I interrupting, Lace?" He manages to suppress his smile, but I can still see it dancing in his eyes. On any other day, I may have seen the hilarity in the situation. All I can think of now is that it could have been anyone, including those guys from yesterday who would have hurt me, perhaps even killed me.

This morning, I had ever so briefly contemplated just staying at home. I had no appointments and could have used the day to do further digging on the file, but the truth is, I'm scared of what I'm going to find if I do. The attack really brought home the danger I'm facing in a horrible way that was all too real.

Then there was the whole scene with Marcus and Evan in my apartment. After Marcus left, I tried to explain to Evan that Marcus is just an ex-boyfriend and that running into him was purely coincidence, but he didn't seem to believe me. Did I even believe it myself? I played the events over and over again in my mind, and the timing just seems too perfect. Him being there right on time to save me. And the way he disarmed those guys so expertly. It was... intense. Like something you see in an action movie. I flush when I think of it, and then push the thought away, a little disgusted at myself. Evan is standing right here, looking at me with his whole heart written on the worried, tender expression on his face.

"How... how did you get in?" I ask. I can't help the suspicious note in my voice.

"Door was unlocked. You didn't answer your phone, so I figured you would be here, especially with Jamie being... " He sees the expression of panic on my face and frowns. "Not here." He shakes his head. "Are you going to tell me what the hell is going on? I didn't want to push you, but after yesterday, with those guys attacking you and Mister Superhero arriving the way he did... and now you nearly jumping out of your skin when I mention Jamie."

I'm feeling so freaked out because Evan is the only other person who knows where Jamie is. If my office is bugged like my apartment is, then him blurting Jamie's location out would be dangerous for her and the boys. I haven't even told my mom yet that the cabin I bought for her is now occupied. I've used it more than she has and never need to ask permission, but still... at some point I'm going to have to tell her *something*.

How am I supposed to keep the people close to me who I care about safe and out of this? I need help. I'm in way over my head, and I don't have the expertise to do this alone. My shoulders sag, feeling the heavy burden of the secret of the file I've been carrying around with me. Suddenly I can't stand it anymore, to be so desperately alone in all of this. I open my mouth, about to tell Evan everything, when he interrupts me.

"I don't want you seeing him again. That guy Marcus. I don't trust him. The way he looks at you, it's clear that he wants you." He rakes his hand through his hair. "Can you at least promise me that you won't be seeing him again?"

I feel my body stiffen, my eyes narrow, my cheeks flush. Is this the real reason why he came over? Not to check on me because he's worried about my safety, but to check up on me because he's feeling insecure? It's much too dog-protecting-his-bone-from-rival-dog for me, and the first time that Evan ever displayed possessiveness. I never cared for the idea of someone seeing me as their property. In fact, I hate it, and every inch of me is screaming at him for thinking he can choose who I'm allowed to have contact with.

"Well, do you trust me?" I ask him in a high-pitched voice that should have been his first clue that this conversation's not going the way he wants it to go.

He looks at me and splays his hands out, palms up. "Come on, seriously? You're going to play the trust card now, after the way you've been acting lately?"

"Get out," I whisper. He steps forward, perhaps to try and repair what is so obviously breaking down between us. Not broken yet, but showing definite cracks. I don't want him to touch me, and I turn away. "Get out of here! You don't dare tell me who I'm allowed to be friends with! That's not how it works between us!"

"Yeah? Well maybe the way it's been working between us is no longer working for me!"

I recoil as if slapped. I'm not ready to have that conversation with him. Not now, not with everything else coming down on me. I turn around, arms hugging myself. I'm about to cry. I can feel the tears threatening to come. Whether from anger or sadness, I don't know. Maybe both.

Evan steps up behind me and puts his arms around me. He kisses my neck, and I feel some of my anger evaporate, turning into lust.

"I'm sorry. Things have been so weird lately." His lips are moving on my neck as he says this. I shiver a little at the feeling of his mouth on the tender skin. It feels so manipulative on his part to be doing this now, while I'm not okay, while I'm still reeling from the turn this conversation took.

I untangle myself from his arms and move away. Looking over my shoulder at him, I say coldly, "I really need you to leave. I still have a ton to do here. As you pointed out, Jamie isn't here, and I need to work. I'm going to be working tonight too."

I see Evan's face fall; we had plans tonight to go and watch a show at the Kennedy Center and have dinner afterward, but I can't imagine facing it with everything else that's been going on. Especially not after what Evan just said. I need some time to myself to process this.

Evan leaves soon after, and I lock the door behind him. Back behind my desk, I try to lose myself in my work, but find it impossible, because now my stomach is churning with guilt and I feel terrible recalling the look on Evan's face. Was I too harsh? Was it really so unreasonable of him to be suspicious of Marcus appearing in my life again after all these years?

The thoughts are tumbling over each other in my mind: Marcus, Evan, the file, Jamie and her kids, the attack of yesterday, Senator Albright. I stand up abruptly, agitated, and pack up my stuff. Then I grab my keys and head to my car. Just before getting in, I stop to scan the parking lot and the busy street in front of my office building. There's a few cars parked close to mine, a few pedestrians walking casually past wearing business suits and drinking from Styrofoam cups or water bottles, or taking bites of their on-the-go lunches. Nobody seems to be paying special attention to me, but I still feel that creepy, tingly feeling on my skin, as if I'm being watched. It's the same feeling I had the day before. Knowing the safest thing for me to do is to get out of here, I get in my car, making sure to lock all the doors before driving home.

In my home office a few minutes later, I'm once more holding the device that I'm certain is used to detect listening devices. I turn it over in my hands, looking for an on switch. I don't see one, and still can't figure out how the darn thing works! Google isn't much help either, and I realize that I need the model number of this device, or at least need to know who manufactured it, to get user instructions off the internet. This one doesn't seem to be on there, though. I give up and place it back in its box on my desk.

Next, I sit behind my laptop and open the file on my computer. Here and there are bits of information that Jamie helped to decode, and now I can read it easily. It's a lot, and most of it is still a jumbled mess. There are a few more names that seem familiar, and when I do a Google search on them, they're revealed to be the names of influential business people or politicians. All of these people have been linked to controversies or scandals in the past.

Just like Senator Albright was.

One of the names in the file, that of an influential entrepreneur and multimillion dollar business mogul, is connected to a sex scandal, while another prominent figure, a daytime television host who is exceedingly popular with frustrated housewives, is linked to a sexual harassment lawsuit from one of her ex-employees. Both stories were all over the internet when they first broke.

Some of the names don't reveal more information when searched for, and I'm guessing these are aliases meant to hide the identity of whoever they are referring to. These people seem to have gone to great lengths to cover up the information, so that even if it's deciphered, the person reading the file wouldn't be able to put the whole picture together.

One thing becomes clear: The name "Senator Albright" isn't only in reference to one person, but seems to be connected to several of the names in the file, including those that are obvious aliases. It looks like Senator Albright's name has become code for a specific sort of operation, one that all these people are involved in or linked to in some way. Interesting.

I notice now how some sections of the file are marked with red flags to underline their importance. I feel my eyes widen seeing that certain words that seem to be directives on how to deal with these individuals are flagged for importance. My heart rate is climbing as one of these directives jumps out at me: *Kill on Sight.* What the hell?

"Hic!" Oh no! Not my damn hiccups again! "Hic!" As I feel my diaphragm contort painfully with each hiccup, I try to calm my racing heart, try to regulate my breathing. *Maybe it's code for something?* I think desperately, but a part of me knows better. The truth of this cannot be denied. "Kill on sight" is not some euphemism—it's meant literally. This conspiracy that probably got Tony killed, not to mention Nathan Shepard and his whole family, is just as dangerous and urgent as I feared. I can't deny it anymore, not even to myself. Why else would these people go to such great lengths to try and cover it up?

"Hic! Hic!" My hiccups are only getting worse. I sound like a farting mouse. Pushing my office chair back so fast and violently that it hits against the back wall, I practically run to the kitchen for a glass of water. I need to stifle these hiccups now! I can feel them making me nauseous.

I get a glass from the kitchen cupboard mechanically. My hands feel cold and detached from my body. In fact, my whole body feels like I'm a moving mannequin. Just before I can fill the glass of water from the tap, there's a loud knocking at my front door. I jump, and the glass falls and shatters in the kitchen sink. I can feel my eyes trying to bug out from my skull.

I walk up to the front door. I look through the peephole, but there doesn't seem to be anybody there. "Hic!" I clap my hand over my mouth, but it's too late. The hiccups are so loud, there's no way the person on the other side of the door didn't hear. Why are they avoiding the peephole? Because they don't want me to see who it is, that's why.

I barely finish the thought when the person on the other side of the door, my surprise guest, moves, and I'm looking straight into Marcus's ruggedly handsome face. "Lacy? It's Marcus! Are you okay?"

Seeing Marcus twice in 24 hours after I haven't seen him in *years*? My mouth is hanging open. I have no idea what to tell him to make him go away. "Uhm, yeah—hic—Everything is fine—hic—Now is just not a great time for me! Hic!"

"I can hear your hiccups through the door! Something sure as hell is up with you. Or did you forget I know all about your hiccups? I remember them only showing up when you were extremely stressed or agitated. After what happened yesterday, I think we need to talk."

God! How can he sound so concerned and so damn smug all at the same time?

A flood of memories wash over me. Yesterday I suppressed them because I hadn't thought of Marcus Grayson in years. I guess I hadn't allowed myself to think of him. That's because he broke my heart, not because he was in any way easily forgettable. We dated for so long, and things were going so well... At one stage, I even allowed myself to think a marriage proposal was in the making.

Then he told me he had been offered a job overseas. The fact that he had even been looking, knowing if he got it things would be over between us, had hurt more than I would have thought possible. Then it was *sayonara! See you never again!* just like that. Now here he is, right at my front door, and I have no idea if I should leave him out there or let him come inside.

CROSSED BOUNDARIES

LACY

*O*pening the door and seeing Marcus standing there, it's the same as yesterday. That same bewildering feeling of unreality washes over me, because on the one hand I recognize him, but on the other, it's like looking at a stranger.

"Hic!" I squeak, and Marcus grins.

"Well, hello to you too."

I turn around and walk back to the kitchen. He follows me after closing and locking the front door. I get another glass and fill it with water from the tap, then take a tentative sip. My stomach is still feeling stretched from the water I already drank, and queasy from the hiccups.

Marcus is watching all of this carefully, quietly. Now he steps forward, grabs me by the shoulders, and forces me to turn around and face him. I'd forgotten how forceful he can be. It's not an altogether unattractive trait, but it makes me flush with irritation now.

"Are we going to talk about what happened yesterday? What the hell have you got yourself involved in, Lace?"

Stepping away from him, I shake my head and put a finger over my mouth. Marcus looks at me quizzically, obviously not understanding what I'm trying to tell him. I motion for him to follow me to my office. There, I take out the package that was sent to me, the box containing what I still suspect is a listening device detector, and show him the note I received.

He reads the note and then picks the device up. Turning it over in his hands, he does a twisty motion with the thing, and now suddenly there's a green light flickering on the device. "How did you..." I begin to ask, but now Marcus is the one shaking his head and telling me to be quiet. My mouth clicks shut with a snap. Being ordered to shut up in my own house by this walking, talking suit of trouble?!

He takes the device and starts sweeping with it randomly around my office. Now it reminds me of those metal detector wands that they use at the airport to look for concealed weapons.

As he moves the wand around, quietly working, I have a moment to silently appraise Marcus. The feeling of nostalgia, a surprising mix of bittersweet memories, washes over me.

He's always been a striking figure. Not as tall as Evan or some of the other men I've loved over the years, but his athletic build and wide shoulders make him memorable. The dark brown wavy hair is achingly familiar. I remember how I used to drag my fingers through it when he lay with his head on my chest. I notice something new: strands of gray in his hair and laugh lines around his eyes and around his mouth. That wasn't there while we were dating. I wonder for a moment what changes he picked up on yesterday when he laid eyes on me for the first time in more than eight years.

He has strong facial features, and obviously takes pride in his appearance. He seems so well put-together, even in jeans and a t-shirt. I've always had a weakness for a well-dressed man. Marcus is what people mean when they say a man is ruggedly handsome. The way he dresses, the way he moves, precise and feline like a tiger, is a holdover from Washington State Military Academy, which his father insisted on him attending instead of a regular high school. Marcus's dad was career army, and the family moving around so much made it difficult for him to make friends and get close to people.

I remember the eight months we dated as being passionate, exciting, and tumultuous, especially when it ended so abruptly. We fought often, both of our stubborn, headstrong personalities bumping up against each other's... but the make-up sex was fantastic.

It took me more than a year after it ended to realize that in the course of our relationship, I shared so much with him about who I was, who my family was, my hopes and dreams. He didn't share that much with me about himself, only the things I managed to drag out of him. He was always a source of mystery, an enigma, and I guess that was at least half the appeal. That sort of thing can be both exciting and very harmful. It appeals more to a younger person, and I'm not in my early 20s anymore.

As if hearing my thoughts, Marcus looks up at me, and I blush because he just caught me staring. He is more concerned with the device in his hands, though, and points down at it, where the flickering green light is now a steady red. There is a scratchy, high-pitched beeping sound coming from the device. I guess Marcus found one of the listening devices that the note hinted at. He digs around in the soil in the potted plant that sits on my desk and pulls out what appears to be a tiny button that was buried in the top layer of soil. I watch as Marcus reaches out and plonks this bug in the glass of water, turning it brown.

Now my attention is fully focused on the task at hand, and Marcus sweeps over every inch of my office. He manages to find three more bugs, and destroys each of them by drowning them in the water. It takes about an hour, and by the end of it, I breathe a sigh of relief and my hiccups have finally subsided again.

"Come on," he says to me. "Let's go for a walk."

I nod and unplug my laptop. I don't want to leave it here and risk it getting stolen. Marcus watches this with a grim expression on his face, and then leads me out of my apartment to the little park in the center of Dupont Circle that basically gave this little residential area its name. There's a beautiful fountain with benches around it. We sit here for a moment, and I turn my face up to the sunshine, just savoring the feel of the afternoon sun on my skin.

When I look back at Marcus, he is staring at me with the strangest expression on his face. Is it... longing? I shift uncomfortably, and he looks away.

"Please tell me what's going on, Lacy," he says, his voice almost pleading. "I can't help you if you don't let me in."

I look at him and fold my arms protectively over my chest. It's the body language of closing up, not opening up to someone, and I see Marcus's face as he takes note of it. Good! He should realize that I'm not to be pushed around like he often tried doing to me eight years ago. I didn't fall for it then, and I sure as hell won't fall for it this time, either!

"First tell me the truth. How did you disarm those guys so quickly yesterday? How did you know where I'd be? Don't tell me it was just a coincidence, because I don't believe that for a second. You want me to trust you with the truth? Fine! You first."

Then I wait, watching to see how he'll react.

He turns to me and puts his arm on the back of the bench we're sitting on. "I don't work for any outfit you'd recognize. I'm a private security contractor, and my client tasked me to uncover suspicious activities connected to some high-ranking officials and business people. There's some sort of conspiracy underway, and I've been tasked by my client, who is an important man himself, to find out what it is. Why he's being targeted, and by whom."

"Who is your client?" I ask, very intrigued now.

Marcus glances around to make sure that there's no one within hearing distance of us. He leans closer, and I can smell his aftershave, feel his body heat. I can feel his closeness, as if it's invisible waves that he's sending out. "Senator Thomas Albright."

The name has the same effect on me that a cup of cold water down my back would have had. Marcus sees this and puts his hand between my shoulder blades, gently rubbing the spot over my shirt with his fingertips. It's a familiar gesture, one that harkens back to a simpler time, and it calms me down. Marcus is still sitting close to me.

"I see you've heard of him." His voice is lower, and I feel a little like I'm being hypnotized.

I nod, and mention what I read about the senator being involved in illegal arms deals.

"He was set up," Marcus says.

I nod, but it's getting increasingly difficult for me to think. The feel of his thumb moving in slow circles between my shoulder blades, the familiar

scent of him filling my senses, the sound of his voice, husky and soothing...
We are cheek to cheek now. I can feel the sandpapery texture of his cheek
against mine, feel the heat of his closeness, the pull of him like a tide. All I
need to do is to turn my face toward him and we'll be kissing. I can already
imagine the feel of his lips on mine. My mouth is dry, my heart is beating
fast, and I'm sure he must be able to hear it going *thud... thud... thud...*

That's when Evan's face flashes in my mind. Kind, sweet, handsome,
and quietly strong Evan, who has always made me feel safe and never
leaves me to wonder what he's feeling and where his loyalties lie.

Reality abruptly reasserts itself, and I move away from Marcus. I feel
a pang of terrible guilt. It seems like Evan was right to be worried about
Marcus. What the hell was I thinking? Getting involved with him would
be the worst possible idea, not least of all because I already have a
boyfriend, and cheating is not my thing.

Marcus gives a shaky sigh. "I'm sorry. It's just, seeing you like this
again... it's not exactly easy." I nod, but don't say anything. I don't trust
my voice yet. "That guy from yesterday... Evan? Is he... are things serious
between the two of you?"

I bite my lip. Are things serious between me and Evan? Do I want it
to be more serious between us than it is now? "It's serious enough that I
wouldn't feel comfortable being with anyone else." I cringe a little inter-
nally at the painfully tactful way I managed to answer his question.

Marcus gives a crooked grin, but turns away from me and places his
hands on his lap. "So now it's your turn to tell me how in the world you
got involved in all of this."

I tell Marcus about finding the file on my home security system and
accidentally downloading it onto my laptop. I tell him that it's still
partly encrypted, but give him a brief overview of what I found out,
leaving any mention of Jamie and her husband out of it.

I open my laptop bag and take it out, then show Marcus the file and
the locations I was able to extract from it.

"So you think these marked locations are sites of actual operations?"
Marcus asks. Now that it's all business between us, it's easier to focus on
what's important.

"Yeah, I want to go to one of them and see what I can find out, but

I've been scared to, because what if I run into an actual illegal operation?" In my mind's eye, I see guys with guns and black clothing patrolling a warehouse. "I have no idea what I'm doing. I don't really know where to start."

Marcus looks over the addresses. "Well, let's go in my car and see what we can see. This one location is practically around the corner from here."

"What? Do you want to go now?"

Marcus seems to reconsider. "How about tomorrow? I'll meet you here at eight in the morning. I need to get surveillance equipment of my own that we can use for gathering evidence if we do manage to stumble onto something."

"Okay, can we go to that one first?" I point to one of the addresses. It's at a shipping yard an hour's drive from here.

"Why that one?" Marcus asks suspiciously. "It's farther away than some of the others on the list."

I shake my head. "It's just a feeling I have." I try not to shift uncomfortably underneath Marcus's searching gaze.

He shrugs as if it doesn't really matter. He walks me back to my place afterward, and when we get there, I see Evan's car parked in front of the gate at my apartment building. As Marcus and I approach, Evan gets out of the car and looks over at us. He has his hands in his pockets, and his cheeks are flushed—not a good sign.

Marcus, either oblivious to Evan's anger or enjoying it, leans over and kisses me on the cheek. "I'll see you tomorrow. Eight a.m. sharp."

I see Evan's eyes pull into little slits, and turn to give Marcus a warning look. Why in God's name would Marcus go out of his way to make things difficult for me? He's definitely enjoying this.

When Marcus is gone, I turn back to Evan. My arms are folded over my chest.

"What's happening tomorrow?" Evan asks. I don't want to lie to him, but I don't want him involved and in danger either. Besides, I don't think he'd approve even if he knew what I'm doing. He'd freak out, tell me it's dangerous, and insist on calling the police. Every instinct is shouting at me what a terrible idea that would be.

Evan looks at me as I stay silent. "Seriously? You're going on a date with your ex-boyfriend and you don't even have the decency to tell me?"

He's beyond furious, and I know I can't blame him for feeling that way. He turns around to get back in his car, and I know I can't let him drive away like that. I grab his arm and tuck my hand into his. Tugging at his arm, my intention is clear: I want him to follow me into my apartment.

We walk upstairs and I close the door behind me, locking out the world. Evan is looking down at me quietly. I reach up and cradle his face in the palm of my hand. He leans into the touch wordlessly, but doesn't touch me back.

For a moment I see the uncertainty in Evan's eyes, the hurt and frustration. How can I possibly make it go away? I want to show him what I feel for him and only him. He is my sanctuary, the place where I feel safe. If anything, my few moments of weakness with Marcus when I almost gave in to nostalgia only underlined the fact that Evan is who I really want.

"It's not at all what you think. Marcus is just helping me with some issues that have to do with Jamie. It's not personal. Our relationship is strictly business."

I stand on tiptoe to kiss him. To underline what I just told him. Marcus isn't important—he is.

He folds his arms around me and kisses me back. There's a few moments where he's still reserved. It makes me wonder what happened to us. We weren't always like this.

Then the heat flares between us, the heat that for the last two years drew each of us in and kept us suspended in so many simmering moments. Evan picks me up and carries me to the bedroom.

As my orgasm washes over me, drowning me in tides of love for this man, there are no other thoughts but of him... of me... of us together. Here, in this moment, I am wonderfully whole.

SHIPPING YARD

LACY

Sunrise has only just crested the tops of the trees, and I'm pacing up and down in the little park in front of the fountain where Marcus and I agreed to meet. I'm shivering. From barely contained excitement or from the chilly morning air, I don't know. My sneakers are making sloshing sounds on the dew-wet grass.

I left Evan sleeping at my place. It was his first time ever sleeping over. It should have been an exciting milestone in our relationship, and I must admit, it was nice having his masculine presence next to me in the darkness of the night, when my worries and fears about today would have been at their peak. Having Evan there was a comfort to me. He made me feel safe, and he was something tangible to reach out to, to hold onto whenever I woke up from the jumble of confusing bad dreams.

I left him a note on my pillow telling him I'll call him later. We didn't speak about Marcus or what the two of us are planning to do today, and I'm glad. I don't want to lie to Evan anymore. Having him involved in this would be the most selfish thing I ever did to him, and I can't stand the idea of risking his life like that. Once that line is crossed, there's no turning back. If I tell him and it turns out it's too dangerous and he doesn't want to be involved, it would be too late. In this case, the cost of knowing the truth is being involved, and without knowing that beforehand... it seems unfair to blindside him like that.

I know Evan is feeling pushed away, betrayed, even. I make a promise to myself as I stand there in the early morning sunlight. When all this is over, I'll seriously examine my own feelings regarding Evan and where our relationship is headed. He may not like the conclusion I come up with, but it's time to be honest with myself and with him. For both our sakes, we can't just keep on dancing this dance without it leading anywhere.

Seeing Marcus's car pull up beside the little park, I'm pulled from my worries about Evan and feel the excited fluttering in the pit of my stomach increase tenfold. I tell myself it's because we're going to visit the locations on the map. That's the only reason I'm feeling excited, isn't it?

I get in the car, and Marcus hands me a dark blue duffel bag. He doesn't greet me, but immediately falls into conversation, as if we're continuing a chat we had a few minutes ago rather than seeing each other after a whole evening's gone by. It's one of Marcus's trademark strange little quirks, one that I forgot about until this moment.

"Here's some of the surveillance stuff I got, along with things we may need. I added two two-way radios there in case we get separated. I've turned the volume on them way down, so they won't make an unexpected noise at an inopportune moment."

In the bag I find the two-way radios, a pair of binoculars, and a very fancy camera. "What's this for?" I ask him, holding the camera out.

"To gather evidence in case we need to go to the police later." It seems so obvious that I feel stupid for even asking. Then again, I'm not used to any of this, and Marcus does seem to be a pro. Marcus told me he's private security for Senator Albright because after the arms deal scandal, the senator realized he was being targeted and that someone was out to get him.

Marcus already has the address of the shipping yard on the GPS. I try to settle in for the two-hour drive, but the silence stretches out between us. Now that we're alone together like this, I can't think of a single thing to say that wouldn't sound like prying. On the other hand, if I don't say anything, the nervousness is sure to overwhelm me. What if I start hiccupping again like an idiot? Then Marcus will know I'm nervous around him.

"So how was Lond—" I start, but Marcus starts talking at the same time.

"How did you and Ev—"

We look at each other, surprised, and start laughing. It breaks the ice between us, at least.

"Go ahead," I tell him. "You wanted to know how Evan and I met?"

Marcus nods. "I guess I want to know who my competition is for your affections." I have no idea if he's joking, only saying that to tease me, or if he's serious. There's a mischievous glint in his eyes that makes it impossible to tell what his true motivations are.

"You left me, remember?" I look out the window. I don't really want to talk about the past and go down memory lane with him. It seems like dangerous ground, full of pitfalls.

"I remember." He says this quietly, and I look at him again. He's watching the road and looking serious, maybe even regretful.

I shift, uncomfortable at the turn this conversation is taking. I tell him about the Halloween party where I met Evan, then naturally move the conversation away from Evan and tell Marcus about Charlotte and Gary, how we became friends.

He asks if I'm still friends with Rebecca. I tell him how she's been, then about my mom. After an hour and a half, I'm thirsty from talking so much. As I take a sip of water from one of the bottled waters that Marcus brought, I realize that he did the same thing to me again that he did all those years ago. He'd ask me questions and get me to talk about myself, about my life, my friends, things that are important to me. Then I'd lose sight of the fact that he isn't sharing anything about himself, not volunteering any information to allow me to get to know him better. It's a very neat trick.

I've had clients try doing it to me too, and I realize their underlying intent before I go down that road. It's always a subversive tactic, when a person doesn't want to tell you something, avoiding all conversation about themselves and making it seem like they are only interested in hearing about you. When most people do it, it's usually a subconscious thing. With Marcus, though, I'm not so sure.

I'm usually very good at steering the conversation in the direction that I want it to go. *Why is it different with Marcus?* This thought carries with it a definite note of chagrin.

"So, how about you?" I ask pointedly. "Any wives, ex-wives, or children?"

Marcus shifts uncomfortably. He shakes his head. "Nope, I never got married, and certainly don't have any children—that I know about." He smiles wickedly in my direction and I roll my eyes, making it obvious that I find this roguish, devil-may-care attitude silly rather than endearing.

"After you, I never found anyone that I even remotely wanted to get serious with, Lacy. I guess you were the one who got away." How is he able to be such a jackass one moment and so endearingly vulnerable in the next? He still has the ability to throw me completely off balance, leaving me unable to think of an appropriate response.

We reach the shipping yard where Tony worked for many years before his sudden disappearance months ago. "What the hell?" I ask sharply, because it seems that the shipping yard is empty.

Marcus turns to me. "You didn't expect them to stick around, did you? I mean, by now they know you're on to them."

Part of me did think that the shipping yard would still be operational, that there would be signs of human life. For them to have packed up shop like this scares me more in a way than finding men with guns patrolling the place would have.

We get out of the car, and Marcus takes the duffel bag with him. I have my own backpack slung across my shoulder. He bends down over his bag, unzips it. "Don't touch the fence," he says as he's rummaging inside it. "I want to make sure that there's no electric current running through it."

He takes out a device that I've never seen before and clamps it carefully to one end of the fence. Checking the gauge, he shrugs. "Seems to be okay. It makes me think this place is a bust, that we won't find anything here."

He glances down at me, at my hands, then takes a pair of black leather gloves out of the bag. "Here," he says, tossing them at me. "If we're going to be digging around, it's probably better not to leave fingerprints all over the place." I only notice now that he's wearing a similar pair. Feeling ill-equipped for this mission, I put the gloves on while Marcus takes a bolt cutter out of the bag and starts cutting away at the links in the fence next to one of the metal poles. He works carefully and quickly, and again I'm struck by how strange it is that he seems to be an expert at this. How often has he done this before? Do I know this man at all?

He bends back the fence, and I step through, then wait as he bends it back again so it won't be obvious that it's been tampered with.

Marcus turns around and leads the way deeper into the shipping yard. We crouch down as we run to the nearest stack of containers, just in case we were wrong and there is security around. Peeking behind the containers, I see a building made from metal sheeting rather than brick. It's one of those semi-permanent structures that's often set up at construction sites for the foremen and other personnel who need an office. I'm guessing it's these buildings that Jamie and the rest of the cleaning staff were tasked to clean when they were assigned to this place.

I'm about to approach the building, still crouched down, when Marcus suddenly pulls me back against him. He doesn't say anything, but points up, and now I spot a camera set up high against the building. We watch it silently for a moment. Then it moves with a soft whirring sound that we wouldn't have noticed if we hadn't been paying attention.

It seems that everything in the shipping yard hasn't been abandoned after all. The camera must be set to a timer. If there's one security camera, chances are good that there will be more.

"Do you have a mirror with you?" His lips are barely moving, but because he's still pressed up against me, I hear what he's asking and understand why he needs it. I lean away and look inside my backpack. I brought a few essentials, like a toothbrush and a comb, in case we end up spending the night somewhere. I find a little compact and hand it to Marcus silently.

Marcus opens the compact and points the mirror so it peeks just past the wall of the shipping container. This allows him to watch the camera and to time it so it doesn't spot us.

When the camera is pointed the farthest away from us, Marcus leads me to the other side of the containers, and then we make a run for it. We go around the side of the building, hugging the wall. Looking around, I don't spot any other cameras. My heart is beating furiously in my chest. It feels as if it's impossibly loud, drowning out all other sounds around me. There's another camera set just above the door. I suspect that directly underneath the door there's a blind spot where it won't be able to see us.

Marcus creeps ahead and tries the handle of the door, but of course it's locked. He takes a little pouch out of his jacket pocket and unzips it. I realize it's a lock picking kit. *Oh goodness, won't it take an awfully long time?* I think nervously, but it seems I underestimated Marcus once again, because the door swings open a moment later. The overhead camera is still moving along its trajectory back toward me. I make it just in time and follow Marcus inside the office. Only when the door is closed behind us do I breathe a sigh of relief. The office is dark, and we can't risk switching on the overhead lights.

I take my cellphone and find the flashlight function on it. I don't use it often because of how fast it drains my cellphone's battery, but at least I'll be able to find my way around. Marcus has a little pen flashlight that he switches on. The office we're in isn't huge. There's two desks facing each other, a huge, ancient copy machine in the corner of the room, a potted plant whose leaves I note are a lush green, and a filing cabinet.

Marcus immediately goes over to the filing cabinet, attempts to open it, and finds it locked. He proceeds to try and pick the filing cabinet's lock, but seems to struggle with it more than he had with the door lock.

While he's busy, I walk over to the potted plant. As I suspected, it's made of plastic, so its leaves being green isn't an indication of how much time has passed since there were people here. The office isn't dusty, and looks way too clean for the place to have been abandoned for long. I hear a click behind me. Marcus has the filing cabinet open and is pulling files out. Next, he takes the camera from his duffel bag and begins taking pictures.

"These ones seem to correspond with the dates you showed me," Marcus remarks. I wonder idly why he's taking pictures of the files rather than using the copy machine in the corner. Then I realize the copy machine will probably be noisier, and we don't even know if it works.

I leave him to take his pictures and make my way over to the two desks. The first thing I take note of is that the computers and phones that may have once been here were removed. Jamie never specified if Tony's boss had a laptop or a desktop computer. It doesn't really matter, because it's gone. I would have loved another bash at extracting more information from it, but obviously the guys running whatever secret and illegal operation this is weren't going to give anyone access to it a second time.

I open the first desk's drawer; there's nothing in there but a dried-out pen, a few random paper clips, and dust bunnies. The second desk's drawer is just as empty. Thinking that I better go and help Marcus take photos of the files with my cellphone camera, otherwise we're going to be here all day, I close the drawer, but frown when I hear something move and fall down behind the drawer to the back of the desks.

I look over at Marcus. He has his back to me, still very much engrossed with taking photos of the files.

I get down on my hands and knees on the floor under the desk to see what it is that fell down when I closed the drawer. There seems to be an envelope of some kind. I see tape stuck to it, and guess the envelope must have been stuck to the bottom of the drawer. I pick it up and feel something inside it, but I don't have time to see what I found. If it was important enough to hide, though...

Standing upright, I stick the envelope in the back of my jeans pocket and make sure my t-shirt is covering the bulge. I don't want Marcus to know what I found until I've seen it for myself.

Marcus is just finishing up. He puts the last of the files away and turns to me. "I have no idea if the pictures I took have useful information, but I think that's as lucky as we're going to get. We'd better get out of here. This place gives me the creeps."

CLOSE CALL

LACY

*A*fter sneaking out of the shipping yard just as carefully as we snuck in, I breathe a sigh of relief when we're in the car again. The whole operation took about an hour, and it's still early. My stomach growls, reminding me that I haven't had breakfast, and I can do with a cup of coffee.

We stop at a drive-through. As Marcus is turned away to give our order through the window, I'm tempted to move the envelope I found from my back pocket to my backpack. Sitting on it, I'm uncomfortably aware of its existence, and the curiosity is like a rodent scurrying across my mind, giving me a painful little nip every now and then. In the end, I don't dare take it out, aware that Marcus will want to know what I found if he sees it.

It feels ridiculous not to trust him. We are in this together, aren't we?

When he hands me the bag of food and coffee, our fingers brush, and I feel that same electric current of attraction pass between us.

Giving in to the feelings it invokes is too tempting, and I pull away, looking out of the window.

We end up eating in the parking lot of the fast food joint. Marcus goes through the list of places that were highlighted in the file. "Where next, Lace?" His color is high and his eyes are glittering. It doesn't take a genius to figure out that Marcus is really enjoying all this. I wonder if that's part of the reason why he went into private security in the first place—because of the promise of excitement. Maybe holding a regular job would have been way too boring for him. He seems like he needs the adrenaline rush.

I point to the address closest to the one we are at now. "This one," I say firmly. "Might as well try to get to as many of them as possible and work our way back home."

He nods his approval, looking at me speculatively. I can't begin to guess what he's thinking. We finish up our meal and our coffee. The food and caffeine makes me feel like I can at least face the rest of the day. As we pull out of the driveway, we mingle with the busy morning traffic. Most people are now on their way to work, so it's gotten a lot busier since we set out this morning.

I check my phone for messages, and sure enough, I have a few to go through. Evan's woken up and asked me where I went despite the note I left for him. I don't want to mention Marcus to him again, so I just tell him that I'm running a few errands and will call him later.

The message from Jamie isn't urgent. She's simply giving me an update on herself and the kids, saying that they're still fine and that she hopes to see me soon. Between the lines, I can read the question she doesn't dare voice: how far I've gotten with my investigation of the file. I tell her all is well and that I'll see her soon.

After catching up with my mom, Rebecca, and Charlotte, I look at my phone's battery and see that I have to charge it soon, otherwise it's going to go flat. That's when it hits me—did I even remember to pack my charger this morning? Shit! I begin digging frantically through my backpack.

"What's wrong?" Marcus asks, seeing my panicked expression. I tell him I forgot to pack my charger, and he shrugs. "So you'll be without your phone for the day. I think you'll survive, don't you? I don't remember you being this dependent on technology."

I realize he's teasing me. He remembers my clumsiness and general weariness of all things electronic. I grin at him. "Yeah, well... we all change in one way or another."

A while later, we pull up in front of the warehouse. It's different than the shipping yard, because here, there's the obvious flurry of activity. We're far enough away parked in Marcus's car that we need binoculars to see what's going on. Through the lenses, I see men in coveralls walking around, one moving crates with a forklift to where a number of waiting trucks sit, ready to be packed.

"I'd really like to know what's in those crates," I whisper, still staring at the hustle and bustle of activity through the double lenses. I don't see any armed men or obvious security, but I'm guessing we won't be able to just walk in through the gate and ask for a peek.

"Hmmm," Marcus says. "How good are your acting skills?" I stare at him, perplexed, as he turns on the ignition and drives around to the back of the warehouse.

"Uhm, I have no idea. I've never had a chance to test it." He parks the car across the street from where huge dumpsters sit just outside the fence. He doesn't explain his plan yet, but gets out of the car and walks across the street to where the dumpsters are. I watch him rummage in them and come back with a crumpled piece of paper and an old employee identification card. He hands them to me and starts the car. Unfolding the piece of paper, I'm a little grossed out, but my curiosity wins me over. I'm disappointed to see it's just what appears to be an internal office memo. An obvious spelling error explains why it was thrown away. The employee security card is from some thick-necked, gray-haired man named Bert Monroe. If this Bert fellow had at least looked a little like Marcus, I would have seen the point of having the identification card, but he doesn't.

I hold it out questioningly to Marcus, who grins at my confusion. He's enjoying being all mysterious, so I sit back and see what happens next rather than insisting on an answer and giving him the satisfaction of holding out on me. I do roll my eyes, though, which makes him laugh. I suspect he has a plan to get us into the warehouse so we can have a look around.

We pull up in front of a hotel. I have no idea what we're doing here. "I'm buying you a drink at the hotel bar. Mainly because we need to sit somewhere with a Wi-Fi signal, and I'm guessing they won't just let us sit here without buying anything."

As soon as we're seated at a table, Marcus opens my laptop and connects to the Wi-Fi. He types away at the laptop keyboard for a good few minutes while I sip at a glass of iced tea I don't want and barely taste. Finally, when Marcus turns the laptop screen around so I can see what he's been up to, I marvel at his computer skills.

I have no idea what program he used, but he managed to create a replica of the security pass. Only now, it's for some woman called Desiree Matthews, and has my picture on it. I know where he got that photo of me. It's from a year ago, and it's on my public business profile. My mouth is hanging open a little at how easy it was for Marcus to create this fake ID. She appears to be a quality control officer for a place called Blackthorn Holdings.

"It won't hold up to a detailed inspection, but should at least get us through the door," Marcus says as he shows me the ID he made for himself. According to this, he's my assistant. "As long as we don't raise any undue suspicion, we should at least be able to have a look around."

"Dressed like this?" I ask, indicating the casual clothes both of us are wearing. We hardly look like a pair of safety inspection officers.

Marcus gives a sardonic wink. "Up for going shopping, Miss Matthews?"

～

ALMOST TWO HOURS LATER, I'M FLASHING MY FAKE ID CARD to a pimply-faced kid who looks about 20 years old. His eyes are large and frightened. I know just by looking at him he's going to get steam-rolled by Marcus.

"Do you have any idea who this is?" Marcus is asking the poor kid crossly. "She's the chief safety inspector for the Washington area, and you're about to buy your company a whole truckload of bad faith by making her stand out here in the sun! If I were you I'd let us get on with our job. By all means, phone the top brass of your company. Ask them why they didn't inform you to expect a visit from us. In the meantime, our patience will be wearing more thin by the minute."

I try for a bored expression, belying the nervous terror I'm feeling in the pit of my stomach. If this backfires on us... if this kid calls our bluff, the whole plan will fall apart.

Finally, something in my eyes convinces the kid to let us in. He opens the gate, and we drive to a parking lot in front of the warehouse. As I get out of the car, I smooth down the tight skirt that stops midway down my calves. I thought the outfit Marcus had chosen for me was a bit much, but I suppose he was right when he said if they are focused on my clothes, their eyes won't be drawn to my face and they won't be able to give a clear description of me afterward. The business suit is professional-looking, but I'd never in a million years wear a jacket of this bright pink. I feel like a wad of chewing gum.

Marcus's suit is dark blue. I understand that our roles for this mission are different. I'm supposed to be the obvious distraction, with my loud clothing, my clipboard, and going "Tut, tut..." whenever I inspect something, writing notes and shaking my head. Marcus will be going around with his camera, looking at what there is to see. Our only contact will be the two-way radios we'll be carrying around.

As we step into the warehouse, I flash my newly laminated identification card around at the workers and demand to inspect the boxes they are in the process of packing. So far, so good. There are a few grumblings, a few glances at my brightly colored clothing, and then they allow me to inspect the goods.

Meanwhile, Marcus takes the opportunity to make his escape, discreetly sneaking away to see if this warehouse is hiding anything of importance. Marcus will be looking for illegal weapons, but there's also the possibility of drugs and, of course, money laundering.

I know very little about health and safety regulations and obviously didn't have time to study up on it before this little hustle that Marcus thought up. I try to keep my comments noncommittal and as vague as possible, but the longer I stay there underneath the scrutiny of the warehouse workers, the more self-conscious and like a fraud I feel.

Finally, after what seems like hours of walking around and looking at random things, taking "notes," and grumbling under my breath, I feel like my time of realistically pulling off this charade is up, and has been for a while. The truth of this hits home when I see a red-faced guy walking over. He's not dressed in a dirty coverall like most of the people here, but instead is wearing what I'd call workman's fancy clothes: a button-up shirt, clean blue jeans over a considerable gut, and construction boots. Behind him, trying to keep up with his fast pace, is the pimply-faced kid from the security boot.

I feel myself wishing the earth would just swallow me whole when a familiar voice says, "Looks like it's time to go." It's Marcus, who has appeared behind me like Houdini.

"What's the meaning of this?!" the guy, who I'm guessing is the foreman of the warehouse, says with spittle flying out from his mouth.

Marcus steps up. "I'm sorry, I'm such an idiot! It seems that we're at the wrong warehouse."

"Excuse me, what?" I can see on this guy's face that he's not going to buy our story so easily. He's not going to be intimidated by Marcus, either. As the rest of the big, burly guys in coveralls gather closer, seeming to want to crowd around us, I realize that Marcus and I could be in serious trouble here.

I look at the foreman's hands. It's easy to check for a wedding ring—he's cracking his knuckles one by one, a gesture that implies he's getting ready to open a can of whoop on someone's ass, presumably ours.

No wedding band, but I think I spot the tan line of one. *Newly divorced, maybe?* When I step closer to this angry, red-faced man, I get a strong whiff of some cheap aftershave, reinforcing the idea that he is recently divorced, on the prowl, and more than a little preoccupied with his appearance. In fact, he reminds me of a bad-tempered cock, strutting his stuff, chest puffed out. Here's a guy that likes to feel important. I put on my best smile and shrug apologetically, casting my eyes down like I'm shy and oh-so-vulnerable. There's no way a man like this can withstand the charms of the breathless, flustered woman.

"I'm so sorry for the confusion, Mister...?"

"Uhm... Wilson. You can call me Lyle."

"Well, Lyle... It explains why my findings didn't reflect what we had on file for the warehouse inspection. Silly me... we're at the wrong address." I give Marcus a withering look, and he pretends to look away, embarrassed by the mistake. I turn back toward Lyle. "Let me give you my number, and we can discuss a date and time when an inspection of your facility will be more appropriate. Maybe over dinner?"

Lyle Wilson blushes and becomes flustered for a moment. Realizing that his subordinates are watching this scene unfold, he barks an order at them to get back to work. That's when I know things are going to be alright, and I breathe a sigh of relief.

He leads us back to our car and watches us drive through the gates. It's only when we stop at the red light at the end of the block that Marcus turns to me, grabs my face in his hands, and gives me a delighted peck on my mouth. "My God, Lace! You missed your calling. You should have been a damn actress! You were wonderful back there!"

I blush furiously at the inappropriately intimate touch, but can't help but laugh at Marcus's boyish exuberance. It's mostly relief that we got away.

We turn right, and Marcus glances in the rearview mirror. I was just about to ask him if he found anything interesting back at the warehouse, but I'm distracted by the sudden shift in mood in the car, the tension coming off Marcus in waves.

I glance back, but part of me suspects what Marcus saw that has him so worried all of a sudden.

"Someone's following us. I swear I saw the gray car behind us pull out of a parking space just outside of the warehouse. Maybe that guy Lyle alerted the top brass about us just after we left, or they were alerted just before he came to send us on our way." Marcus hits the steering wheel with his hand in frustration. It makes me jump a little. "Dammit, and I thought that guy Lyle was so charmed by you that he wouldn't think to mention our visit to his boss!"

"Guess not," I say glumly, and then ask Marcus, "Can you lose them?"

Marcus nods. "It depends on how determined they are to keep up."

MOTEL HIDEOUT

LACY

I'm pushed back in the seat, and scramble trying to clutch onto anything I can get ahold of so I'm not thrown sideways as Marcus suddenly accelerates and then takes a random turn. Luckily, my seatbelt prevents me from falling into Marcus's lap.

"Hold on, Lace!" he calls, and I can hear by the almost gleeful note in his voice and see by the glitter in his eyes that he's more excited than scared. Wish I could say the same, though. My heart is hammering in my chest, and my stomach gives a painful lurch with every second that ticks by. We're whizzing past other motorists, and it's the speed at which we're driving down the road that scares me almost more than the idea of a bunch of thugs chasing us like the ones who cornered me a few days ago.

"You're going to get us arrested for reckless driving!" I shout, and Marcus grins at me.

"They may get arrested before we do," he says, and then laughs at the look on my face. I can't believe he is this blasé about the situation, as if he's involved in a high-speed chase every other day!

"You're right, though. We can't just keep on driving like this indefinitely. I just want to get far enough ahead so we can park in a crowded place and then lose them on foot."

To me, that makes no sense. If we abandon the car, won't it be easier for these guys to catch us? I have no choice but to trust Marcus's obvious expertise in this situation. We drive around for another 40 minutes, trying to outmaneuver the guys following behind us. Finally, Marcus manages to lose them, and he quickly turns and drives into the underground parking of a huge department store. We park in one of the spaces and quickly grab our things from the car. There's a truck parked in a parking space just a few paces further away. We just manage to crouch down behind the truck and peek from behind it when we see the two guys in the car that's been following us stop with a screeching halt.

Marcus and I are hidden by shadows, and see one of the guys with his windows rolled down scan the parking area, hoping to spot us. He's a burly man with long, tangled hair in a vivid shade of orange. He has a wild beard and bushy eyebrows in the same shade as his frizzy hair. He reminds me of a fluffy ginger cat. "They couldn't have gone far. Must be around here. Probably took the elevator and are roaming around upstairs. Call the other guys. We have to sweep this whole area."

They drive off, but I don't feel any sense of relief because I know they'll be back soon with reinforcements.

The words the guy spoke, talking about other guys looking for us as well, makes me realize that we're trapped since we have no idea what the second set of guys look like, who to watch out for. It feels like the walls are slowly closing in on me. What the hell are we going to do?

Marcus motions for me to be quiet. He gets up and takes his lock picking kit out of the pocket of his pants. I get up too, and just before he can start fiddling with the lock, I stick my hand out and press down on the handle. I don't know how I knew it was unlocked, but I'm glad, because maybe, just maybe, we can stay in the back of this truck until it leaves and it will take us outside and away from these men.

The truck is filled with crates covered with tarps. There's space inside to move around. Marcus climbs up and holds his hand out to help me climb on the back of the truck. When he closes the door, the

LETHAL LIAISON: THE LACY LANGFORD CHRONICLES

darkness that envelops us is total. The smell of peaches, fresh and sweet, fills my senses, and I don't have to guess what's in the crates.

Once or twice, I stub my toe in the dark, but keep from calling out in pain by reminding myself that the men may be closer now and will be able to hear if I do. We make our way to the back of the truck, carefully crouching behind the stacks of crates.

Everything is eerily quiet. I can hear the beating of my heart, my own breathing, even the subtle swish of my own blinking eyes. Next to me, I can hear Marcus breathing too. It feels like an eternity that we're there, suspended in time. Somewhere far off, I can hear a car alarm go off, faintly warbling, and my overexcited imagination serves up vivid images of the thugs going from car to car, searching for us. It gets so bad that my body starts trembling. Marcus, sensing my fear, pulls me close and folds his arms around me.

He has his mouth close to my ear, and whispers now, ever so softly, "It's okay, they won't find us here." I shiver at the feeling of his closeness, his lips tickling my ear. All I keep thinking about is that if they do find us, we're trapped, two sitting ducks.

Suddenly we hear footsteps approaching. My breath catches in my throat when I hear the sound of a click and the door of the front cabin of the truck opening. With an enormous rumble, the truck's engine roars to life, and then we're thrown against the back wall of the truck as it starts moving. I've been crouching down so long that it's a relief when I unfold my legs, sitting down with my back against the crates.

We're moving, and that's all that matters. We're getting away from the guys that were chasing us. We did it!

While the truck drives around, Marcus tells me that we have to take a chance at some point and jump out of the truck, but he wants us to be as far away from the men that were chasing us as possible when we do. All I can imagine is opening the doors of the truck and discovering we're on some freeway, and jumping would be risking getting run over by cars.

In the end, I think Marcus has the same fears I have, because it's only when the truck comes to a complete halt, the engine is switched off, and we can hear the driver exiting the car that Marcus stands up.

It's now or never, and Marcus opens the door of the truck. I blink, blinded for a moment by sunlight suddenly streaming in from the open door. When we step out of the truck onto a tar road, I blink, a little surprised at the change in scenery. We're in the middle of a small town, away from the hustle and bustle of Washington.

Sitting in the back of the truck, surrounded by darkness, time lost all meaning, and I wonder for a moment where the hell we are. Sunlight has seeped out of the day, and it's late afternoon. Evening is fast approaching.

Marcus closes the door of the truck. When we step out from behind it and look up, the question of where we are is immediately answered. Evidently, the truck driver went into the diner whose sign proclaims that it serves the best breakfast in Boonsboro.

"We're in Boonsboro?!" I say, surprised. We must have been in the back of the truck for almost two hours.

"Looks like it," he grumbles, and I wonder briefly where he expected us to be for him to look this disappointed now. Then his face clears, and he turns to me. "Let's get a bite to eat. I don't know about you, but being chased always makes me hungry."

I don't know about best breakfast, but the diner serves the best tuna melt sandwiches with fries that I've had in a very long time. It's only when I take the first bite that I realize how hungry and exhausted I am. Over dinner, Marcus and I don't say much.

"I guess we better find a place to stay for the night," Marcus says quietly to me after we've finished the last of our food. "We can make a plan to get back to Washington in the morning." When our waitress comes to our table with the bill, Marcus asks her about motels within walking distance of the diner. She recommends a place just down the road. I'm glad, because I can't imagine walking very far in the high heels and business suit I'm wearing.

The room we end up getting has two twin beds in the same room. I can't help but feel relieved that I won't have to spend the night with Marcus in the same bed. As he pours each of us a drink from the mini fridge, I excuse myself to go and have a shower.

Mostly I'm just dying to get out of this scratchy, ugly suit I'm wearing. The shower is heavenly, and serves to get the last of the sweat from the day's excitement off me and relax my overworked muscles. It's been a hectic day, but I feel strangely alert as I finish drying my hair with the

94

towel. I've put on a fresh set of clothes, a t-shirt and a pair of jeans, because I won't be sleeping in the same room as Marcus wearing just a t-shirt and panties.

Being in his company is distracting enough as it is without complicating matters further. All day, there was way too much touching and too many moments of intimacy that made me aware of him in a way that I wouldn't have been otherwise. Thinking back on what I felt in those moments makes me flush with an uncomfortable guilt.

I wonder suddenly if Evan will be worried not hearing from me, and what he thinks I'm doing. He knew I was going somewhere with Marcus, and no matter how innocently things play out tonight, it's still guaranteed to look bad to Evan.

There's not much I can do about it now, so I push the thought away. As I'm digging in my bag for a pair of socks, I feel something hard in the back pocket of the jeans I was wearing earlier. The envelope! In the excitement of being chased, riding in the back of a truck like a hobo, and ending up two hours from my home, I forgot all about the envelope I found in the desk drawer at the shipping yard.

I go over to the wash basin and turn on the tap so the running of the water will mask the sound of the envelope I'm tearing open. I tip the contents out, and a man's wallet slides into the palm of my hand. Something else falls to the floor with a clang and skids to one corner of the bathroom, and I pick it up. It's a plain golden ring. I try putting it on my finger, but it's way too big for me. The man's wallet I found would suggest that the ring belonged to a man as well. Is it a wedding band?

I open the wallet with my heart hammering in my chest. A secret part of me, perhaps instinct or woman's intuition, whispers what I'm going to find when I open the wallet. My fingers are shaking, afraid of what this will mean if I'm right.

I open it and slide out a driver's license, presumably from the owner of the wallet. The name on the license is that of Tony Kaplan, Jamie's missing husband. The wedding ring suddenly feels like it's burning my finger. I take it off and put it in my pocket. I open the wallet and see that there's a few dollar bills in there. The edges of the bills are stained a dark maroon, and I wonder if it's dried blood. I can imagine this wallet lying in a pool of blood, soaking it up. Then someone collected it, along with the victim's wedding ring. The picture forming in my mind is way too plausible, and fills me with a sick sense of dread.

In another compartment, I find a single photo of Jamie holding her two boys. Looking at it, at their smiling faces, I remember Tony, and tears sting my eyes. Finding these very personal items surely means that Tony is dead. I'm going to have to return them to Jamie, and then she'll know what I know—that her husband, the father of her children, is most likely gone forever, and that the chances of finding his body are very unlikely. Whoever killed him must have disposed of his corpse in a clever, permanent way, because he wasn't found, and I know Jamie tried calling hospitals and morgues to find out if a John Doe matching her husband's description had been found. She came up empty-handed every time.

Something is gnawing at the back of my mind, though. Something about this feels all wrong. Why wouldn't the people who killed Tony have disposed of this evidence? Someone decided to keep it, but who? And why? They hid it carefully away. Was it Tony's boss, Derek Phillips? The one who told police that Tony had gone back to Turkey? Is there a way to question him about it without exposing myself and getting killed?

All these questions tumble around in my head, but I know I can't stay in the bathroom much longer. I still don't want to share this information with Marcus, or the location of where Jamie and her children are hiding. I put the wallet in the back pocket of my jeans, gather my stuff, and step out into the room.

Marcus comes over holding a glass with whiskey and soda. I accept it gratefully after throwing my backpack down at the foot of one of the beds. I take a sip of the slightly burny alcohol and then look up at Marcus, who is standing right in front of me, too close. He's staring down at me with an intense expression that isn't that difficult to read.

After the intensity we just experienced, facing all the excitement and danger together, it's only natural that we should be feeling bonded, drawn together. There's also the very real memories of our past relationship to contend with, the fact that we were intimately involved. Marcus and I—we weren't just one very hot and passionate fling in the heat of a moment. What we had was real. I loved him once, and I still believe that he loved me, too.

That makes him uniquely dangerous to me. I feel it in every bone of my body, how easy it would be to just give in, to surrender to him and to this feeling pounding through my veins.

Instead, I step away from him. Just one step, but it may as well be a whole canyon that exists between us now. Sometimes one little step is all it takes.

He nods his head sadly, as if answering the unspoken question between us. "I guess we better get some sleep. I want to be out of here early tomorrow morning."

I put my drink down on the end table next to my bed. Marcus is taking off his shirt and pants, clearly meaning to sleep in his boxers. I can't help but glance at his very alluring body. He is still one of the most compellingly sexy men that I've ever met, and that, of course, is half the problem. It's one of the reasons why I have to keep him at a distance if my relationship with Evan has any chance at all of surviving all of this.

Sighing at my own treacherous thoughts, I get into bed with all my clothes on. I switch off my bedside lamp just as Marcus is switching his off too.

My eyes are already closing, heavy with the feeling of finally being able to rest. As they shut and I feel myself being pulled down, one thought flickers across my mind and is gone as sleep claims me: Marcus never shared with me what evidence he found at the warehouse. I guess he doesn't trust me completely, either.

A SHOT AT NORMALCY

LACY

I step onto the familiar porch, and the wooden floorboards creak underneath my feet. As I put my bags down next to the front door, I glance over at the porch swing. It's a rickety old structure that's part of my childhood, a relic from a time when I lived here in Mount Union. I remember times I would sit next to my mom, underneath a blanket if the night was chilly, and we'd talk for hours. Sometimes we'd reminisce about my dad, recalling fond moments with him, and other times I would complain about school, share teenage drama, or breathlessly tell my mom about a boy or girl I liked.

Now here I am again, when my life feels like it's drifting away from me like flotsam, and I need someone to be my anchor.

I ring the bell as I always do, because I don't live here anymore. It only takes a few minutes before my mom opens the door, and she stands there, looking at me with a surprised smile.

"Oh my goodness, Lacy! I didn't expect you today!"

I step up and hug her tightly, smelling her floral perfume. She's a few inches taller than I am, her eyes are chocolate brown instead of blue, and her hair is peppered with gray, but otherwise we look very similar. She folds me into a hug, and I rest my head on her shoulder for a moment, closing my eyes and savoring the moment.

When I pull back, my mom's delight has turned to worry as she regards me closely.

"Come in, I'll put some coffee on and you can tell me all about it."

Those words, "You can tell me all about it," are achingly familiar as well, and something my mom says often. I follow her inside the house, closing the door behind me. In the kitchen with the faded yellow linoleum floor, I pull out a chair and sit down at the small breakfast table, letting my handbag slide down to the floor.

What exactly am I going to tell my mom? Just like with all the other important people in my life, telling her everything would be putting her in danger. I need her, though, her wisdom. That's why I came here. In times of trouble, I can usually depend on my mom to give me advice.

This morning, Marcus and I got a taxi to take us back to the shopping center where his car was parked. After Marcus dropped me off and was on his way, I looked around at my apartment, and it felt like someone had been in my house while I was away. I know Evan had been there, but his presence wouldn't have accounted for the creepy feeling I had that all my things had been touched, all my belongings had been rifled through with strange fingers by faceless men searching for something.

That's when I knew I had to get out of there. My phone was charging, so I quickly called Evan, who was relieved to hear from me. After updating him about the situation as much as I dared, I told him I was getting out of town to visit family for a few days. Evan got quiet, and then asked me to call him tonight to let him know I'm okay. Over the phone, he sounded reserved and accepting. I have no idea what this means for us in the long run, but at least he's not pushing me anymore for answers that I can't give.

I packed my bags and headed here. Not in my car, but with the city bus. The bus ride was boring and uneventful, giving me a chance to think about what I want to do. Usually I like public transport, because one of my favorite pastimes is people-watching. I sit and look at the many different people and try to make up stories about who they are and why they're here. It's a silly little game I've always liked playing, but not this time. This time I had too much on my mind, and I barely saw the faces of the other passengers on the bus.

I knew that I wanted to go and see Jamie as soon as possible. I need her to decrypt more of the file. I also need to find some way to tell her what I found at the shipping yard where Tony worked and give her back Tony's belongings. I don't think I want to do this alone, though.

My mom hands me a cup of steaming coffee and then sits across from me, sipping quietly on her own. She's waiting for me to tell her why I've come and why I look so anxious.

"I need a break from work and everything else. I feel a bit burned out. Would you like to take a trip with me to the lake? We can stay for a day or two, and it will give me a chance to unwind."

My mom looks at me quietly, then nods. "Sure, I'd love that."

I know she's not completely convinced by the explanation I gave her for the state I'm in, but she's willing to go along with the plan.

After our coffee, I help my mom pack her bags and load them into her car with my luggage. Then we're on our way. It's a two and a half hour drive to Deep Creek, and on our way I tell my mom that Jamie is staying at the lake house with her two kids. My mom has met Jamie, and they get along really well. In the end, I don't say outright that Jamie is hiding from an abusive spouse, but that's the impression I leave her with. I know Jamie would hate that, but we don't have any other choice, because it's the best cover story there is to explain why Jamie and her kids need to hide away like fugitives.

As we leave the city behind, it feels like I'm shedding at least some of my worries like a coat. I feel lighter, more relaxed. I find an oldies station on my mom's relic of a car radio, and pretty soon we're singing together to Juice Newton's Angel of the Morning. My mom has a much better singing voice, but I'm not bad, either. It doesn't really matter how we sound. We're having fun as the two of us harmonize with the sweet-as-treacle love song that I've always adored. Then a track by the band Wilson Phillips comes on, and I'm delighted. The singing and being together is a sweet moment, and makes the time seem to fly by.

We pull up in front of the lake house. It's a beautiful, balmy day. I sent Jamie a message to expect us, so she comes out of the house looking pretty as a picture in a floral print shirt and a pair of shorts. The kids come out to greet us as well. My mom, always the schoolteacher who loves kids, is swept up by the two rambunctious, chattering boys. She takes them into the house after giving me a meaningful look. She senses that I need a moment to talk with Jamie alone. Though she doesn't know why, she's attuned enough to my emotions to know that the boys need a distraction while I take Jamie for a walk.

We walk down to the lake and sit together on the pier. I take off my shoes and put my feet shin-deep into the cold water. After the long drive, it's soothing. I close my eyes for a moment, and then I turn to Jamie. She has her legs pulled up, her arms folded around them, hugging them to her. It's a defensive posture, and it's a reaction to what Jamie senses: that I have something difficult to tell her.

I tell her briefly about Marcus and about our trip to the shipping yard. I tell her about the mysterious envelope I found. Jamie listens to all of this intently, her dark eyes full of fear. Silently, I hand her the wallet and Tony's ring.

She clutches them for a moment, looking down at them, and I have no idea what she's thinking, what exactly she's feeling. The only thing I can compare it to is how, after my dad died, I would go into his and my mom's room while she was out, open his closet, and let my fingers roam over his shirts hanging neatly in a row. Sometimes I'd press them against my face, feeling their rough texture on my skin, and smell the ghost of him. The tears that fell then would scald and scourge, as the tears of gut-wrenching grief often do.

Jamie presses the wallet against her chest, the ring dangling from her index finger. She looks up at me, and I can see the grief turning like a knife in her gut. "He was dead all this time..." she says breathlessly.

I don't know what to answer, so I just let her talk, let her voice her confusion and pain. "All this time, a part of me hoped that I would find him alive. But now..." her voice breaks, and she starts sobbing. All I can do is hold her while she leans her head against me. We sit that way for a while, watching the lake, where a swarm of beautiful, snow-white egret are taking flight.

~

After I leave Jamie at the lake, I go back to the cabin and join my mom in entertaining the kids. When Jamie has gathered enough of herself to join us again, my mom and I get our few belongings from the car. Jamie moved the boys' stuff to her room. At first I wanted to protest, but then I realized that she wants her kids close to her, to find comfort in them after the news she just heard. I have no idea how or when she'll tell them that their daddy is never coming home, but I don't blame her for putting it off until she's dealt with it herself.

After unpacking my stuff, we go for a swim and have fun in and around the cabin. Jamie makes spaghetti and meatballs for dinner, and the two boys are quiet and subdued after their bath. It doesn't take long after Jamie tucks them in for both of them to fall asleep.

My mom sits outside on the porch with one of the books she brought, enjoying a nightcap while reading by the bright porch light, where a few insects are buzzing around the bulb. Every now and then there's a *tick! tick! tick!* as one of the bugs flies into the glass of the lightbulb.

I've set my laptop up on the desk in my room, and Jamie busies herself with decrypting more of the file while I pour each of us a drink. By the time I join Jamie again, she is poring over a section of the file. She looks startled by my sudden appearance, and I wonder uneasily what has her so intrigued that she didn't hear me entering the room.

I sit down on the bed next to her, and she shows me while she takes a big swallow of her gin and tonic. My own eyes scan the contents of the file. It's a message that was released about a summit meeting. I feel my breath catch a little as the importance of this dawns on me.

The summit meeting is going to be held in a few weeks at the Grand Washington Hotel. The list of attendees alone peaks my interest. There are names of important political and business figures, global leaders, intelligence agencies, and important figures in security and defense. Some of the names are those of Senator Thomas Albright, General Peter Hawkins, and CEO Lydia Carter. The file also mentions a special guest appearance, a briefing session that will be run by this person the day before the actual summit meeting. The name of this mystery guest isn't mentioned in the file.

A few phrases jump out at me, like "finalizing alliances" and "disrupting opposition," suggesting a plan for a massive deal or operation. The nature of this operation or deal isn't apparent in the file, but the idea of all these prominent figures meeting so secretly, deciding a course of action that will affect the rest of the world, gives me the creeps. It has all the hallmarks of that "single new world order" that conspiracy theorists often talk about. It seems like something crucial will be revealed during the summit.

I can see by the look of urgency on Jamie's face that she agrees with me that this is an important event. "That guy Marcus you told me about, he's private security for Senator Albright, isn't he? Can he get you into this event?"

I shrug. "I can ask, I suppose." Jamie mentioning Marcus like that throws me off. She looks at me quietly for a moment, and a knowing look comes into her eyes.

"Is everything alright between you and Evan?"

I shift uncomfortably. "Yeah, of course. Why do you ask?"

Jamie shrugs. "I don't know, you guys seem to be drifting apart, and have been for a while now. And the way you talk about this Marcus guy..." She sees the look on my face, and shakes her head. "Never mind, I guess I was mistaken."

Her words give me something to think about, though. After Jamie copies the rest of the decrypted file on a memory stick and I place it in the bedroom safe, she says goodnight. I join my mom on the porch.

My mom looks up when I sit down and places her book facedown on her stomach. She's lying back in the recliner with her feet up, her shoes lying abandoned on the porch floor. I kick off my shoes and lie back, too. The lake is almost completely dark, and all there is to see really is a firefly here and there, twinkling on and off like flashlights sending messages in morse code. The symphony of the night creatures is unseen, but loud out here.

My mom and I sit for a few moments like this, and then she turns to me. "Everything okay, sweetheart? A bit better now?"

I know I can't tell her everything that's been happening because the truth is dangerous, but there's one part, at least, that she'll understand.

"Marcus Grayson recently made an appearance out of the blue again. We've sort of... reconnected, become friends," I say quietly.

"Ah," my mom says, as if that explains everything. I look at her questioningly, waiting for her to elaborate. She clears her throat, and it's obvious that she's thinking carefully on what to say so as not to hurt me.

"I'm guessing Evan isn't too pleased with this newfound friendship that you and Marcus have."

I give a little sarcastic laugh. "You can say that again."

"Well, honey, I'll tell you the truth. I was a little relieved the first time when Marcus left. I knew it broke your heart at the time, but I always felt like there was something... missing in that boy. Something that other people are born with and just naturally have that he doesn't."

"What is it?" I ask, intrigued.

My mother thinks carefully. "I don't know, exactly. I just always got the impression that it was this missing part of him that he was searching for in you. That's a dangerous thing. People often talk about completing each other, but I do feel that's wrong. I was a whole person when I was married to your father, and he was a whole person too. We complemented each other, worked together as partners and loved each other very much. He was my best friend, but he didn't fill some empty part in me. Expecting another person to do that only sets both of you up for disappointment. Another person can't complete you—only you can do that."

I'm quiet for a moment, considering all the differences between the two men. "And Evan? You feel like he's a whole person?"

My mom actually smiles. "Yes. Evan has a quiet strength that I've always admired. He knows exactly who and what he is. I really like Evan." Then she looks at me. "That doesn't matter, though. Do you still like Evan?"

I feel my eyes suddenly burning with tears at this honest question. "Yes, I love Evan. I just don't know if I can give him everything he wants."

"Well, the only thing you can do is do your best by him. If that's not enough, then at least you gave it your all, didn't you?" She shrugs carefully. "As for Marcus, just tread carefully. I don't mind who you decide to be with; man, woman... as long as the person is a real partner to you, loves you, and treats you right, it doesn't matter who it is. You know that. Just be careful of Marcus. I'd hate to see you lose a good person like Evan and then have Marcus break your heart and disappear again."

After that, we fall quiet and just bask in the sounds of the lake at night; frogs and crickets, a hooting owl close by. There's about a million stars in the sky and a bright moon riding in the night like some virtuous avenger. As I look at the bright face of the moon, a lonely heron calls nearby, and the sound gives me a chill down my spine.

UNDERCOVER TENSION

EVAN

I stretch my hand out, my tightly clamped fist raised to knock on the door of Lacy's apartment. My hand hesitates, and I'm struck by how much things have changed in just a short amount of time.

When she got back from visiting her mom, she seemed more relaxed, more like the old Lacy. Her going on the trip out of town in the first place was so unexpected, the timing suspicious. It was just after she went God-knows-where with that Marcus creep, and I'm not gonna lie, to me it seemed like she was running away. It left me feeling more insecure than ever, wondering what happened on her outing with Marcus, if she maybe did something she regretted and didn't want to face me.

When she returned, she was the same as before, and I suppressed the urge to interrogate her about what happened. We went on like we always have, and things seemed to be getting back on track. Then I realized she was still seeing Marcus, still in contact with him, and my own misgivings returned with a vengeance.

The worst of it is, I think Lacy was about to tell me the truth once, weeks ago, when I went to her office to confront her about the guys attacking her and about her ex-boyfriend's sudden appearance back into her life. I think she wanted to confide in me what's really been happening in her life that has her so stressed, worked up, wild-eyed, and neglecting her health...

Then I opened my big mouth and actually tried to forbid her from seeing Marcus. Big mistake, I know. A woman like Lacy does not respond well to the alpha male tactics. It's one of the reasons why I find her so unbearably, undeniably intriguing. The fact that she is her own person, completely sure of who she is, what she wants, and how to get it, makes the littlest of victories I win with her taste more sweet. The fact that she doesn't let just anybody get so close to her makes the ground I've won over the last two years seem all the more precious for the effort it took to win it.

Since she got back, I've felt like the trip must have done her some good, because she seems more herself. I've been careful not to let my jealousy of Marcus, the feeling that he's trouble and that he's trying to get between us, show. It sure as hell hasn't been easy. I'm trying to be the understanding, accommodating boyfriend, trying to encourage her to confide in me again.

Then yesterday, Lacy tells me that she and Marcus are going to a black-tie event tonight—together! Without giving me any indication what it's all about, mind you! I think most guys in my situation would have seen red. I stormed out of here and ignored Lacy's phone calls for the rest of the night, and for most of today. Only a few minutes ago did I decide to swing by her place. If I can't talk her out of going off to some fancy to-do with her ex, maybe I can at least get her to tell me what it's all about, maybe repair some of the damage all this is causing in our relationship.

Setting my shoulders back with determination, I knock.

Lacy opens the door, and my breath catches in my throat. She's wearing a wine-red evening dress. Her hair is tied back from her face and hangs in a thick, intricate braid down one shoulder. The bodice of the dress hugging her perfectly proportioned figure is peppered with sequins. It's low-cut enough to be alluring, but still looks tasteful. With her blue eyes dusted with sultry makeup, her lips painted the same shade of wine-red, she is stunning, and I feel my eyes just drinking her in.

"Nice of you to finally show just as I'm about to go out," she says sarcastically, in reference to her failed attempts to get ahold of me today. I realize I'm just staring at her like the village idiot, and I close my mouth and shrug, awkwardly brushing through my hair with my fingertips. I had this whole speech planned out, but now, seeing her like this, it just flew from my mind.

Exasperated at my lack of a response, Lacy turns around and walks away from me into her apartment. That's when I get a look at the back of her dress. The low-plunging back, revealing all that creamy, olive-toned skin, like soft caramel. From experience, I know exactly how it feels. I've traced my fingertips down Lacy's naked back on many occasions over the last two years, and my hands are itching to do so now. My mind is like an empty wind tunnel, howling without a thought. My lust for this infuriating woman reaches its peak, and can't be held back any longer.

I step into her apartment, close the door behind me. Then I step forward and grab Lacy by her arm, turning her around, grabbing her by her waist, and bringing my lips down on hers in one fast, fluid motion. We crash into each other, hungrily grabbing. The taste of her lipstick, the feel of her soft lips on mine, her wet, slippery tongue in my mouth...

It makes the roaring in my mind louder, makes the need to consume her, to claim her as mine, stronger until it's an unstoppable force. My hands roam over her naked back, my fingers digging into the soft skin, the supple flesh beneath my fingertips. It's just as velvety soft as I knew it would be, and my senses drown in her warmth, her flowery scent, her body yielding against mine.

Lacy's hands are locked behind my head, and she's kissing me back just as hungrily. We are like two drowning people clutching at each other for dear life. My hands move further down, grabbing her soft, luscious bottom. The fabric of her dress swishes, whispering secrets as I pick her up in my hands. I'm pressing her closer to where my rock-hard need for her is burning the most.

She responds to this by grabbing onto me harder. I lift her up, and she wraps her legs around me. I walk with her like that in the direction of her bedroom, wondering idly if I'll even be able to make it all the way there. I want her so goddamn much! Distantly, I hear her shoes clattering to the kitchen floor.

We only make it to the living room, where I place Lacy carefully down on her feet. Then I reach behind her neck and find the ribbon tying back the halter neck of her dress. I grab it and pull, and then the top of her dress falls down her front. The dress doesn't lend itself well to wearing a bra, I suppose, and I'm grateful for it when Lacy's beautiful breasts, naked and alluring, greet me.

Afterward, as I'm slowly regaining thought, I roll off of her and lie with my head back. I'm trying to catch my breath. Lacy is also lying back, panting. We stay that way for a moment, and I'm just starting to wonder if this was a mistake with everything being so confusing between us, if I just muddied the waters even further with this moment of unbridled, mindless passion. She leans over and kisses me, her lips smiling wickedly.

"You know, you're not going to get away with acting like a jerk every time by distracting me with great sex!"

"I'm not?" I growl and grab for her, but now she pushes me away firmly.

She stands up, tying the dress up behind her neck once more. "I have to get ready."

As she rushes off to fix her hair and reapply her makeup, I stare after her disbelievingly. I stand up and pull my pants back up, straighten my own shirt. I walk through to her bedroom, watching her as she puts on a fresh layer of lipstick. "You're not seriously still going to this event, are you?"

I can't believe that after what just happened between us, she immediately wants to run off with another guy!

She looks at me, her eyes large and worried. "I've told you before, it's not a date. Marcus is just helping me with some stuff. It's purely business between us."

"So what exactly is it your ex is helping you with, Lace? Explain it to me." My voice has gone dangerously quiet, and I feel the pounding of my anger in my temples, behind my eyes, grinding like glass.

She flushes, ignoring me, and I watch as she puts on another pair of panties and goes through to the lounge to pick up the torn pair still lying discarded on the couch. She's just thrown them in the garbage when the doorbell rings. She looks up, and then glances guiltily at my face. She still hasn't answered me, and I can't stand not knowing where she'll be tonight.

"This is fuckin' ridiculous!" I bellow. Swearing is not something I do often, and she flinches at the ugly sound of it.

I watch helplessly as she opens the door. Marcus is standing there, dressed in some expensive designer suit. He leans over and kisses Lacy on the cheek. Looking behind Lacy, he spots me, and gives me a smirk when he notices the living room is still in shambles, Lacy's lipstick still smeared on my face.

By his darkly dancing, merry eyes, I can see he can guess what happened between Lacy and myself just before he arrived. He's telling me, not in so many words, that it doesn't matter—he'll be with her for the rest of the night.

Marcus looks down at Lacy, and the way he drinks her up with his eyes, the same way I did a few moments ago, makes me want to pound his skull in for him. It's not that I'm afraid of this guy, but I am afraid of doing something reckless that will make me lose Lacy forever.

Pound... pound... pound... The throbbing in my head just behind my eyes makes it difficult to think, and I know I don't have long before I lose all self-control. I have to get out of here.

"I'll call you when I'm home later." Lacy's voice is just a tiny squeak, not very much like she usually sounds. The tension in this place is so thick, it sounds like she's almost choking on it.

I walk to the front door, meaning to just get out of here as fast as I can. Walking past Marcus, he still has that hateful smirk on his face. "We may be a little later than you expect, though." He's taunting me, I can hear it in his voice. I'm just seeing red, and next thing I know, Lacy is yelling for me to stop it, and I'm grabbing Marcus by the front of his suit, pushing him up against Lacy's fridge hard enough to make it knock against the wall behind it and make the contents inside shake and rattle.

I'm looking down at him, about two seconds away from pounding his head to pulp, and he's still bloody laughing up at me with his hands palm-up.

"If you so much as touch a hair on her goddamn head, I'll kill you,

LETHAL LIAISON: THE LACY LANGFORD CHRONICLES

do you hear me?!" I'm hissing this into his face. Even now, I can see he's not scared of me—he's enjoying this immensely. I'm doing exactly what he wanted, losing control in front of her like this, showing her exactly what sort of animal I can be.

"I promise I won't do anything she doesn't want me to." His words are dripping with innuendo, and I can hear Lacy hiss at him to shut up.

I know if I stay here, I'm really going to kill this guy. I've never been this angry before, and the feeling scares me. It's seeing for the first time what I'm truly capable of, seeing the possibility of it, and realizing it's something about myself that I never even would have guessed at.

I can't really kill him. It may be satisfying in the moment, but the repercussions are not something that I'd want to live with.

I put him down, disentangling my hands from his suit jacket. Then I walk blindly away from both of them, deaf to Lacy's protests calling me back to try and explain. I'm deaf to everything but the pounding of rage in my head.

I have no idea how I got back to my car, how I drove away from there, but I come back to myself a while later. It's pitch-black outside my car windows, and for a few moments I have no idea where I am.

Then I realize I'm somewhere in downtown Washington. It takes me half an hour to get back to my own apartment building. At least the long drive helped clear my head. My stomach is churning, and I feel sick because I think I've finally reached the end of my tether when it comes to me and Lacy. I can't believe the last two years will end like this, with that jackass stepping in between us and whatever madness going on in Lacy's life that she's feeling so protective over pushing us apart.

I still love her desperately, but enough is enough. I can't do this anymore. She finally succeeded in pushing me away.

I take my keys out of my pocket to unlock the door to my apartment. From the corner of my eye, I see two men appearing from the shadows. Startled, I jump back a little. Then I relax, because they have their hands held up, trying to put me at ease.

One of the guys is white and the other is Black, but other than that, they may as well have been factory produced and rolled off different production lines, they are that similar in being nondescript. They're wide-shouldered and square-jawed. Both of them are wearing similar suits, and they both have a buzz cut.

"Evan Steele?" the Black one, who is slightly taller, speaks up.

I nod carefully, because I'm still reeling from my encounter with Lacy and Marcus. I know I don't have the patience for any more drama tonight.

The stranger reaches slowly into his pocket, being careful to keep his other hand where I can see it. He takes something out, and part of me is not very surprised when it turns out to be a badge. What does surprise me is that these two are not detectives, as the cop-air and their body language would suggest, but FBI agents.

It all feels so unreal that I don't respond, just wait for them to tell me what this is all about.

"Can we come in? We'd like to speak to you about your girlfriend, Lacy Langford. We believe her life is in danger, and you may be the only person who can help us get her out of it."

THE SUMMIT MEETING

LACY

I watch from the window as Evan's car tears out of the parking lot of my apartment building. Then I furiously turn back to Marcus. He is standing there, quietly watching me.

"Why did you goad him like that?!" I ask, yelling now. "Are you trying to break us up? What for?!"

Marcus shrugs. "Come on, Lace. The guy is obviously insecure for reasons of his own. It's got nothing to do with me."

I huff at Marcus, brushing roughly past him. I walk through to the lounge and pick up the couch cushions, straightening the mess of Evan and I's passionate tryst. It was wonderful, right up to the moment when it wasn't—then it suddenly became horrible. I sit down on the couch. My hands are still shaking from seeing Evan push Marcus up against the fridge. Mild-mannered, easygoing, always-smiling Evan... He's only ever expressed aggression when in the hockey ring, and that is always... controlled, in a way. Never like this! I've never seen him furious like this, and would never have guessed at this aggressive aspect of his personality. *Is it my fault? Did I cause this?*

As if sensing my thoughts, Marcus quietly pours each of us a drink. The one he hands me is quite a bit stronger than the one he poured for himself. He then sits down next to me, reaches out, and squeezes my shoulder. I have a mind to shake it off, but I feel tears of frustration—and, let's face it, fear—threatening to spill down my cheeks.

"Maybe it's better that you're seeing his true colors now, when you can break it off. A woman like you can't be owned. You're a free spirit just like me, and for a guy like Evan... Let's just say I've seen guys like him before. He'll always be insecure when it comes to someone like you."

Evan, insecure? No... that doesn't seem right. I need time to think about this. My mom's words about Evan and about being careful of Marcus are clanging around in my mind, but now is really not the time to be caught up in self-reflecting and mulling over the slowly deteriorating relationship I've held dear for over two years now.

"We should probably get going. Doesn't the event start soon?" I stand up and put my drink on the coffee table. My nerves are frayed, and I have to pull myself together. I can't afford to dull my senses with alcohol before the meeting has even started.

After retrieving my handbag and locking my apartment, Marcus holds the door of his car open for me. My treacherous senses take note of how nice he smells, how handsome he looks, and I feel a flush rising from the pit of my stomach all the way to my cheeks. I get the impression that Marcus is acutely aware of the effect he has on me, that he's doing some of it deliberately. Is he actually enjoying it, seeing me so unsettled?

I shake the feeling off as we drive down the street and mingle with the evening traffic. The Grand Washington Hotel is located in downtown city center D.C., so by the time we get close, darkness has fallen and the streets and buildings are aglow with city lights. We park in front of the hotel, and a valet opens the door for me. Marcus is there to take my hand, and I feel like I'm Cinderella going to the ball. I've been to lavish parties before, but nothing quite like this.

In the foyer of the hotel, I see men and women milling about in their evening wear. My eyes are wide looking at some of the people I recognize from news stories and television, the kind of people I would never meet in real life.

One of the women catches my eye and smiles. She's a tall, dark-haired beauty with a distinctly haughty look. She's easy to recognize, and it's impossible to mistake someone else for her. Her high cheek-bones and full lips are set off by a sharp, hawklike nose and cold, calculating eyes. The champagne-colored dress she's wearing accentuates her curves, sticks to her body like a second skin. Not only is she a fashion icon, but she's also the host of her own talk show.

I recognize her as the one and only Cindy-Mari Hunter. She also happens to be the sworn enemy of Yulanda Coolidge, the woman who was charged with the sexual harassment of a former employee. Since the charges, Yulanda's ratings have gone down the hill and her show was cancelled, whereas Cindy-Mari's show's popularity has gone through the roof.

Seeing the one person who benefitted the most from Yulanda's destroyed reputation here, smiling, makes me feel sick to my stomach. Yulanda Coolidge was one of the people mentioned in the file linked to the code name Thomas Albright, and I can't help but feel that important people are being destroyed as a favor to some other powerful people... but to what end? Is it so these powerful people from all walks of life will owe a favor to the one orchestrating these attacks? Or is it rather a single world order kind of deal, where these powerful figures move in the shadows, destroying those who are not aligned with the greater plan and pushing forward those who are?

Before I can chase down these thoughts and decide which of these very frightening possibilities seems more likely, Marcus leads me into the ballroom and grabs a glass of bubbly from a nearby tray. He leans over and whispers in my ear, "Shall we work the room and see what information we can gather?"

It's a good plan. Marcus and I part ways, and I watch him as he disappears into the crowd. My strategy is simple: hanging around at the edges of conversation and gathering snippets of information here and there, like a butterfly flitting about but never quite lighting on a single flower.

Soon this strategy pays off when I stand close to Lydia Carter, the

CEO of Luxworth Holdings. After seeing her name on the guest list of attendees, I did a bit of digging and realized that her company bought out multimillion dollar business mogul Sean McNealy's, the man who was linked to a sex scandal a few months back. It was suggested that Sean McNealy had relations with a girl who was underage at the time. The victim never came forward and the charges were dropped, but it was enough to ruin McNealy's business, as his stocks plummeted, and Lydia Carter swept in and made a killing.

Just like with the two talk show hosts, I find it very suspicious that the person who benefitted from the destruction of McNealy made it onto the guest list of this event.

I stand close to Lydia Carter. Her back is turned to me. I can't see the person she's talking to, but the snippet of conversation I hear has me pricking my ears, holding my breath in anticipation.

"You should have joined the game long ago instead of blowing off those who could have helped you. Now Barbara is moving in as the favorite choice, and you'll be left out in the cold."

"I'm here to pay my dues like everyone else, Lydia," a man's tired voice says, and when Lydia moves aside, I see it's Senator Albright. I was a little surprised to see him on the guest list in the first place, seeing as he was targeted by whatever clandestine force is behind these social and political attacks. "I can't help it if they feel like Barbara is a better candidate than I am. She's a viper, and hopefully the constituency will see through her."

Lydia Carter gives a mean little laugh that makes the hair on the back of my neck stand up. "The voters are sheep, Tom, nothing but sheep. They'll believe whatever the organization tells them to believe."

With a cold feeling in the pit of my stomach, I realize they must be talking about Barbara Pierce, the leader of the opposition party that was the most vocal in their damnation of Thomas Albright following the arms deal scandal. *What the hell is really going on here?*

Lydia moves away after giving Thomas a withering look of pity. Evidently, she saw someone else here at the event that she can either cozy up to or belittle. *I do not like that woman.*

My eyes meet with the Senator's, and I realize that I've always liked this man. At least from what I saw by reading articles about him here and there, he always gave the impression that he was a man of the people. I've never been one to be super involved in the goings-on of political figures, so it was easy to forget his name until I saw it in the news months later.

When the news broke of the illegal arms deal, I was shocked and angry, just like everyone else. I wrote him off as just another dishonest politician, and basically forgot all about him until this mess started and I read his name in the file.

I can see now that whoever went out of their way to ruin the senator did a brilliant job. *Maybe Lydia Carter is right,* I think with bitterness. *Maybe we are all just sheep.*

The senator moves closer, holding out his hand, and we shake. I introduce myself to him, wondering if Marcus would have told him about me, that I'm trying to help uncover the conspiracy that destroyed his reputation. He gives no indication that he recognizes my name.

We make small talk for a while, and I wonder what he's doing here. Is he trying to get into the good graces of the very people who tried to destroy him, hoping to join their operation now, whereas before he refused them? The snippet of conversation I heard between him and Lydia Carter would suggest this is exactly what he's doing. I'm burning with the sudden desire to tell this essentially good man something, anything, that will make him go home, that will keep him from throwing his convictions out the window.

Before I can say anything, I see Thomas's attention drawn to a person behind me. His eyes widen ever so slightly. His face goes rigid, like he's carved from stone. Curious as to who he saw that would have this effect on him, I'm about to turn my head, but then someone steps up and stands next to me.

I look up into the face of a tall older man. From what I can see of his thick, carefully styled gray hair, he's a gentleman in his early 50s. He obviously takes care of his appearance, evident in his neat, manicured nails and hands that I get a glimpse of as he shakes Thomas Albright's hand.

"Good evening, Thomas. It's so good to see you. How have you been?" The newly-arrived stranger has a pleasant, baritone voice, and sounds sincere asking after Thomas's well-being, but by the look of fear on Thomas's face, it's clear that there is something else going on here.

Thomas unsticks his tongue from the roof of his mouth and answers this man in a soft, carefully controlled voice. They fall into conversation, exchanging pleasantries and giving me the opportunity to regard this man more thoroughly. His strong jawline in his handsomely chiseled face gives an air of sophistication and privilege which his gentile way of speaking also hints at. I get the distinct impression that this man, in his perfectly tailored suit, is someone of importance and power. Thomas's reaction to this man, his reverence, would also suggest this.

After a few moments, he turns to me and smiles. I notice how this charming smile doesn't seem to reach his piercing blue eyes.

"Who is your lovely friend?" the stranger asks. He takes my hand and squeezes it in both of his. "You certainly have a knack for standing out, my dear. I thought I knew all the names on the guest list for tonight's event, but yours seems to have slipped my mind."

"I'm Lacy Langford, and I came with a friend of mine, a Mr. Grayson. Marcus Grayson." I glance over in Thomas's direction as I say this, and I'm surprised that there's no flicker of recognition that betrays the fact that he is Marcus's employer. Confused, I turn back to the newcomer.

"Victor Calloway. I'm a guest speaker here tonight for something I'm intimately familiar with—security consulting." He laughs as if it's a little joke.

"Victor is being modest," Thomas chimes in drily. "His company is the leading firm in security and private covert surveillance techniques."

"Really?" I raise my eyebrow. I'm about to ask what this entails, but Victor laughs it off.

"Now, now, Thomas. Don't be giving away all my secrets." I see by Thomas's face that he's as confused about this comment as I am. "The walls have ears, after all."

My stomach drops all the way to my shoes. The note I received with the listening device used that exact phrase. The stationary—expensive, fancy... I can imagine a man like this using stationary like that. Is he trying to tell me he sent me the note? Does he know I have the file?

LETHAL LIAISON: THE LACY LANGFORD CHRONICLES

I smile, trying to scramble together an appropriate response to gauge how much this man knows about the file and what it contains.

Before I can think of something to say, Victor Calloway leans in and says, "Do you find your work satisfying, Miss Langford? As a relationship advisor, I mean. I can only imagine what it is like to help people with their personal problems."

I swallow at the sudden lump in my throat. Neither Thomas nor I had mentioned what exactly it is that I do for a living. Yet Victor knows. Worst of all, he wants me to realize that he knows exactly who I am. I give some generic response that I normally give when people ask me about my line of work. Victor nods as if he's very interested in what I have to say.

"And you don't find that sometimes perhaps you get a tad too personally involved? Trying to help people that really don't want or deserve your help? Taking it too far and sacrificing too much along the way? Behavior that is sure to raise a number of red flags if you were to decipher it?"

He's definitely referencing the file, trying to gauge how much I've been able to find out about it. He's looking at my face closely, trying to see when what he says strikes a personal chord with me. It's a technique I'm very familiar with, and I don't appreciate it being used on me.

Setting my resolve to not give him the answers he is looking for, I shrug. "Everyone deserves help, Mister Calloway. Be it a lowly dock-worker, a single mother, or a politician struggling with personal issues, everyone deserves someone to listen and give them advice on how to navigate treacherous waters."

I see his eyes narrow a bit on the last one. The cold look he gives me is there and then gone. "You are right, of course." He reaches into his pocket and brings out what I assume is a business card. "Why don't we schedule an appointment for some date in the future? I'd love to pick that interesting mind of yours further and discuss morality, and the personal cost of it, some more."

He excuses himself and walks lazily away from us. Looking down at it, I see that it's a business card, printed on the same stationary as the note I received with the listening device detector. I feel so confused. All this time I assumed that the note and device were sent from some force of good out there who wanted me to find the listening devices that the people behind this conspiracy had planted in my home. Now I'm not sure what to think.

I open my handbag and throw Victor Calloway's business card in there.

I turn back to Thomas, who finishes his champagne in one nervous gulp. "Who was that man really?" I ask Thomas quietly.

He shakes his head, as if unable to comprehend that I don't know. "He's the son of Alfred J. Calloway, an important political figure with deep ties to Washington's political elite. Victor's father wanted him to go into politics as well. With the money from his mother's family, old generational money, it would have been a cinch for Victor to have one of the best political campaigns in history, but Victor had other ideas. He grew up in the lap of luxury, attending private schools and excelling academically. After high school, he attended a military camp. Some may see that as enduring a hardship, but I think it appealed to Victor's meticulous and structured nature. After high school, instead of attending college, Victor Calloway disappeared from the social scene."

"Disappeared?" I whisper. "Well, where did he go?" Thomas had leaned in close to tell me these things. I am thoroughly intrigued. We may as well have been here alone, for all I took note of the different people conversing privately in their own little groups around us.

"I don't know," Thomas says, and straightens up. "There's rumors and speculation, of course, but I think that's all I want to say on the matter of Victor Calloway."

Now Thomas takes me by the arm and leads me away to an even quieter corner. He leans in again, whispering urgently to me. "It's obvious to me that you don't belong here, my dear. I don't know who you are exactly, but I suggest you rethink your presence here. You're already on Victor Calloway's radar, and it's only a matter of time before you'll be escorted out of the building."

I flush, feeling caught out and guilty. Before I can protest, Thomas continues his appeal. "Victor is a dangerous man. Being thrown out will be the kindest conclusion to your unwanted presence here, if you catch my meaning. Soon those doors will be opened, and everyone else will walk through. Then the real reason for this meeting will start, and I suggest you get out of here before that happens. You won't be allowed to walk through those doors, you hear?"

I glance over at the doors he is talking about and see two security guards standing there with clipboards in their hands. By the bulkiness of their suit jackets, I would guess that they're armed.

When I look back, I see Thomas has left me and is walking through the crowd. He's probably right. It seems I've overstayed my welcome. It's time to find Marcus. I walk through the room looking for him, wondering if his evening has been even half as eventful as mine has.

I spot Marcus standing out on the balcony with his hands in his pockets. He seems to be looking out across the downtown Washington skyline. I'm just about to walk out and join him when another person comes into view. Someone is out there talking to Marcus.

I can just hear what the two men are saying—they're standing far away, so I have to really strain my ears to hear them.

"Are we ready to proceed with moving certain pieces off the board?" Calloway asks Marcus.

It's clear that they know each other. Marcus assures Calloway that "the board is set," whatever that means. As I watch, Victor Calloway slaps Marcus on the back, and Marcus turns his face. I can see Marcus is smiling at Victor. The two of them start to turn around, and I suspect that they're going to come this way at any moment. I duck out of the doorway and stand with my back against the wall. I see them walk past me mere seconds later. Since I'm hidden by the French doors, neither of the men see me. As they walk back into the crowd, the two of them part ways, and now Marcus is scanning the room, looking for me.

RELUCTANT OPERATIVE

EVAN

$\mathcal{T}$his feels surreal, sitting in my lounge with two FBI agents across from me. I got a beer from the fridge as soon as I closed the door to my apartment. I offered them something to drink, but they declined. I guess they wanted to press upon me the urgency of whatever it is they want to discuss with me.

The agents introduce themselves as Qual and Helmsley, no first names. Qual, the white detective, takes the lead once I'm seated across from them. "We have reason to believe Miss Langford's life is in danger."

"Yeah, you already said that. Why, though? Is it about those two guys who attacked her the other day?"

They give each other a meaningful look. I get the impression this is the first they're hearing of the attack. Helmsley takes a pen and notebook out of his pocket. "When was this?"

I give them the exact date and a rundown of the events. "I have no idea what they looked like, or why Lacy didn't want to go to the police, but she was adamant about it. Of course, Marcus was there to save her, so I guess it turned out okay." I say this last part with a note of bitterness in my voice.

Qual looks at me, one eyebrow raised. "Marcus Grayson?"

I nod, a little surprised that they seem to know immediately who I'm talking about. "Who is he? Is he an agent too?"

Helmsley shrugs, looking uncomfortable. "He's not an FBI agent, no. His connection to this is a matter of national security."

Oh, great, I think. *Now they start with this national security nonsense.* I had hoped that keeping information close while still asking for someone's help was just Hollywood BS. Guess the movies got the arrogance of the FBI right. I put my beer down on the coffee table and fold my arms across my chest.

"I guess you better tell me what this is all about."

Helmsley answers, "We believe Miss Langford inadvertently got mixed up in a dangerous conspiracy. She seems to have been investigating the nature of it, and we're afraid that if she keeps on doing that, she'll get hurt."

Qual then leans forward. "The conspiracy seems to be tied to global security and could result in significant harm. Already in the Washington social and political structure, key players are being targeted, removed, and replaced with others who we think are connected to the conspiracy themselves. It started with allegations brought forward against Senator Thomas Albright. He was accused of being involved in illegal arms deals. Do you remember reading about it or hearing about it a few months back?"

I nod. I take a keen interest in politics. The allegations had come as a complete shock to me. Before that, I used to be one of Albright's supporters.

"Those allegations proved false, and the information brought forward was investigated, but ultimately proved as thin as vapor. Unfortunately, the damage to Albright's reputation was already done, and it's believed that was the intention." Qual's face is flushed as he says this, almost as if he takes what was done to Albright personally. I get the impression he's more of the hothead between the two agents.

"That is just one example of how a powerful individual was brought down by an organization that moves in the shadows, gaining power by any means necessary. We've been unable to establish who is running this organization."

"And you think Lacy is involved? How? She's a relationship consultant, for Pete's sake!"

"We don't know how it happened, but we're sure that it has to do with a file one of Miss Langford's employees got hold of. You know Mrs. Jamie Kaplan, don't you?"

I'm startled, but don't want to say anything. I know where Jamie is. She's living at Lacy's vacation house. Since admitting this could get Lacy in trouble, I keep my mouth shut.

Qual smiles, as if reading my thoughts. "It's okay. We know you helped Miss Langford to move Mrs. Kaplan to the lake house at Deep Creek. It's the best place for Mrs. Kaplan and her children at this time. Obviously we can't go into specifics about the entire investigation, but we believe that sooner or later the people behind the conspiracy will try to eliminate Mrs. Kaplan, and that will be our shot at catching them, if we can control the situation."

"So why reach out to me? Why not talk to Lacy herself?"

Qual shrugs, obviously a bit irritated. "We tried to advise Miss Langford to leave the investigation alone. We sent her a note saying that she's involved in things she shouldn't be. That only seemed to fuel her curiosity further. Then we tried installing listening devices in her apartment, but since then, they've all been found and destroyed."

I look at the two agents with my mouth hanging open. Then I burst out laughing. I just couldn't help it. One woman outsmarted two agents? "Yeah, you guys obviously have no idea what you're dealing with."

Helmsley nods. "That's become apparent to us as well."

"So if subtlety didn't work, why not just approach her directly?"

"It's gone beyond that, I'm afraid. Do you know where Miss Langford is tonight?"

I look at Helmsley. "She went to a black-tie event with Marcus Grayson."

Helmsley nods. Obviously they already knew this. "It's a top secret meeting where we believe some of the people involved in this conspiracy are getting together to discuss ongoing strategy. We tried to get an undercover agent in there, but we failed. It seems that the guest list is tightly controlled. Yet Miss Langford and Mr. Grayson managed to get in. We want to know what she found out at this meeting. That's where you come in."

Qual picks up a bag that he brought with him that, until now, was lying forgotten on the ground at his feet. "We want you to install new surveillance equipment in Miss Langford's home and around her office. Ones that will not raise an alarm with most surveillance equipment detection devices. You know her best, so you'll have a better chance of firstly, having access to her place, and secondly, knowing where to place these bugs without raising Miss Langford's suspicion again." Qual places a tiny listening device on the table between us. "Then you'll need to monitor her and report your findings back to us."

I look at the two agents incredulously. "You want me to spy on Lacy and report her movements back to you? I won't do that! It's wrong! Lacy trusts me!"

Helmsley smiles bitterly. "Which makes you the best candidate we have to do this." He sees that I'm not going to budge. "Look, until now, we've moved under the assumption that Lacy is innocent in all of this. Unfortunately, her being able to get into the summit meeting tonight looks suspicious to those we report to. Not only do we have to know what she finds out at this meeting for the sake of national security, but also to clear her own name."

"So if I don't agree to help you spy on Lacy, you'll charge her with a whole bunch of federal crimes? Destroy her name and reputation, her whole life?! Then you're just as bad as the people that you're trying to stop!" I'm angry now, but more than a little scared as well. Never in my wildest dreams could I have imagined being placed in a situation like this. All that keeps clanging around in my head is that Lacy is in trouble and that she needs me.

"Whether or not we charge her with anything when all this is over depends on your cooperation, yes. However, you're missing the most pressing point. We won't be able to charge her with anything if she ends up dead. Moving forward, we have to assume Miss Langford is working with these people, and she may very well end up in the crossfire between our two organizations."

I take a long swallow of my beer and think about what these two guys are saying. My hands are shaking. If Lacy's life is in danger, then of course I'll do whatever is in my power to help. "Lacy is not allowed to know that she's being monitored, is she?"

Helmsley shakes his head. "No. We don't believe it's in the best interests of the operation to warn her anymore. We're changing tactics, and need to know what she knows while maintaining her safety and that of Mrs. Kaplan and her children, who are also innocent victims in all of this."

Finally, I nod. It takes a while for the two agents to run me through the plan, the listening devices I have to install, and how to contact them after I've done so.

～

STANDING IN THE DARKNESS OF LACY'S APARTMENT LATER that night, I feel a nervous but undeniably excited tingling all over my body. *Is this what people normally feel when they enter other people's houses without the homeowner's knowledge? Is this dark thrill, knowing it's wrong, part of why they do it?* Although I know my intentions for being here are pure, I can't help but feel gleefully guilty all the same.

Just do what you came here to do and get out of here. It's good advice, and I decide to follow the instructions of that internal voice.

After putting Lacy's spare key that she entrusted me with months ago back in my pocket, I switch on the flashlight I brought. I'm careful not to shine it on the windows, because someone from the neighboring apartments could see it and report a break-in.

The last thing I need is to be arrested for breaking and entering. They didn't say as much when they gave me the instructions, but I got the distinct impression that I'm basically on my own in this part of it. If I get caught, then the two agents will have no problem with hanging me out to dry.

It takes me longer than I would have thought to find the appropriate locations for the listening devices. Helmsley had given me a layout of Lacy's apartment where the previous bugs had been placed. Obviously they were found and destroyed, so I have to find new locations for both the listening devices and the cameras so I can watch Lacy's apartment in real time.

I suspect Marcus helped Lacy with finding and destroying the first lot. It's frustrating not knowing how or why he's involved in all of this, but the very fact that he is proves that he's not what he seems, maybe not at all the person Lacy thinks he is. I feel a little bit vindicated knowing I was right not to trust him and that it has nothing to do with being jealous of his shared history with Lacy.

I have no idea how long Lacy will be gone, how long this event is supposed to last. Every second that ticks by feels like I'm about to be caught red-handed.

By the time I sneak out of Lacy's apartment, I'm drenched with sweat. I know I'm not out of the woods just yet. I still have to sneak downstairs without being seen. There's a moment when one of Lacy's neighbors almost catches me. In the last second before the lady coming up the stairs would have looked up and spotted me, I manage to blend in with the shadows underneath the spiderweb-infested bottom of the staircase. Luckily, this lady was too preoccupied with her phone, and I suspect a little drunk as well. She stumbles slightly before turning the corner and walking up the stairs.

I parked the unmarked white van I was issued away from all the other vehicles in the parking lot, and back behind the steering wheel, I breathe a sigh of relief. I still have to make sure that the surveillance equipment actually works.

My whole body goes rigid when the lights of an approaching car splash across mine and illuminate me for a second. I duck down and peek over the top of the dashboard. The car parks in one of the spaces marked for visitors that sits in a pool of light. The car doors open, and on the passenger side I see that it's Lacy. She and Marcus just got back from their night out. By her body language, the rigid set of her shoulders, and the fast pace she's walking in, she doesn't look happy at all. I have a sound amplifier, a device with a disk at one end, pointed in Lacy and Marcus's direction.

Through the headphones, I hear Marcus speak. "Lace, wait. Dammit, will you just wait?!"

He grabs her by the arm and stands in front of her. Lacy is folding her arms protectively across her chest. I notice all of this with a sense of satisfaction. *Looks like Mister Perfect isn't so perfect after all.*

"What is it?" Lacy asks coldly. She's definitely pissed off about something.

"You tell me. Did something happen at the meeting? You haven't said two words to me since we got in the car. What's wrong?"

"Why did Senator Albright seem to not have a clue who you are? When I mentioned to him that I was there with you, there was no reaction whatsoever."

So Albright was at the summit meeting? What the hell? Didn't the two agents say only those connected to the conspiracy would be attending? If Albright is so innocent, why was he there? Luckily, the recording device attached to the amplifier is picking all of this up.

Marcus laughs. "Well, it's not as if he's going to advertise that he hired me, is he?"

"I think you're lying," Lacy hisses. "What about the pictures you took at the shipping yard? The ones you took at the warehouse? Were you ever going to share with me what you found there? Don't you trust me?"

I have no idea what Lacy is talking about, but I suspect it has something to do with the two of them spending that day together just before Lacy went to visit her mom. I swallow down a lump in my throat. I never asked Lacy about it, about what may or may not have happened between them on that trip. I guess part of me was afraid of the answer. Part of me still is, and suddenly I'm torn between ripping the headphones off my head and listening to see if one of them lets something slip about that day.

My curiosity wins, and I lean forward, sweat dripping down my forehead. I'm hardly breathing.

"When we got to the motel, both of us were too exhausted to do anything, if you can recall. The next morning you were desperate to get back home, so there wasn't any time for me to go over the footage. After that, both of us were so preoccupied with this summit meeting that there wasn't time for anything else."

I don't love the idea that Lacy spent a whole night in a hotel room alone with this guy, but at least it doesn't sound like anything happened. I feel like an idiot for thinking otherwise. Lacy's never been like that.

Marcus leans forward and takes her hand. "Maybe tomorrow night I can bring over some Chinese, and all the stuff I found. Then we can go through it together."

The way he's talking to her, almost purring... my jaw is clenching painfully as I bite down on my teeth in frustration.

Lacy shakes her head, but it seems like a reluctant refusal. "I'm going out with Rebecca and Charlotte tomorrow night. I haven't seen them in ages. I can really use a break from all of this, to be honest."

Marcus nods. He is rubbing his hands up both of Lacy's naked arms. He moves closer. "Maybe I can come up to your place? We can open a bottle of wine and I can tell you what I found?"

From what I'm feeling right now, I may as well be trapped in one of the nine circles of hell. Seeing Lacy like that with Marcus... it's a knife to the gut. I would have preferred to stop listening to this, but I'm trapped.

Luckily, Lacy steps away from Marcus and shakes her head. "I can't. I have an early morning ahead of me. Busy... clients to see. I better get going."

She leaves Marcus standing there, looking after her with his mouth hanging open. I want to shout and pump my fist in the air, I'm just so damn happy. All this time part of me really thought there was something going on between them. More than Lacy was admitting to me.

Sure, I watched Marcus try his luck, but can I really fault him for trying? Lacy is a beautiful, intelligent, deeply compelling woman. Maybe if the roles were reversed I'd try my luck as well, even if she was with someone else.

The most important thing I witnessed was how Lacy handled herself. She rejected his advances successfully. It makes me feel sort of guilty for that scene in her apartment earlier. I should have known that she can handle herself.

I watch as Marcus gets into his car and drives away.

Now I turn off the sound amplifier and instead listen through the headphones to what the bugs I planted are picking up inside Lacy's apartment. I can see her on the little monitor, unlocking the door. This is almost as good as being right there.

She closes the door behind her, and I hear a light thump as Lacy presses her back against the door and slides down onto the floor.

Now she's sitting there, quietly sobbing with her hands over her face. For the first time, knowing what I now know about what she's been dealing with, I realize how awful it must be for her to feel like there's no one in the world she can confide in.

UNDERNEATH THE SURFACE

LACY

*CW*hen the front doorbell chimes loudly, echoing through my apartment, I sit with the mascara wand clutched in my hand, staring at myself with frightened eyes in the mirror.

Although I'm getting ready for a night out with Charlotte and Rebecca, the first time I'll be seeing them in weeks, I know it's neither of them that arrived at my apartment, because I'm meeting them at the club.

I've been super on-edge the whole day. I went into the office, and instead of working, I did some research on Victor Calloway. He's every bit as mysterious as Thomas Albright said he was. Over the years, a few amateur internet sleuths interested in exposing shady dealings of high-profile people had put together information on Calloway in a way that would fit different conspiracy theories about who he is and his dealings with other influential people, both socially and economically. Calloway, being from both old money and the political elite, fit the bill as someone these people would be interested in.

Most of the conspiracy theories are completely outlandish, often involving things like the illuminati and lizard people. Trying to tread through this obvious junk to find something credible was a difficult and treacherous business. Interestingly enough, the conspiracy theorists who suggest Calloway is an assassin, a killer for hire to the elite, make the most compelling arguments for their case. These people managed to compile photo and video footage evidence of Victor over the years when he was "missing," in which he showed up at functions and exclusive parties, rubbing shoulders with powerful people in London, Paris, Germany...

The conspiracy theorists suggested that at each of the functions that Victor Calloway attended, some VIP ended up dead shortly afterward. Looking into it, I realized that the supposed deaths were all linked to natural causes and tragic accidents, and in some cases the people who supposedly died are still very much alive, leading me to believe that Calloway isn't in fact a killer for hire and that the deaths following his presence at these parties were nothing but coincidence. Still, Victor's presence at these functions would suggest that he's at least a person who socially and politically plays different fields.

In the end, I felt that although he's probably not some highly paid assassin, he at least works for some clandestine organization, and represented this organization's interests by attending these super elite functions and parties. He was never photographed with a companion, suggesting that for him, this was work. He seems to be a singularly focused individual, not partaking in the normal distractions of building romantic relationships.

One little piece of info I gathered was from remembering an offhand comment Thomas Albright made that Victor Calloway attended a military academy instead of a regular high school. I had my suspicions regarding his connection to Marcus, and found it. Both of them attended Washington State Military Academy. A few years apart, because Victor is more than 10 years older than Marcus, but it's a connection nonetheless. One that Marcus failed to mention.

He's been calling me all day, wanting to get together so he can share what he found at the shipping yard and at the warehouse, but after seeing his interactions with Victor at the summit meeting, I really don't know if I can trust Marcus anymore. I think I need to pull back from him for a while. I need to ask Jamie for help with doing research about Calloway and trying to uncover the connection between him and Marcus. I've already messaged her the details. She'll look into it for me.

Now, as nervousness clenches my stomach, I'm afraid it's Marcus at my front door. I stand up from behind my dressing table. On my way there, I tie my robe more securely around my body.

I open the door just a sliver, and I'm glad to see that it's only Evan. "Hey Lace, mind if I come in?" He looks at me uncertainly. That wariness certainly wasn't always in his eyes. *Dammit! Why did my life suddenly become so complicated?*

I hold the door open for him and make sure to lock it again as he walks in through the kitchen. In the lounge, I sit down on the couch. I'm glad to see Evan, and I'm hoping to talk this thing out, what happened last night and that ugly scene with Marcus. I thought for sure that it was over between us, that Evan was never going to speak to me again. His presence here suggests that he still wants there to be an us, even after all that happened.

Instead of sitting down, Evan is pacing around like an agitated tiger. I watch this for a few moments in silent wonder. I've never seen Evan like this. The night before, I had never seen him so angry, either.

I open my mouth to start the conversation, but before I can say anything, he walks over and bends down in front of me. He takes my hands into his and looks earnestly up into my face.

"I don't know what's been going on with you, what you've gotten yourself involved in, but I think you should stay home tonight. Just stay here in your apartment where it's safe."

How on earth did he know I'm getting ready to go out? Then I realize he would've noticed my makeup, the earrings I'm wearing, the way my hair is done. I squeeze his hands, trying to give him some reassurance. "I'm just going out with Charlotte and Rebecca. That's all. I'll be perfectly okay. Please, don't worry."

Instead of calming him down, it only seems to agitate him further. He has a wild, panicked look about him. He disentangles his hand from mine, reaches out and touches my face gently. He's cupping my face in both of his hands. I feel the familiar heat rising because of his touch, but I don't think a passionate encounter is exactly what he has in mind.

"Please, for once, just listen to me. I have the most awful feeling about you going out tonight."

I sigh heavily. I can see the genuine concern in his eyes, but I just can't cancel my plans with the girls last minute and disappoint them again. Things have been so hectic lately—I haven't been a good friend. I have to maintain some semblance of my normal life, because if I don't, when all this is over I'll have nothing left.

I'm about to tell Evan some of this, but he gives a frustrated grumble and starts pacing again, leaving me to stare after him, perplexed. "What's gotten into you all of a sudden? I tried calling you last night after I came back home, but you didn't answer any of my calls or messages. We haven't even talked about that scene yesterday, you almost beating Marcus up, and now you come here acting like... I don't know what."

He gives me a helpless look, as if he's dying to tell me something but can't possibly bring himself to. I stand up and go over to him. He grabs me around the waist and hugs me to him tightly. "I just want you to be safe. I'd die if something were to happen to you. You don't know..."

I don't know what? Did Evan somehow find out about the file, about Victor Calloway and the conspiracy? I've been careful to keep him out of it after he helped me take Jamie to the lake, so how could he possibly have gained new information? I dismiss the idea. This is probably just Evan reacting to Marcus as the perceived threat.

Well, he's not exactly wrong, is he? The thought is filled with chagrin. No, Evan isn't wrong about Marcus. I don't think I can trust him at all. I push that thought away as well. I really don't want the thought of Marcus to taint any moment between me and Evan anymore. I reach up and kiss Evan. It's meant to be a tender kiss, a *thank you for worrying about me* kiss.

He takes me by surprise when he responds, not by kissing me back softly like I expected him to, but by grabbing me, crushing his body to mine, and hungrily devouring my lips with his.

Soon, both of us are panting. My face feels warm, my body tingling with want. I know he wants me, too. I can feel the hard, throbbing rod of need against my stomach. He picks me up and lays me down on the couch so I'm sitting up. I reach for him, meaning to undress him, and he takes my hands and pushes them back against the headrest.

"Keep them there," he warns, and I can feel a clenching between my legs. I've always loved it when he takes charge like this.

He takes the belt of my robe in his hand and pulls, letting my robe fall open to either side, unwrapping me like I'm a gift. I have a pair of lacy black underwear on underneath. He looks down at my body, caresses every inch of me with his eyes. I can see by the way his pupils dilate, his eyes darkening, that he likes what he sees.

Afterward, I still have my eyes closed, needing a moment to recover. I feel Evan move, and he's adjusting my underwear for me, closing my robe. I open my eyes and push up so I'm sitting upright on the couch. I grab his hand, meaning to let this moment between us drag on, giving back some of what he just gave me. I can see he's still hard, still wants me.

He bends down and kisses me on the forehead. "Take care of yourself, Lacy. Please." Then he pulls his hand out of mine, turns around, and leaves. I hear the front door open, and then close again a moment later. I'm left there, basically still in pieces. Evan just left.

What the hell just happened? Why didn't he stay? Nothing's been resolved between us! Nothing! In this moment, I feel so confused, so lost. I pull my legs up on the couch, curling up into a ball. I fall to my side as the sobs start racking my body. I've never felt so abandoned before.

As I wipe the tears from my face away, I realize this isn't quite true. I felt like this years ago, just after Marcus left. That was a watershed moment for me, for sure. Feeling like that, I promised myself that I would never let another man or woman do that to me ever again. Since then, I've never let anyone get close enough to me to hurt me, to make me feel so lonely, so desolate, when they leave.

I don't know exactly how long I lie like that, crying. I don't hear the front door open, don't hear someone walking across the tile floor of the kitchen, or hear them discover me in my moment of utter despair. I just become aware of someone touching my hair tenderly, stroking it gently, comfortingly. Someone is kneeling down in front of me. With the tears obscuring my vision, this person is a shattered image, a broken prism of a man. It might have been anyone at all that I'm reaching for now, lost in my sorrow.

135

I grab him around his neck, and he picks me up, holds me tightly. His strong arms fold around my shaking body. He's saying nonsensical words to me as he holds me, as his hands move over my back.

"Shhh, it's okay. It's okay, Lace. I'm here, and I'm never leaving you again, never."

I desperately want to hear those words, desperately want those reassurances. All the loneliness and the feelings of isolation of the last few weeks come bubbling up. The man is still talking, telling me everything that I need to hear.

"You're not alone, darling. You don't have to be alone ever again. I'm here for you, I'm here."

I'm lying with my head on his chest. My hand is travelling up his chest, and now my fingers are stroking his neck, his jawline. I hadn't realized it, but this moment, bursting at the seams with emotion, is turning into something else, something more than just taking and giving comfort.

I feel the stubble of beard, smell his spicy, musky scent, and realize suddenly that it's Marcus's voice urgently whispering. Marcus... and not Evan. Before I can do anything to stop it from happening, Marcus's lips come crashing down on mine. It's a furious kiss, rough and unsuppressed, every bit as passionate and wild as it was all those years ago.

The moment seems to fold in on itself, and I'm suddenly transported back to a time when this man, this confusing, enigmatic, powerful man, was all I wanted. I'm just out of college again, hungrily experiencing the world in little bittersweet bites as Marcus would allow.

The moment stretches out between us, and I feel his hands moving over my body, exploring, squeezing, stroking... just like Evan's did a few minutes before. *What the hell is happening to me?!* I try to push Marcus away as reality reasserts itself, as Evan's face appears behind my closed eyes. This is crazy, and terribly wrong!

I try to push Marcus away, but either he doesn't care or he's mistaking my fluttering hands as a sign of the passion and wanting that I so stupidly displayed a short moment before. He's not responding to my protests, and I have to find some way to make him hear me. With nothing else to do, I bite down hard on Marcus's lips that are still assaulting mine, bruising them with the intensity of his lust.

He yelps and moves away from me, surprised. He brings his hand up and touches his lip. His fingers come away bloody.

I stand up, pushing him aside. Now I'm standing across from him, a good distance away. I'm hugging myself with my arms. I swallow hard. "That... that was a mistake. I'm sorry." I can feel my eyes are large. I'm shivering from the shock of what almost happened between us, from what *did* happen. I'm not used to losing control like that.

All the previous tenderness and concern for my well-being is now gone from Marcus's face. He smiles, his teeth covered with blood from his broken lip. It's gruesome, and my stomach gives a disgusted little lurch. *He looks like a shark regarding its prey.*

The thought is there and then gone as Marcus slowly gets to his feet. I hug myself, all too aware now of how sparsely I'm dressed. Marcus doesn't try getting close to me again. He regards me for a moment from the other side of the room.

"You naughty little tease," he says, and then laughs. "That's okay. I now know you still want me. I'm a patient man, Lace. I have some time. I'll wait for you to make up your mind."

Marcus strolls to the archway leading to the kitchen. He pauses, turning with a finger raised, like a teacher correcting a slow student. "Just remember, my patience isn't infinite. Sooner or later it will run out."

I hear him leave, and breathe a sigh of relief. I stand there alone in my living room, my thoughts swirling around in a whirlpool. Then I remember Charlotte and Rebecca, my night out with them. Shit!

I rush to go get ready, but before I do, I lock the front door so there will be no more surprise visits.

THE COST OF DUTY

EVAN

*W*hen I get back to the van, I'm shaking. I had to get out of there. The moment between me and Lacy, that mindless encounter of passion, left me reeling. If I had stayed, I would've spilled the beans, told her all about the danger she's really in and how the FBI recruited me to help them keep track of her. That would've been dangerous for both of us, so I left. My need for her is still coursing through my veins like a flash flood.

I take a few minutes to gather myself. Then I switch on the monitor connected to the cameras inside Lacy's apartment. What I see there shakes me to my core. She's still lying on the couch, but now she has her legs pulled up to her chest in a fetal position. It's so vulnerable, so unlike the woman I know, that I struggle for a few moments to believe it's really Lacy. Through the listening devices, I can hear her loudly sobbing.

Shit! That's not how I wanted to leave her! Having sex had come as a complete surprise to me too, but I thought she understood that I meant her no harm, that I love her and only want what's best for her.

Feeling guilt clench my stomach into a tight ball, I reach out to open my car door, meaning to go back there, to take her in my arms and apologize for leaving her in such a state. Though I don't understand why she's crying, what she's feeling, it doesn't matter. Obviously she's hurting, and I need to make it better.

Movement on the monitor catches my eye, and I see someone entering Lacy's apartment. I see Marcus's familiar hateful form move through the kitchen and then appear in the entryway to her living room. He notices Lacy on the couch, regards her for a moment, and then moves forward, obviously about to give the comfort that I wanted to give, that I should be giving.

Part of me wants to jump out of the van, sprint up the stairs, and interrupt this scene as it's unfolding, but I'm suddenly powerless to move. It's like watching a car crash unfold before your eyes and being unable to look away.

I see Marcus stroking her on her head, and then I see Lacy sit up and reach out, grabbing Marcus around the neck and sobbing with her arms around him while he lifts her up. *What the hell?! Why is she allowing this to happen?!*

I see with eyes that feel like they are burning how Marcus is now pawing at her. How the interaction is slowly turning from giving comfort to something else entirely. As his hands move down her back, cupping her bottom where the short robe lifts up to reveal her thin lace panties, the bitterness of jealousy and rage fills my mouth.

How can she do this to me? I can still smell her, still taste her. Now I'm watching as another man is getting ready to make love to her. He's kissing her hard, and she seems to be kissing him back. It feels like a knife to my heart, twisting, turning. I breathe out, all the hurt of seeing that carried on one breath. I'm unable to make a sound—thankfully, because had I shouted my anguish, the world may have shattered from its sound.

Then Marcus lets Lacy go suddenly. I see him reach up to touch his mouth, and think Lacy must have bitten him to make him stop. Now she's standing on the other side of the room, hugging herself. *Good!* The thought doesn't carry enough conviction, though. I had seen too much before she finally ended it.

I hardly take note of the promises he makes to her, hardly take note of his departure or of Lacy rushing to get ready. Of course she's still going out with Charlotte and Rebecca. Of course she's not listening to a word I said.

I'm in no rush to follow Lacy. The night Lacy left her phone at the office, the FBI installed spyware on her phone so it would act as a GPS. They've since handed the tracker over to me. I know I can catch up with Lacy in a minute or two once I'm ready.

I need a few moments, because I'm still shaking with anger and frustration. I have my hands over my eyes. All has gone quiet in the apartment since Lacy's departure. It's a few minutes later when I hear a stealthy little *click* through the headphones.

I look up, and see on the monitor through one of the cameras, Lacy's apartment door swings open. Three men enter, their hands covered with black gloves. Otherwise, they are dressed in normal, everyday clothing. The one walking in front has a lock pick in his hand. Evidently, he just finished quietly breaking into Lacy's apartment. Seeing them there, so soon after Lacy left, gives me a chill down my spine.

The leader turns to the other two and quietly says, "Boss wants us to look for any evidence or clue that will suggest where the Kaplan woman is hiding. He's done playing games. He wants her found and eliminated. We should've done something before Langford ran her and the kids out of town."

My hands clench on the steering wheel. These men mean business. I realize two things as I sit there, helplessly watching as they rifle through the files in Lacy's office: The first is that finding the connection to Deep Creek won't be difficult. Lacy bought the place for her mother, but she's still paying water and utilities, and probably receives a bill every month. The second thing is that even if I call Helmsley and Qual to report that Jamie and the kids are no longer safe, they won't move the little family to safety. They want to use them as bait to lure the men working for whoever is behind this conspiracy. For both sides, Jamie and her two little boys are just collateral. Too often in a situation like that, the bait gets hurt, sometimes ends up dead. Men like Helmsley and Qual would write these deaths off as a sacrifice made for the greater good. That's how they do certain things and are still able to live with the consequences.

That doesn't sit right with me, never will. Especially not where two little kids are involved. I know I can't drive to the lake house and move Jamie and the kids myself. Sure, Jamie has met me before and we were always friendly. She knows I helped Lacy to move them to safety by Lacy borrowing my car, but it's Lacy she trusts. Especially after the world recently turned on her so viciously. If I just show up there, she won't give me her cooperation. I need Lacy.

I bring up the spyware tracker app and see that Lacy is at The Rose Petal Lounge, a posh champagne bar that transitions into a full nightclub after 12 a.m. It's a favorite place of Rebecca and Lacy's where they've hung out countless times in the past. I've joined them on a few occasions, and was unsurprised when Gary and Charlotte made their escape each time just before it went full club mode.

I'm glad that the place where Lacy went is at least somewhere I know. Only problem is that it's large and the interior is very dark, as these sort of places are. Every second that ticks by is another moment of opportunity lost to get Jamie and her family out of harm's way before the guys who are supposed to eliminate her as a witness arrive.

As I speed away from Lacy's apartment, my emotions are in overdrive. I drive blindly, feeling as if I'm moving through treacle, as if time became something rubbery trying to hold me back. How will I feel if we're too late and the little family ends up dead? I have no idea, and don't even want to entertain the thought. I can't begin to imagine how Jamie got involved in all of this, but I'm positive that she got roped in against her will, not because she's done something bad.

Finally I get to the club, park the car, and walk up to the roped-off doors. There's a line of people standing there, waiting impatiently. They are dressed in designer suits and cocktail dresses. Dammit! There's a wide-shouldered, surly looking bouncer in a suit outside, checking reservations on a clipboard. I look down at my faded t-shirt and jeans and know I'm not getting in there dressed like this, even if I bribe the bouncer with a wad of cash. Maybe I should have taken the time to swing by my apartment and put on a suit, but it would have taken time that I certainly don't have.

As I contemplate my predicament, wondering what to do, I see two familiar faces exit the club. Gary is leading Charlotte out, his hand on the small of her back. They're smiling as they're walking out. I walk over, feeling relieved. "Hey bud, how are you guys?"

They look up, surprised to see me. Gary and I exchange a few pleasantries as I walk with them in the direction of their waiting car. Then I turn to Charlotte. "Would you mind getting Lacy for me? I just need to run something by her quickly. I would've gone in there myself, but..." I shrug, pointing down at my inappropriate clothing.

Charlotte grins. "Sure, just hold on. I'll ask her to come out here." When she disappears inside, there's a few grumblings from some of the people standing outside who have been waiting for more than an hour to get in. The bouncer barks at them to shut up.

Gary and I stand around awkwardly, waiting for the women to come back outside. "What's been going on with you and Lacy?" Gary asks quietly. "She's been all over the place for weeks now, and it's no secret that you've been missing practice sessions too. It looks like both of you are hell-bent on destroying your careers."

I look at Gary, and I really don't know what to say. I understand now why it's been so difficult for Lacy to keep the people close to her safe. They want explanations for why you're acting strange, not realizing how dangerous the truth can be. I mumble something about personal issues, but I can see Gary's not buying it. I've missed two practice sessions in the last few days. It's not only because keeping tabs on Lacy is a full-time job, but to be honest, hockey just seems so much less important in the greater scheme of things since I learned about the conspiracy. I can't tell Gary any of that, and I feel a helpless, impotent frustration. Gary is a good guy, a friend, and he deserves more than what I'm giving him.

Finally, Lacy and Charlotte come walking out of the club, saving me from having to answer more of Gary's questions. He and Charlotte don't linger, sensing that Lacy and I need a moment to talk in private. We say goodbye to them, and then it's just me and Lacy, and I have to face the music and do what I came here to do.

Lacy is giving me a careful look that breaks my heart, but I push it aside, as well as the feelings of resentment I still have after seeing what happened between her and Marcus earlier tonight.

I lead the way to a more private spot where the chances of us being overheard are slimmer. Then I turn to Lacy. Before she can say anything, I grab both of her arms so I can keep her from turning away when she hears what I have to say.

"All this time, you've asked me to trust you while you were dealing with... things that you wanted to keep me out of. I haven't been able to do that, but I want you to know that I do. Despite everything, I do trust you. You don't have to tell me anything, but I need you to please do the same for me. Can you do that, Lace? Can you trust me?"

She's looking up into my face, wide-eyed, for once at a loss for words. She nods as if in a daze.

"Right now there are men at your house, looking for evidence of where Jamie and the kids are."

She shakes her head. "What are you talking about?! That's... how can you possibly know that?"

"It doesn't matter. We have to go to the lake house and warn Jamie. She and the kids should pack up and go. The sooner, the better. They can stay at my place while this is being sorted out, or you can put them up in some anonymous hotel. It doesn't matter, as long as you don't use your credit card to pay for it. I have some cash that you can give Jamie."

"Evan, how are you involved in all of this? What do you know about it that you're not telling me?"

This time I'm the one who is shrugging and looking away. "This is where the trusting me part comes in, Lace. You know that no matter what, I'm on your side, don't you?"

She nods. "Of course, but..."

"No buts. It doesn't matter how I know. What's important is that I know that Jamie and those two boys are in danger. We can stand around and argue, or we can get them to safety. Time is running out."

I think it's the last thing I said about time running out that really gets to Lacy, because she nods. "Alright, let's go."

I lead her to the white, unmarked van and open the door for her. She hesitates for a moment, then shakes her head as if arguing with herself. I see her glance at the surveillance equipment and see her make a decision not to ask questions about it. I'm just glad that I turned it off; otherwise, she would have seen footage of her own apartment on the display, and that probably would have resulted in a whole bunch of questions, perhaps even angry accusations.

I walk around the van and get in on the driver's side. I glance over at Lacy. "Better buckle up. We have a long drive ahead of us."

THE CLEANING CREW

LACY

*W*e drive for a while in silence, me carefully regarding Evan from the corner of my eye. The van, this equipment... nothing is making sense anymore. Is everyone in my life different than I always thought they were? I thought I knew everything there was to know about Evan. Now, it seems like he's hiding this enormous thing from me, and it seems directly connected to the conspiracy, to Victor Calloway. I can't even begin to guess how or to what extent. The question is, can I trust him, and am I safe with him?

In my gut I feel that although Evan's involvement is a complicated puzzle and he's not about to share the details with me anytime soon, I can in fact trust him. These latest developments haven't changed the feeling of security I get when I'm around him.

I still have so much to figure out. About Victor Calloway and the conspiracy, about feeling watched all the time and what it may mean. About me and Evan, and what our future together is supposed to look like.

That last point is laughable, since being involved in stopping this conspiracy means both of us could end up dead, and then we won't have a future together or apart to worry about. A few times I consider just asking the questions shaking around in my mind point-blank, but Evan asked me to trust him. He used my secrecy since I downloaded that damn cursed file as an example of how we both have our secrets, both have our reasons for not telling the truth to the ones we care about, because knowing the truth is dangerous.

. If it's the truth, if Evan is in the same predicament, then pushing him into a corner to confide his truths in me seems like a terrible idea, especially since I'm not ready to share all the crazy twists and turns my investigation has taken since I started looking into the file.

After a while he seems to sense my reluctance, my inability to start a conversation. He smiles hesitantly before moving his eyes back to the road. "I hope you didn't think earlier that I came over just to seduce you. I... I was in a bit of a state, to be honest, and didn't really want you to see me like that. Not after Marcus and I almost got into a fight right there in your kitchen."

I blink, surprised at the subject he chose to talk about and the careful way he seems to be phrasing his words. "Uhm... that's okay. I... uhm... I was a bit distressed as well. I guess I've been a little... uhm... stressed lately."

He looks at me and rolls his eyes. "A bit, yeah. Just a tad." *Under-statement of the freakin' year*, I can imagine him thinking. We burst out laughing together, and it's a sweet moment. It feels good to be in sync again for once. After that, the silence between us doesn't feel so uncomfortably desperate anymore.

We called ahead from Evan's phone to warn Jamie what was happening. When we reach the lake house, all is quiet and dark but for the moonlight and the sounds of insects and birds that call this part of the world home. We warned Jamie to get the boys ready as quietly as possible and not to switch on any lights, as we don't know who may be watching the house. If it looked to them that Jamie was going to flee, it could push them into attacking. Evan and I know we'd never be equipped to handle a head-on confrontation with these people, so our best bet is to sneak Jamie and the kids away before the men coming for them get wind of what's happening.

Evan and I park the van a distance from the lake house, on the side of the winding dirt road leading past most of the houses. Then we travel on foot the rest of the way. We have flashlights but are too afraid to use them, so we rely mostly on moonlight to illuminate our path.

When we reach the back door of the lake house, Jamie opens it before I can knock. She must have been watching for us from the back kitchen window. I give her a quick hug and a few whispered reassurances, because she looks terrified. She doesn't say much, maybe because she'll only believe things will be okay when she and the boys are able to go back home again to rebuild their lives.

The boys are asleep side by side on a couch in the living room. Even woken up in the dead of night by their nervous mom telling them to get dressed doesn't seem to change the fact that they are still only little boys who need their sleep.

Evan carries Sam, and Jamie picks little Billy up, who barely stirs awake before lying his head back down on his mommy's shoulder. I carry as many of the suitcases as I can. Most of their belongings will have to stay here at the lake house since we can't carry it all down to the van. I'll have to bring Jamie and the kids some new clothes and supplies once they've been settled and I'm sure I'm not being followed by Calloway's men. In my gut, I've already made up my mind that Victor Calloway is the mastermind behind all of this.

We're a very subdued little group as we drive to the AMTRAK train station in Cumberland. It's just over an hour's drive, so by the time we get there, it's the early hours of the morning and the sun is at least up. We find a small diner where we can have some breakfast and kill time, as the earliest bus back to Washington D.C. is leaving just after 8 a.m. Evan pops over to the ticket window to buy bus tickets for Jamie and the kids. While he does, I inform Jamie about Victor Calloway and how I suspect he's part of the conspiracy, maybe even the mastermind behind it. Jamie agrees to look into it once she and the kids are safe.

They're going to take an Uber from the station to Evan's apartment, where they'll be staying for the foreseeable future. Since I'm still being watched, it's the safest place we could think of for Jamie and her sons. Since I have a target on my back, my place wouldn't have been an option.

We say goodbye to Jamie just before they get on the bus. I hug her tightly and feel a momentary surge of black, pitiless anger at the faceless people who disrupted our lives to the extent that Jamie's family—what's left of it—needs to flee like criminals just to stay alive.

As the bus disappears up the hill and around a corner, Evan turns to me. "What now, Lace? What do you want to do?"

I still feel that hard little marble of hate in the pit of my stomach. I've never been this angry. I guess it's the injustice of it that bothers me the most, how a happy little family like the Kaplans can be torn apart by a group of powerful people like they mean nothing. The fact that my own life, my career, everything that I've worked for, is hanging on by the barest of threads is secondary to the feeling I had just now, watching Jamie and her kids get on that bus.

"I want to go back to the lake house," I hiss through clenched teeth. "I want to see if these people show, and what they look like."

Evan looks at me quietly, noting, I think, the furious determination he can see on my face. He doesn't say anything as we make our way back to the parked van. The drive back to Deep Creek is quiet and tense. I wonder if Evan is as nervous as I am, wondering what we'll find when we get there. Maybe this isn't such a great idea, going back. Maybe we're walking into a trap. I know I, for one, won't be able to relax until I know Jamie is safe and I'm far away from this place that suddenly feels like it's surrounded by watchful eyes and an ominous cloud.

Evan parks the van in an even more secluded spot, and I wonder how we're going to get out again once this little detour is over. As we open the doors and step out onto the shin-length, wet grass, we navigate our way down to the cabin. I have no choice but to walk very slowly, as I'm still dressed in my evening wear of the night before. My shoes have already been ruined hours ago, during our first trip down to the cabin.

We're just about to break through the tree line surrounding the cabin when Evan pulls me down to a crouch beside him. Luckily, we've been quiet up until now, so the guys moving around inside the cabin didn't notice us approach. The back door is standing wide open, and I can see a guy with a gun standing in the doorway, just obscured by the shadows of the dark interior of the cabin. He's standing so quietly that I never would have noticed him if I wasn't looking. I'm guessing it's the noise that the men inside the cabin are making that alerted Evan to the fact that the cleaning crew is already here.

That's the only way I can think of them—as a cleaning crew. I must have heard the term from some action movie, but it fits the situation. They are here, after all, to clean up any evidence of the conspiracy they can find. Most importantly, the witnesses. By the sound of breaking glass coming from inside, I'm guessing that they're really angry and frustrated by the fact that the witnesses disappeared.

Silently, Evan and I watch and listen, waiting for the men to appear so I can get my look at them. There's no car parked nearby that we can see, and I'm guessing they did the same thing as us and parked their car a distance away so as not to alert anyone of their arrival. It takes about another 20 minutes for them to conclude their search of the cabin. Then one guy appears in the doorway next to the man standing guard.

"There's nothing here. Can't believe she slipped away. She was here for weeks, and we didn't think to check the records of relatives tied to the Langford woman." Hearing my name mentioned is a shock to my system. I feel my stomach lurch, and I clap my hands over my mouth. I'm terribly afraid my hiccups will start. This is a tense situation, and it would be just my luck for my hiccups to start.

Evan, sensing my distress, reaches out and squeezes my shoulder with one hand.

"You think someone warned Kaplan? Langford herself, perhaps?"

I see the other guy shrug. In the dark interior of the doorway, it's just a slightly darker moving shadow. "How could she know? No, something's going on here. I told the boss before that I think someone, maybe more than one person, is playing a double game. That's the only explanation I have for this."

I can't help but give Evan a glance from the corner of my eye. He knew they were about to find evidence that Jamie and the kids were stashed at the lake house. If what this guy is saying is true, then only people in the inner circle of the conspiracy were aware of it.

Evan's not part of the conspiracy, though. Right? I mean... that's ridiculous, isn't it?

My attention is drawn away from these sickening thoughts as the guys finally come walking out of the cabin together. They put their guns away. My stomach clenches painfully as I recognize all three of them. Besides the two guys who chased me in the alley that day and were fought off by Marcus, there's also the orange-haired guy who forced us into riding in the back of a fruit truck. It's the one who so forcefully reminded me of a bad-tempered ginger cat. Now, seeing him again, it's still the same. I like cats, so it should've made him maybe less scary, but instead I suddenly have an inkling of what a mouse must feel like.

Luckily, the three men parked somewhere that requires them to walk to the front of the cabin, in the opposite direction of where we are hiding. Evan and I, after pulling back and hiding behind a tree, wait another 10 minutes in complete silence until the three men are a distance away before we make our move. Then, when we are sure they're gone, we go up to the back door and walk into the cabin.

When I get into the dark kitchen, I hear and feel glass crackling under my feet. I look down and see the whole floor is littered with pieces of glass. At first the source for all that glass confuses me, as I see that all the windows are intact. Then I look over at the cupboards, see them all standing open, and realize that one of these guys threw all the glasses and coffee mugs down on the floor, shattering them. There's no reason for it. It was done out of pure malice.

Crunch! Crunch! Crunch! I hear our footsteps echoing in the silence of the kitchen. It's quieter when we move to the living room, but here, my heart breaks a little as well. My mom and I furnished this place bit by bit. Every bit of furniture, every piece of art was carefully chosen for this place, brought here and given a home because we liked it, because in most cases they meant something to us. The result was a lovely mish-mash of both our personalities, not clashing but harmoniously blending. Now, it's all been either overturned or destroyed. Even if I pick up the pieces again at some point, I doubt if I'll ever feel the same about this place again. Maybe it will be tainted forever now.

I don't have the time to mourn the loss of this place. I know that we have to leave soon. I disappear into the bedroom I recently shared with my mom on our last visit here. I already decided that I'm not going back to my place tonight. I don't want to be alone, and I'm scared that if I'm there, Marcus will show up again.

Evan's place is out of the question as well. He lives in a very nice apartment, but it's really more of a bachelor pad. With Jamie and the kids staying at his place, there won't be room for me or Evan.

Stepping into the room, I see with a sinking feeling that they touched everything here too, pulled the items out of the drawers and scattered them everywhere. Deeply annoyed and saddened by all of this, I manage to find an empty gym bag and retrieve most of my clothing that I keep here at the cabin from the floor. I quickly change out of my cocktail dress and put on a pair of jeans, a shirt, and some flats.

A few minutes later, I find Evan. He's carrying a suitcase and a paper shopping bag. He sees my questioning look and explains, "For Jamie and the kids." I can see some of the boys' toys peeking out from the top of the shopping bag. Knowing vaguely how kids are, I'm sure the boys will love getting their toys back. I smile at Evan, feeling that warm and fuzzy feeling seeing how thoughtful he is, how he cares about the plight of Jamie and her two children.

We're standing in the lounge, and something behind Evan catches my eye. There's a blinking red light in the bookshelf. I should have noticed before that given all the destruction to the rest of the cabin, with everything else in a state of chaos and disarray, it's strange that this one bookshelf is untouched, or seems that way. I brush past Evan to walk over to the bookshelf standing in one corner of the room.

"What is it?" Evan asks, and then follows me as I walk over to inspect it more closely. If not for the gloominess in the room, the fact that the heavy curtains are drawn and the lights haven't been switched on, I wouldn't have noticed the blinking light at all.

I peek between the books, and sure enough, there's something that was placed in the shelf. I pull the books out for a better look, letting them fall to the floor. What I reveal looks like some sort of electronic alarm system where the face of the clock should show the time. The light is still blinking red underneath it.

"What is this thing? Do you know?" I ask Evan uncertainly. As we watch, the clock counts down some more. Evan pulls out the books on one shelf lower, and now I can see it's attached to little packets of a substance I don't know.

I'm still confused by this, but Evan's eyes go wide, and I can see the color draining from his face even in the dark. He grabs me by the hand and pulls me away, heading for the door.

Realization suddenly hits me, and I feel my whole body going cold. "Is that...?"

Evan doesn't stop to answer my question, and that's answer enough. We start running for the back kitchen door. If we're right, and it really is a bomb that the guys set up before leaving the cabin, we only have a few minutes before it's set to explode.

Evan and I run out the kitchen door and away from the cabin. We've just made it to the tree line when there's an explosion, louder than I would have thought possible. I feel warm air gushing, engulfing me, making my hair and clothes blow forward. Now we're in the tree line, and we duck behind a tree as we hear windows shattering. I throw my gym bag down and kneel behind the tree, cowering with my hands over my head.

Evan is right there, holding me to him with his hands over mine, sheltering me with his body. I have no idea how long we sit like that, but eventually I smell burning, and we're coughing from the smoke. I sit up. Evan and I both peek out from behind the trees at the cabin, or what's left of it. It looks like a hollowed-out husk. Amazingly, most of the walls and the roof are still standing, but the windows are all broken, and a fire is burning merrily inside. It seems like the explosion pushed out through the windows; the clearing in front of the cabin is littered with half-burned, and in some cases still-burning, debris. Seeing the smoke rise into the sky, I know that we only have a few minutes before the fire department will show. I don't think we want to be here answering questions when they do.

Evan seems to be thinking the same thing. He stands up and holds his hand out to me. "Come on, Lace. We have to go."

TAKING COMFORT

LACY

As Evan opens the door, I feel dizziness wash over me, and I reach out one hand to steady myself on the side of the van. Large, black spots are dancing in front of my eyes. What I keep coming back to is how close Evan and I came to being obliterated just now. Was that their intent? Did they somehow know I was coming back to the cabin and try to eliminate me, or was it just a case of covering all their tracks since they couldn't find the evidence they were looking for?

I can't think straight, and all these thoughts are making the feeling inside me worse. From somewhere far off, I can hear Evan's voice, concerned about me, asking if I'm okay. I can't answer him, because my stomach lurches painfully again, making my gorge rise. Then I'm stumbling blindly through the tall grass and bushes. I'm about to be sick, and I don't want to do it all over the van or my own gym bag. I bend over, and the sound of retching sounds far away, like it's not even coming from me.

When it's over, I feel better. Evan is there to hand me a Kleenex and a bottle of water. In the distance, we can hear the warble of a firetruck, maybe emergency vehicles as well.

Evan helps me into the van and then walks around to put the bags in the back. While he's busy, I glance again at the monitor in the front of the van, whose screen is black. For all I know, it could just be a very fancy GPS, but I have a feeling it's not. I have the urge to try and switch it on to see what's on the screen, but I don't, and Evan is climbing in behind the steering wheel.

"I think we should find a hotel in Maryland instead of trying to drive back to D.C. just now. What do you think?"

It makes sense. We've been up all through the night, and it's been a stressful time. I can see by the pallor of his skin, by the bags under his eyes, that Evan is just as exhausted as I am. I nod quietly. I don't care where we stay, as long as it has a shower and a bed.

We find a little four-star hotel that looks like what people mean when they say a place is quaint. It's out of the way, and quiet at this time of the year, when it's not even close to tourist season.

Evan opens the hotel room door with a key card. I'm glad, because I don't have the energy to lift my arms. I sway a little on my feet as we step inside. I feel like I'm in a daze, like I'm walking through a dreamworld with fuzzy edges. After putting our stuff down, Evan notices my sluggish movements, the white pallor of my skin, and how unsteady I've become. He picks me up in his arms and carries me to the bedroom. I'm clutching him around his neck with my face turned to his chest. *After everything we've been through, he still smells good*, I think.

The room is crisp and clean, and has an enormous king-size bed. He puts me down on top of it. I get up to pull the covers back and almost fall down again when I kick off my shoes. Evan steadies me with his hand and guides me back onto the bed. I fall down onto the pillow, and it's blessedly soft. My eyes are already closed. I feel Evan's hand in my hair, stroking the strands back from my face.

"Sleep now, Lace."

That's exactly what I do. I feel my body twitch slightly as I remember the explosion, the *whoosh* of warm air that lifts my hair up and blows it forward. Only, in my dream—because that's what it is, not memories exactly, but a dream—the explosion is so much bigger. It consumes the tree in front of me, engulfs it in flames, and I realize too late that I'm part of the fire. I'm one with it, and I'm disappearing within its crackling, furiously hot embrace.

~

BEFORE I'M ABLE TO CLAW MY WAY TO COMPLETE consciousness, I become aware of the smell of food. The fact that I haven't eaten in nearly 14 hours is probably why I felt so faint and dizzy earlier. That coupled with the emotional stress, me puking my guts out at the side of the road—it's no wonder that my body just needed to shut down for a few hours. I check my watch and see that it's already after four in the afternoon. I almost slept the whole day through.

My stomach gives a tremendous rumble, and I sit up in one fast, fluid motion, like I'm a vampire rising. *Yeah, a ravenous vampire*, I think with a grin. I desperately need a shower too, but feeding the growling monster in my gut is my first priority. Somewhere in this hotel room, there's food, and I'm going to find it!

I get up, and I'm about to open the bedroom door when I hear Evan's familiar voice on the other side, talking to someone. I have no idea where exactly he is, but I suspect he's on the phone. I can't make out what he's saying; he's talking quietly, and I suspect it's because he thinks I'm still asleep. Then I remember that, despite how wonderful he's been, how caring, I still don't know how he's involved in all of this. My curiosity gets the better of me, and I open the bedroom door just a few inches to quietly peek at the lounge area on the other side of the door.

Evan is pacing up and down, clearly agitated. It reminds me of when he came to my apartment to warn me not to go out.

"Yes, she's still sleeping. But honestly, once she wakes up, I don't know for how much longer I can keep her here."

He's quiet for a moment, and then barks at the person on the other end of the call, "And how the hell am I supposed to do that? Tie her up like this is damn 1940s Germany and I'm the secret police?! If you'd just let me tell her why she's in danger, why those guys are after her and almost killed both of us..."

I close the door softly, afraid Evan will glance toward it and see me staring at him. Honestly, I've heard enough. Obviously he's not working for the people who blew up the cabin, the ones after Jamie and the kids, but he's certainly working with someone, and I have no idea what to think. Standing there, biting my lip, I'm torn about what to do and where to go from here.

Then I realize I'm being ridiculous. This is Evan, after all, and whatever else he is, he's been a rock to me these last few hours. Actually, since this whole mess started. Maybe I was wrong to be so reluctant to involve him. Maybe I should have confided in him ages ago. I decide to just handle it casually and see if he shares his part in it with me first.

I open the door of the bedroom and yawn tiredly while I stretch, as if I've just woken up. Evan is putting his cellphone away, and I think he abruptly finished his call when he heard the bedroom door open. He looks up at me and smiles, but it takes a while for the smile to reach his eyes.

"I bet you're hungry. I had room service deliver a few things." With this he walks over to the cart standing to one side. I hadn't noticed the cart before, but it's the source of the wonderful smell that woke me up. As he uncovers tray upon tray of food—pancakes with maple syrup, bacon, sausage, eggs, sautéed mushrooms, hash browns, steak and fries, apple pie, fruit salad with cream—I burst out laughing. There's enough food for an army.

Evan smiles sheepishly. "I wanted to make sure you got something you like. I didn't know if your internal clock would prefer breakfast, lunch, or dinner... but I guess I went a little overboard."

"Doesn't matter. It looks delicious." I take a plate and start dishing up. Truth be told, I don't think my internal clock is running the show at the moment, because I don't care what time it is; I take some of everything. When we're settled with a plate of food each on the couch, Evan finds a nice relaxing rom-com we can watch. The fact that he's going out of his way to put me at ease doesn't go unnoticed. I appreciate the gesture, even though I can't be sure if it's just because of his general concern for me, because he's in love with me, or if he's doing all of this because he was tasked to by persons unknown.

Regardless of motivation, after a while it has the desired effect on me, and I start relaxing and enjoying the movie. By the end of it, Evan and I are curled up together on the couch, laughing about the characters' delightful misunderstandings that keep them from finding romantic bliss. After the movie, we end up chatting.

"Whoa, that's a big yawn for someone who slept for so long," Evan remarks as my eyes are watering after I gave a big yawn. He's not being sarcastic; I can see he's genuinely concerned.

I check my watch and see that it's just past seven. If I go to sleep now, I'll probably be awake in the early hours of the morning.

"Would you like some coffee? I think the water is still hot."

I look over at the cart longingly. Coffee would have been the perfect way to finish off the meal, but I do want to sleep again eventually, so having coffee now would be the worst idea. I shake my head reluctantly.

"Nah, I guess I'll go and have a shower."

I excuse myself and get my things ready, glad that we booked into a hotel room that provides things like complementary toothbrushes and toothpaste, because it's the one thing that I didn't have extra of back at the cabin.

I brush my teeth first, since my mouth feels like some animal crawled inside it and died. Then I turn on the shower, and by the time I'm standing there naked, the water is the perfect temperature, so hot it makes the bathroom mirrors fog up.

I stand underneath the shower and let the warm water beat down on my tired back muscles. I close my eyes, savoring the exquisite feel of the warm, silky water pouring down on me. Inside the shower, it sounds like I'm standing under a tin roof during a thunderstorm.

I don't hear the bathroom door opening, or the determined movements of Evan as he undresses. I open my eyes when I hear the door of the shower sliding open, and then he is there behind me, folding his arms around me, pressing his naked chest against my wet back.

I lean my head back against him, feeling myself melt against his welcoming masculinity. His hands are traveling up my soapy, slick body, hungrily exploring, cupping my breasts and then kneading them. My heart pounds faster, my breath comes in shorter gasps.

He spins me around and kisses me, his lips hungrily claiming mine, not asking but demanding. It's a demand I willingly give in to as I fold my arms around his neck, as I taste his tongue, as I let my body mold into his.

After a while, he puts me back on my feet. We wash each other silently, falling into this other rhythm that's as natural to us as the first. How many times over the last two years have we showered together, washed each other? Many times, too many to remember the exact number, anyway. It's a pleasantly intimate ritual that somehow never made me feel uncomfortable despite my insistence that I have issues with commitment. It's interesting that in this one aspect, when other people may feel vulnerable and exposed, I feel close to Evan, and have no problem at all with that closeness.

We find warm, fluffy robes that we dress in and Evan pours each of us a drink from the minibar. As we sit on the couch, sipping our drinks in the post-glow of lovemaking, I notice he has dark bags under his eyes and is looking rather pale.

"Did you sleep at all this afternoon?" I ask him.

"Uhm, a bit, yeah," he says, but he avoids my gaze, and I'm guessing that he didn't sleep much.

I stand up and hold my hand out to him. "Let's go to bed."

Evan seems relieved. It's my turn to take care of him a little now. We take off our robes and get in bed together, naked. I love the feel of his body skin to skin with mine. It's a comfortable, homely feeling, since sex is the last thing that either of us are thinking about right now.

Holding Evan, my head resting on his chest, I feel the moment when sleep claims him. His whole body relaxes, his breathing becomes deeper and evens out. I try to relax, but I'm too alert. Despite the evening we just spent together, the part of the conversation I overheard earlier is scratching at the back of my mind. I want to brush it off as nothing, I want to forget about it and take comfort in Evan's presence.

This whole ordeal has taken its toll on me, left me feeling desolate, scared, and terribly lonely. It's only natural that I want—no, *need*— some solid ground to stand on. Part of me realizes that it's not in my nature to just turn a blind eye. I need to solve this mystery. Otherwise, I'll never have peace.

Quietly, I get out of bed, making sure not to disturb Evan. I find some sweatpants, a t-shirt, and a pair of flip-flops. As I take Evan's car keys quietly from the end table next to his side of the bed, there's a moment when he shifts in his sleep. I stand there, frozen in place, watching him turn over. When I'm certain that he's still asleep, I sneak out of the bedroom quietly. The thick, luxurious carpet in the master bedroom guarantees a silent exit.

I let myself out of the hotel room and walk down to the parking lot. I manage to find the white van that Evan so mysteriously acquired and switch off the alarm. Then I get in the driver's seat. I have my cellphone in my hand, and put it down on the dashboard. I decided that if Evan wakes up while I'm snooping, I'll just tell him that I came out here to find it. It's a flimsy excuse, but it's the only one I have.

When I turn to the mysterious monitor set up in the front console of the car, my heart is hammering in my chest. Hic! Dammit! It's been awhile since the nervous hiccups showed up. I've been in plenty more dangerous situations since the last time I had them, and I hoped I was finally rid of them, but—hic!—seems like I'm not.

I decide to ignore the hiccups. Maybe they'll go on their own if I do. I look for a button to switch the monitor on. After what feels like an eternity's fruitless searching while berating myself for not knowing more about this kind of stuff, I finally find a button on the bottom of the screen.

An image flickers into view, and I see the whole screen is split into different sections. It takes me a moment to figure out what exactly I'm looking at. When I do, my heart drops all the way to my shoes, and I'm pretty sure my mouth drops open as I recognize my apartment.

Every little screen is showing my apartment from different vantage points. Suddenly, the feeling of constantly being watched even after Marcus destroyed all the bugs in my place makes sense. What also makes sense is how Evan suddenly appeared at my apartment yesterday, nervous about me going out. He knew before I told him! I wrote it off as him just noticing that I had special makeup on and that my hair was done up as I only occasionally wear it, but now I realize that he wouldn't have taken note of those small details, not like a woman would.

With an ice-cold feeling starting in the back of my spine and moving all through my body, I realize that Evan must have seen that moment between me and Marcus as well. How I cried after Evan left me, how

Marcus almost took advantage of my distress. He saw and said nothing, not a damn word!

Under normal circumstances, I probably would have felt ashamed, but now I feel violated and very, very angry.

One good thing about this latest shock: It chased my little bout of hiccups away. *Good,* I think. I need to be quiet when I go back to the hotel room to get my stuff. The last thing I want is a drawn-out confrontation with Evan. He had his chance to tell me about this, to come clean about it and explain it to me. Instead, he kept quiet and allowed me to trust him. It's a mistake I won't be making again anytime soon.

TRUE COLORS

LACY

I arrive back at my apartment in the quiet early hours of the morning. Once I retrieved my belongings and managed to leave the hotel room with Evan still sleeping, I had to call a taxi to take me back to Dupont Circle. It was one of the longest and most expensive taxi rides I've ever taken, but at least I got away from Evan.

Now I'm standing here with my keys in my hands, wondering what to do. Knowing there's cameras all over my apartment makes me feel creeped out. Standing there, deliberating with myself about what to do, I nearly have a heart attack when someone suddenly speaks up behind me.

"Excuse me, Miss Langford?" I turn around, cowering against my own front door. A man steps out of the shadows who I know I've never seen before.

"My name is Derek Phillips. I believe you're helping Mrs. Kaplan?"

Derek Phillips? Tony's boss, the person who Jamie downloaded the secret file from? I'm so surprised to see him here you could knock me over with a feather. "Uhm, I'm sure I have no idea what you're talking about."

The thin, reedy man in front of me is sweating profusely. He looks scared out of his mind. "We don't have time for this. Look, can I come in and talk to you?"

I look at my front door, knowing that if we have this conversation inside, Evan and whoever he's working for will hear everything. I'm not sure I want that. I'm very aware that I'm somehow caught between two opposing factions, and I have no idea who the good guys or the bad guys are. All I know is that neither side really cares about me as a person. If I want to survive this and make sure the people close to me survive it too, then I have to protect my own interests.

In the end, I lead Derek Phillips to the little park in the heart of Dupont Circle. It's where Marcus and I came to have our little chat just after he found and destroyed the bugs in my apartment.

I sit tiredly down on the bench. At this time in the morning, there's no one around. We pretty much have the entire park to ourselves. I put my backpack down on the bench next to me and lean back, ready to hear Derek out.

He doesn't sit down, just stands nervously, fidgeting with something in his hands. After a few seconds of this, he hands it to me. I take it, and see that it's a memory stick. I look up at Derek questioningly.

"Marcus Grayson is not who you think he is. There's proof on there that you can't trust him."

"How... How do you know I'm involved, and that Marcus is? What's going on?"

He shifts uncomfortably. "I know about the file that Jamie Kaplan downloaded from my computer. Her husband Tony and his friend Nathan stumbled onto something they shouldn't have—a high-powered individual who was framed for illegal weapons trading. The organization I work for tried to pin drugs trading on this high-powered man first, but in the end, only the weapons trading got enough attention to destroy him. I don't know all the details. I'm very low on the totem pole of people involved. Nathan and Tony were just... they made a mistake, and paid for it with their lives. Their families are innocent bystanders."

"It doesn't explain why you've come to me. If these people are really that dangerous, why risk bringing me this?"

"Because it's gone too far. Innocent people have been dying, and I don't know what to do to stop it, because I know there are more deaths to come. I tried to protect Tony's family in my own way by directing the police away from his wife and children, to make it seem like they were at odds, but she wouldn't leave it alone. I tried to hide evidence that Tony was murdered, but it's since disappeared." Is he talking about the wallet, Tony's wedding ring? I found that stuff in Derek's office, hidden away. Now Jamie has it, but I'm not about to tell Derek that.

"I heard your name mentioned. I know that Grayson is pretending to help you. There's a video file on that memory stick. It's the last bit of evidence I have. Watch it, and if you want to talk, I'll be at this address for a few days." He hands me a card with the name of a hotel and an address. "After that, I'm gone. I'm getting as far away from here as possible."

I'm regarding Derek quietly, my mind turning. On the one hand, there's so much I want to ask him. On the other hand, I'm not sure if I can trust him. He worked for these people, and it's only now that he feels the need to turn on them. Nathan and Tony disappeared months before I found the file on my home system. Why—if it was really because of innocent people dying—did it take him so long before he decided to turn traitor against this organization?

I'm about to ask this, risking alienating him, when the loud, jarring ring of my cellphone shatters the silence of the park. I only switched the sound of my cellphone back on a few minutes ago after exiting the taxi, and haven't had a chance to look at missed calls or messages. Uneasily, I wonder if it's Evan who woke up and found that I was gone. I'm so flustered by Derek's revelations, his warnings, and what I found out about Evan that I don't look at the caller ID before pressing the answer button and putting the phone to my ear.

"Hello?" I answer hesitantly. When I look up, I see that Derek is gone. He melted into the darkness again, pretty much the same way that he appeared at my apartment.

"My God, Lacy! What... why didn't you answer your phone? What's happening? I've been trying to reach you for hours." It's my mom, and she's absolutely hysterical.

"Mom, I'm okay. I've just been..." I was about to say I was busy, which would have been the lamest excuse, considering the situation. I should have called her, I should have known that the fire department would contact her about the explosion at the cabin and that she'd be worried sick.

For the next few minutes, I do my best to apologize for not calling, for not assuring her that Jamie and the kids were gone from the cabin when it exploded and that I was safe as well.

"The fire department is saying it was a gas leak," my mom says quietly. The device that Evan and I saw at the cabin flashes into my mind. It was a bomb, and it would have left evidence behind. Someone paid the fire inspector off to say that a gas leak was the cause. By now, I shouldn't be surprised at the reach these people have to bribe government officials, police, even the fire department, but each time I see evidence of how powerful they are, it comes as a shock.

I can hear, though, that my mom is not buying it. She knows I'm involved in something dangerous, something that's been causing me a fair amount of agony. "Lacy, what's going on with you? Please tell me. I can't help you if I don't know what's wrong."

Those words from my mom are so reminiscent of childhood and depending on her to make everything okay again that I feel tears fill my eyes. "I think this one is a little outside of your jurisdiction, Mom," I say, laughing a little cynically. "It feels like I'm surrounded by people who have their own motivations. Some of those motivations are dangerous for me, and I'm finding it difficult to know who to trust."

My mom is quiet for a while, and I give her a chance to formulate a response. This is one of the things that I appreciate most about her; she never speaks thoughtlessly. When she offers advice, it is always only after considering all aspects of the situation carefully.

"You listen to me, Lacy Langford!" I know she's using my full name like that to make me pay attention. "You are one of the people I know who have the keenest insight into human nature. You do this naturally, instinctually. It precedes your training as a relationship advisor, so it's not just what you were trained for—you gravitated toward that line of work because you have a natural talent for knowing what people are all about. In this situation, I think you got blinded by other factors, and now you feel lost and out of control. To solve this problem you should get back to what you're good at, listen to that keen gut instinct of yours, and play to your strengths."

As usual, my mom's advice strikes a deep chord inside me, and I know she's right. I have lost sight of what I'm good at, and I've been running on fear and in a state of panic throughout most of this.

I assure her I'll take her advice and think of a way to use that to get myself out of this mess. We talk for a little while longer, and I tell her the insurance should have no problem paying out to have the cabin rebuilt and refurnished, since it was just a gas leak. We both know it wasn't, and she gives a rueful little laugh. "Someday soon, you're going to tell me exactly what happened here."

I guess I will, but that day is not today. There's still too much at stake. I think at the moment, my mom believes that the fire at the cabin was set maliciously by someone out to hurt me by destroying something that I hold dear. If she knew the truth, that some clandestine organization of powerful people are behind it and that it may have been done to actually kill me, she wouldn't have been this calm about it, or this willing to let me sort it out myself.

We chat for a few more minutes, but it's really early in the morning. My mom was unable to sleep for fear of my safety, but now that she knows I'm okay she starts to yawn, and the conversation starts lagging. We say our goodbyes, and I go upstairs and finally let myself into my apartment.

I've decided I'm not spending another night here while the cameras are up. I won't be able to relax knowing I'm being watched. I start packing up a few things, moving around from one room of my apartment to the next. While I'm busy, daylight breaks, and birds start chirping in the tall trees outside my apartment windows.

The ringing of my front doorbell about 20 minutes later makes me glance up from packing one of my suitcases. Is it Evan? Did he come over, realizing that something went wrong last night and perhaps wondering why I took off?

There's a hard little gem of determination in the pit of my stomach.

I guess that if Evan wants to, I'm more than ready to give him a piece of my mind. We can discuss things like snooping, crossing boundaries, and breaking trust.

I open the door, fully expecting Evan to be standing there looking at me, ashamed of what he did. Instead, it's Marcus, and he looks anything but shy and embarrassed. I had planned to watch the video file on the memory stick when I made it to the hotel room, because I didn't want the people watching me to know that I have it. Not until I know exactly what it is that I have. Now it feels like the memory stick is burning a hole in my pocket.

Derek Phillips said the video is evidence that Marcus is not really on my side. That can mean anything, really. Now what? Do I turn Marcus away, or try to continue the facade that I trust him?

Marcus doesn't give me a chance to decide. He steps up to me and grabs my face in his hands. "Where were you? I was worried sick!" He kisses me on the side of my mouth and pushes me further into the apartment, then closes the door behind him.

"Look, the time has come for us to stop playing games with each other." He says this seriously, as if he's about to tell me something I don't know or haven't considered yet. "I think your boyfriend is working for whoever is behind this conspiracy. He's working with someone, and it's come to my attention that he's been tasked to remain close to you and find out what you know."

I look at Marcus carefully. "Really? And how did this information come to you?"

"Come on, Lace. You know I can't reveal my sources. You know I'm on your side here, maybe the only person left you can trust. I'm the only one who can protect you now."

My mom's words from our conversation a few minutes ago whisper to me like a ghost, setting off all kinds of alarms inside me. Marcus is trying to manipulate me to think I have no one left in my life who I can trust. Naturally, he wants to be the one to fill that void, to ensure I gravitate toward him.

He's wrong, though. There's a whole bunch of friends and family I trust, people I've known for years who I know for a fact have my best interests at heart. My mom, Rebecca, Gary, Charlotte... and Evan, I realize with surprise.

Despite everything, my gut tells me that I can still trust Evan. However he's involved in all of this, whatever the reasons are for him monitoring me without my knowledge, he's not my enemy.

I look at Marcus and realize how manipulative he's been through all of this, ever since he showed up in my life so unexpectedly. I now believe that those thugs that attacked me in the alley work for Calloway, and considering what I saw at the summit meeting, I believe Marcus is working for him as well. Maybe the whole attack in the alley was a setup just to give Marcus a reason to get close to me. He's certainly tried to do his best to alienate the people close to me so he'd have me all to himself. Especially Evan.

Marcus must have seen some of what I'm thinking flit across my face, because he steps up to me as I retreat, and then he has me trapped between himself and the fridge. He reaches out and touches my face tenderly, stroking it with one index finger. Over my cheek, down to my lips... he's looking down at me with that familiar fire in his gaze that I remember all too well.

"You need me, Lace. You can't do this without me. Please let me help you." He's purring the words, trying to mesmerize me. Now that I've seen behind the mask, realized what he's trying to do, I see Marcus as he really is.

I try to push away from him. "I'm not interested in having a physical relationship with you, Marcus. We can't be that ever again."

Instead of letting me go, Marcus bends down and angrily kisses me on the lips. He's crushing me, and I'm finding it difficult to breathe. Behind me, the fridge rattles as stuff falls over inside.

Finally, I can't take it anymore, and I slam my foot down on Marcus's toe with all the force I can muster through the thin soles of my tennis shoes. It doesn't hurt him, but the shock makes him loosen his grip, and I wrench myself free.

I stumble back, my breath heavy, gripping my phone like a lifeline. Anger simmers beneath the surface as I glare at him. "Get the hell out, Marcus! I'll call the police if you don't, I swear I will!"

Shaking his head, he laughs. It's a low, mocking sound. His eyes are cold. "There will come a time, Lacy, when you'll wish you listened. And next time you fall, I might not be there to catch you."

The slamming of the door has its own finality as I'm left alone in my kitchen. I know I need to get out of here. I need to go somewhere where I can recuperate and actually think. For now, though, I'm reduced to sliding down the wall, to sitting with my arms over my head to try and restore some semblance of calm and control to my shaking body.

TROUBLING DISAPPEARANCES

LACY

*A*ll the way from Dupont Circle to the Intercontinental Hotel at the wharf, I'm glancing nervously behind me in the traffic, afraid that Marcus is following me, stalking me. Now that his mask has slipped and I've finally gotten a good look at the real man behind it, I know he's cruel and dangerous, and not someone I should have ever gotten close to.

I don't have the energy to face Evan, either. I know he must be looking for me, but I'm tired of both of us being a pawn in someone else's game. Right now, I need to get to a place where I can safely go through the evidence that Derek Phillips left me with and decide then if I have enough of an upper hand to take down Calloway.

I park in front of the hotel, and the valet gives me a strange look as I hand him my car keys. At this moment, I don't look like the fancy, upper-class clientele they usually get at this hotel, but I needed somewhere with excellent security so I can feel safe and know I'll be afforded the privacy I need to figure out my next move.

It takes some convincing, but I get the receptionist to accept cash for the room. Luckily, I had some emergency cash in my safe at home, and this is an emergency if there ever was one. The room I get, luxurious, open, and airy, isn't home, and can't begin to make up for the fact that my beloved apartment in Dupont Circle feels tainted after everything that happened there—not to mention that my every move was being monitored and my privacy so grossly invaded.

At least it's somewhere safe, and I feel a sense of relief wash over me as I lock the door, set my few belongings down, and start setting up my laptop. I'm determined to solve this puzzle once and for all. I take the mysterious memory stick out of my pocket and regard it as my laptop is booting up. I'm burning with curiosity about what it contains. It must be explosive, to warrant the sick fear I witnessed in Derek when he gave it to me.

I put the memory stick into my laptop's USB port. When it opens up, I see that there are multiple files on the memory stick. The first one seems to be a video file, and there's an audio file as well.

Since it's first on the list, I double click on the video file. There is no sound, and it seems to be a grainy black and white video, like the kind you get from security cameras. It takes me a moment to figure out what I'm looking at. The vantage point of the camera is from higher up, supporting my theory that it's from a security camera. The setting is somewhere industrial, and looks like a warehouse of some kind. I can make out containers and an unmanned forklift standing in the background. The metal sheet building is huge. From looking at it, I can't tell if it's a factory warehouse or maybe that of a shipping yard. When Marcus and I went around to the different locations in the file, both places we managed to get into had buildings like these.

The place looks mostly empty but for the two central figures in the foreground. There's a man tied to a chair, and another one standing to the side. With a surprised lurch in my stomach, I realize that both men are familiar to me. The one standing to the side is Derek Phillips. The man tied to the chair is Tony Kaplan. He looks petrified, and by the way his lips move, he's talking to someone off-camera.

The front of his shirt appears to be wet, and is much darker than the rest of his clothing. He struggles in the chair, his neck straining, and I can tell he's yelling at someone. *My God*, I think, *am I about to see Tony's last moments?* The thought makes me sick, but I'm not allowed to look away. Derek Phillips risked his life to bring me this. It's my duty to watch.

I see Tony cowering back in the chair as the third person, the one that was off-camera, steps forward. By his neatly combed back dark hair and his telltale body language, I can tell it's Marcus even before he takes off his suit jacket and turns sideways to place it on the table that Derek Phillips is leaning against. There are other items on the table that Marcus now picks up: a rag and a bottle of water. He seems to bark an order at Derek.

Derek goes around to the back of the chair, grabs hold of Tony's head to steady him, and pulls his head back as Marcus places the rag across Tony's face. Marcus then proceeds to spill the bottle of water out slowly over the rag, wetting it and making it stick to Tony's face as his body is jittering, trying desperately to break free.

It's sickening to watch, because through my own morbid curiosity I've read up on this particular torture technique that many secret intelligence agencies across the world have admitted to using in the past. Including different agencies in the states.

Watching Marcus waterboard a helpless Tony, watching Derek help him torture Jamie's husband, is one of the worst things I've ever had to sit and watch. It feels like I myself am drowning, struggling to breathe. It's an empathic reaction to watching another human being suffer. I have to close my eyes until it's over.

When I open my eyes again, the rag has been removed from Tony's face, and Marcus is talking to him again. I have no idea what's being said as there's no audio, but it's clear from Marcus's body language that he's using a softly soothing tone of voice now, trying to mesmerize Tony into submission, like he's done to me as well.

The video cuts out, and the last scene shows Marcus with his back turned to Tony, who is clearly pleading for mercy.

My stomach is a sick, squirming ball after watching that. Derek is right; Marcus is certainly not who I thought he was. If not for the last of my illusions about him being shattered because of that scene between us a while ago, then this would have done it for sure. I have no idea what

Marcus's role in all of this is, but I don't believe he's private security hired by Thomas Albright.

For one, Thomas didn't seem to have a clue who Marcus was. His expression didn't falter from politely interested at all when I mentioned Marcus's name to him at the summit. Secondly, he seemed way too comfortable and familiar with Victor Calloway.

Speak of the devil—the first audio file on the memory stick is a recording of Victor's voice. The recording is soft, and I get the impression that Derek Phillips either recorded it himself on a hidden device or obtained it from someone who got the recording that way. I have to turn the volume on my laptop way up to hear what is being said.

"Albright has outlived his usefulness. It is time for him to be moved aside, forcibly if necessary, to make space for those who are more willing to be a team player."

Now another voice speaks up, and I recognize it as Marcus's. "I think it's safe to say that Albright will no longer be a problem. After the arms deal scandal—" He doesn't get a chance to finish as Victor interrupts.

"That was a start, but as long as Albright is around, there are those who will follow him out of a misguided sense of loyalty. No, we need a more permanent solution than merely destroying his name."

The recording ends, and I sit there feeling cold from head to toe. What are they talking about? Destroying the man's reputation is not enough? Does Victor mean to get Albright arrested and put away on some trumped up charge? Is that the permanent solution he means, or is there an even more sinister meaning behind it?

I nearly jump from my skin when the sudden ringing from my cell-phone shatters the silence in the apartment and my own racing thoughts. It's Jamie, and I'm so glad to hear her voice. She tells me that in the last two hours while the boys were asleep, she managed to dig into Calloway as I requested. I ask her what she found out, and her response chills me.

"I think I'd better show it to you rather than tell you over the phone, Lacy. It's important. This man, he's more dangerous than I think you realize."

Intrigued, I agree to drive over there in the next few minutes. I can hear the two boys in the background and cartoons on Evan's TV. Either Jamie doesn't want to get into it over the phone because the kids are awake, or there's another reason she wants to tell me about it in person. I don't tell Jamie that I'm not at my apartment, so it will take me a few minutes longer to get there. Hopefully, if what Jamie found now is enough, I can take all this information to the police, and it will be over soon for both Victor Calloway and Marcus Grayson. It will be a relief to have this matter resolved.

I leave my laptop as is, grab my keys and handbag, and go downstairs to get my car. The drive takes an hour and a half since it's early morning traffic on a weekday, and most people who still have normal lives are on their way to work.

I pull up in front of the stylish, modern apartment building where Evan has lived for the last three years. He moved to Washington a year before I met him. I sit in the car, drumming my fingers and wondering what I'll do if I get upstairs and he is there with Jamie and the kids. What will I do if he arrives once I'm there?

I don't know how I'm supposed to act, and what he would expect from me. Perhaps things between us have degenerated too far to ever be saved, but he remains one of the few people who I know I can trust, who will be there for me if I call on him. I decide that if a confrontation with Evan is inevitable, then I will share all the information I have with him. Maybe I should have done that long ago.

My thoughts are preoccupied with Evan as I step out of the elevator and into the hallway leading to Evan's apartment. The hallway is very quiet. Maybe that should have alerted me to the fact that something is wrong, but I'm used to it, as Evan's apartment building, though nice, spacious, tasteful, and comfortably upper middle-class, isn't the sort of place a lot of families with small kids elect to buy.

Jamie's kids are usually very noisy, and I should have heard them and the television chattering from the other side of the door as I stuck my hand out to knock. The door swings open, revealing the empty apartment on the other side.

I feel my stomach twist and a cold finger move down the back of my neck. "Jamie!" I call out, and my voice echoes through the apartment. There's no answer. I walk through the hallway and reach the lounge area and open-plan kitchen. The television is paused, and there's the remains of breakfast scattered around the breakfast table. Jamie is fastidious about keeping a place neat and tidy. She wouldn't have left Evan's place with dirty dishes and pans scattered around his kitchen. I vaguely register the child's drawing of a little pig stuck to the fridge with magnets of colorful fruit and vegetables. It's strange seeing that sort of stuff in Evan's usually pristine and minimalist-style kitchen. It's like in the short time they've been here, the kids have completely taken over and stamped their presence on nearly every surface. I'd be lying if I didn't admit that it makes the place look welcoming and... homely?

But where are they? She was expecting me, so she definitely wouldn't have left. I take out my phone and try to call Jamie, but it goes directly to voicemail.

I walk through the whole apartment, checking every room. It's clear that whatever else happened here, Jamie and the kids left in a hurry. In the bedroom, clothes are peeling from a suitcase that was half-packed and then discarded. Maybe because they were running out of time and couldn't afford to wait? There's also the fact that Jamie doesn't have a car to have easily packed up and left on her own with suitcases and two small kids, one of whom actually still needs to be in a baby seat, according to law.

This is horrible, and I think I'm in shock. This hasn't hit me yet, not as hard as it will once the unreality of the situation has faded. Were Jamie and her kids abducted by Victor Calloway's men? If it was Calloway, then they're as good as dead. All I can do then is mourn the loss, but that doesn't feel right for this situation. For one, I don't see Jamie's cellphone anywhere. Sure, it's been switched off, but I don't think Calloway's men would have let her take it along at all. For another, there's no sign of a struggle, just signs that they left in a hurry.

I walk back to the living room. Jamie had information for me, important information about Calloway that potentially could have saved us all. Now I'll never have it, unless I somehow track Jamie down —but where do I start? The hopelessness of the situation is threatening to overwhelm me. My knees buckle out from under me. Luckily there's a couch just behind me, and as I sit down, I feel something hard underneath my butt.

Pulling it out, I see that it's a pink little pig sitting on its haunches and rubbing its round little belly. I throw the plastic pig to the opposite side of the couch and hear a strange rattling sound as it lands on the scatter cushion.

Frowning, I retrieve the toy again for a better look. On the top, between the pig's ears, I see a slot. *Oh,* I realize after a moment, *it's actually a piggy bank!* I shake it and hear that same noise of something rattling inside it. Checking at the bottom, I see that there's a plastic cap where a hole would give a person easy access to the coins placed inside the pig. Taking my nail and lifting the cap out, I peek inside the pink plastic depths of the pig. I see what it is, and turn the pig over in my hand, letting the memory stick slide out onto my palm.

Looking at it in amazement, I remember the drawing on the fridge that I dismissed as a cute kid's drawing. Actually, thinking about it, it may be too sophisticated a drawing for Jamie's two boys, but Jamie leaving it in a hurry as a message for me? That suddenly seems not only possible, but like exactly what happened.

UNMASKING THE TRUTH

LACY

*B*ack at my hotel room, I take the other memory stick out of
my laptop's USB port and replace it with the one that Jamie
left me. The fact that Jamie left it at all suggests that she wasn't fearing
for her life or the lives of her children when they left, because as loyal as
Jamie is, as committed to fighting for this cause as she is, I believe her
children would be infinitely more of a priority to her than this. If their
lives were in danger, she would have focused on that rather than leaving
me this final piece of the puzzle.

Waiting for my laptop to read it, I'm practically jumping up and
down in the chair from nervousness and excitement. My hands are
shaking and I'm hiccupping like mad, but this time I don't really worry
about it because there's no one here to notice but me.

When the files on the memory stick finally display on my laptop's
screen, I see that there are multiple articles and photos downloaded
from the internet. I'm amused to see some of them are the same stuff
that I found already about Calloway presented by numerous conspiracy
theorists. Just like me, Jamie dismissed the outlandish claims of illumi-

nati and lizard people and focused on the ones that seemed at least plausible, and not like the musings of a person caught in delirious fever dreams.

Jamie, with her knowledge that's a lot more extensive than mine, went a few steps further, and from her notes, I read that she found most of this information on the dark web. I'm impressed, since I myself have no idea how to even access it.

Some of the photos Jamie found are from some place known as the Farm, where clandestine officers train from different intelligence agencies. There's not supposed to be any recording equipment or cameras allowed at Camp Peary, but evidently some of these undercover agents-in-training see sneaking them in as an extra challenge to test their capabilities. The result is a slew of grainy pictures featuring future agents-in-training, and yes, in the pictures Jamie downloaded, I recognize Victor Calloway. Since Victor is 53 years old, I'd guess these pictures are from about 30 years ago.

The pictures after that are of Victor Calloway photographed at different international summits and other public appearances. He was photographed dressed in his finest, mingling with important and powerful people, and I would guess that his upbringing and years spent in private school would have made him someone who could perfectly blend in among people like that. In one of the photos, I see Victor subtly handing a device to what appears to be an aide. A newspaper article published shortly after that event links a mysterious death to one of the guests attending that particular party.

I feel a thrill of recognition race through me. The aide is also easily recognizable. Even in a black and white newspaper photo, the man with the red hair, neatly trimmed and clean-shaved, one I've recognized on multiple occasions. That means that he was an agent as well, but now works for Victor Calloway.

It makes much more sense now: Victor was never an assassin like the internet investigators suggested, but a special agent from one government organization or another. This is both interesting and terrifying at the same time.

There's one or two newspaper articles from the mid 2000s, when Victor would have been an agent for more than 10 years. Those articles indicate botched operations in foreign countries that resulted in diplomatic scandals. Victor wasn't named in the articles, as all of the agents' identities would have been protected, but one of the grainy newspaper articles shows disgraced agents leaving a plane. Most of them are hiding their faces from the cameras, but Victor, easily recognizable, looks like he's refusing to do that, feeling perhaps that the criticism was unjustified and that he has nothing to be ashamed of.

As I read about these botched operations, of speeches that Victor seems to have given years afterward, a picture starts forming in my mind of who this man really is. Obviously arrogant and self-assured, I think that Victor at some point became disillusioned by the government agency he was working for. Perhaps he was fired, but I think it's more likely that he broke away on his own and has since then been working diligently to bring down the very government he feels betrayed him, humiliated him.

Is there some way to use this information to my advantage? I think there must be. A plan of how to bring Victor Calloway down is slowly starting to form in my mind. Before I can put my plan into action, there is one person I have to contact. I have to go and see Derek Phillips and confront him with this information, see if my suspicions are correct. Not just about Victor Calloway, but about Marcus too. I think Victor hired Marcus to get close to me since I discovered the file. I want to see if Derek knows who Victor Calloway and Marcus Grayson really worked for, and how they are connected.

I take my car keys again and my handbag and head out the door. I have the address that Derek Phillips gave me; it's a seedy little house in a poorer and more run-down part of Washington that I don't normally visit. I guess that's the point. Derek probably thinks that it's a good place to hide, and that neither Marcus nor Calloway would think to look for him here.

As I drive past the run-down homes and littered streets of Woodland in Ward 8, a wave of desperation washes over me, like the hopelessness here is seeping into my skin. My hands on the steering wheel are all sweaty. My hiccups have fled for now, but I know that if my stress levels amp up another notch, then they're sure to return.

I find the house where Derek Phillips is supposed to be, and it's as if a dark cloud of foreboding is covering the entire place like some toxic sort of gas, making it difficult to breathe. I don't like this at all. Cold rivulets of sweat are running down my back as I push the little garden gate open. It gives a tremendous squeak that is unsurprising, as the hinges are caked with rust. My shoes make loud crunching noises on the dead leaves and loose rocks as I walk up the narrow garden path that hasn't been swept in ages. Clutching my handbag tightly like a shield, I walk up to the front door of the brown brick house with the peeling off-white roof and the dirty windows.

I ring the doorbell that sounds in the deep bowels of this hulking house. I wait for more than two minutes, but there's no answer. Trying the doorbell again, I suddenly feel very conspicuous standing there. I try to count until 100, but have barely reached 50 when I decide to just try the door. The handle turns in my hand, and the door creaks open.

Entering the house, it's the same feeling of nervous trespassing that I felt at Evan's place, and the same feeling of abandonment that hangs in the air. Only here, I can see that there definitely was a struggle. I have no idea how long Derek Phillips lived here, but it's clear by the overturned table, the droplets of blood I find on the kitchen floor, that something violent happened here. There's broken glass everywhere, and the TV is busted in.

Knowing that I won't find Derek here, I turn around and turn tail, desperate to get out, because I know it was a mistake to come here.

The door slams shut behind me, and I run to my car. I struggle to get my car key out of my handbag because my hands are shaking so badly. I almost drop them when a voice suddenly speaks up behind me.

"Hey lady, do you know what that guy did?"

I turn around and see an African American teenager standing with a skateboard in his hand. He's pointing to the house I just vacated.

"What guy?" I ask, but I think I already know what this kid's going to tell me.

"Guy that lived there. He moved in a week ago and got arrested this morning. SWAT team took him away."

"A SWAT team? How do you know they were?"

"Because they were wearing their tactical gear. All black, just like on Counter Force. Duh." He rides away on his skateboard, and I watch him, nonplussed, for a moment before I get into my car, wondering what the hell Counter Force is. It's only when I'm a block away that it dawns on me that the kid was probably talking about a computer game.

Well, whatever team of guys came to take Derek Phillips away, I doubt they were police officers. *Unlike Jamie and her kids, Derek put up one hell of a fight*, I think, remembering the broken glass and the droplets of blood on the kitchen tiles. It scares me to realize that Victor Calloway has these resources behind him to organize a professional abduction like this, but I should have expected it given what I found out. He has all the money in the world, connections, and special training, and me... I feel small and ill-equipped to handle this situation.

For the next while, I drive around in a daze. I feel numb and alone. I hadn't realized how much I had depended on Derek to answer my questions and to give me guidance on what my next move should be. With him gone and most certainly dead, I have no idea what to do. I feel like I'm floundering.

It's early evening, and the sun is setting by the time I get back to the hotel room. I'd like nothing more but to crawl into bed and forget all of this, but I know that if I tried, I wouldn't be able to sleep. I throw my car keys and handbag listlessly down on the coffee table. I would have avoided looking at my laptop if not for the notification sound that suddenly chimes from it.

Still feeling dazed, I go over and sit down in the chair. Poking at the touchpad to get rid of the screensaver, I see that the notification is from a news report that just came in. I frown, wondering what happened. I've set up an automatic alert to sound if a news story comes up on a subject I'm interested in. Most of my automatic alerts have to do with changes to government policy or labor practices connected to my line of work, but as I open the news article, my eyes grow wide and my chest suddenly contracts painfully as I read what happened earlier tonight.

The news article proclaims: "Disgraced Senator Dies in Tragic Car Crash." I scan the article wildly, then read through it again more carefully. A few phrases jump out at me, and between the lines, I can see that the police suspect either foul play or suicide. Apparently, Thomas Albright crashed his car on his way to his Washington home on a non-slippery, well-lit road early this afternoon. Early bloodwork indicated that he wasn't driving under the influence, and there was no one with him in the car.

The article reiterates details about the case from a few months before, when Albright was implicated in the arms deal scandal. The reporter hints heavily in favor of suicide, and it makes me wonder if this reporter was paid for his "unbiased reporting" by Victor Calloway.

I know in my gut that Calloway is behind this. I keep coming back to the recording I heard earlier, how Calloway stated that Albright outlived his usefulness and needs to be permanently dealt with. I remember thinking that Calloway meant getting Albright arrested. I should have known he meant to kill Albright. Hasn't Victor proven time and again that he has no problem with arranging for someone to be murdered?

Of course, he never gets his own hands dirty. No, he gets others to do his dirty work for him. And therein lies the problem: If I go to the police with this information, it's doubtful whether they would even arrest him on suspicion of conspiring to commit murder. Victor is a powerful, well-connected man with heaps of money. I can only imagine what the type of attorney he can afford will do with the evidence I have.

On the other hand, I can't just sit on this knowledge and hope it goes away. It won't, and neither will Victor. He has a personal vendetta against me now, and he won't stop until I'm dead. Besides, I still feel I owe it to Jamie and her kids to help her get their lives back. Days ago, I forgave her for dragging me into this unknowingly, and since then I volunteered myself again and again as the person who will try to help her.

Then there's Thomas Albright to think about. What about his wife and their children? Since the scandal broke, they've stood by him, but now, if his death is written off as a suicide, then he'll look guilty, and it's like their support means nothing then. No, his family deserves to know the truth.

Before I can land on a realistic course of action, the choice is taken out of my hands when my phone rings. I answer it eagerly, hoping against hope that it's Evan.

Evan, whom I ran away from before hearing his side of the story, I think, with guilt once more churning inside me. If I get out of this alive,

I'm going to have a few things to explain to Evan. He's another person who is owed the truth.

Unfortunately, it's not Evan on the other end of the line.

"Hello, Miss Langford." With a chill, I instantly recognize Victor Calloway's silky, baritone voice, his drawling way of speaking. I can't answer, though—my mouth is suddenly too dry.

"I'm guessing by now you heard about the tragedy that befell poor Thomas Albright? Such a waste, wouldn't you say? I saw how friendly the two of you were at the summit meeting. It's a shame that you couldn't help him. He could have benefitted from your specific area of expertise."

"You unimaginable bastard!" I hiss through clenched teeth.

"Now now, Miss Langford. There's no call for being rude. If there's one thing I can't stand, it's common rudeness."

"What exactly can I do for you, Mister Calloway?"

He gives a polite chuckle. "It's more about what I can do for you, my dear. For instance, I can return the confidential client files that have recently come into my possession. It seems someone broke into your office and stole them from your company hard drive."

My stomach turns. If those were to come out—privileged, confidential client information... I'd be ruined!

"I'm listening." I refuse to give him more. He can't know how much it rattled me, hearing what he has. If he releases that information, my reputation will be ruined, but the lives of the people I work with will be too.

"Why don't you meet me at Sterling House Rooftop Garden? We can share a drink and talk about a suitable conclusion to all of this. One that will benefit both of us."

I grin, remembering what the significance of that location is for Victor Calloway. He doesn't know it yet, but his incessant need to control and impress makes him exceedingly predictable, and I suddenly know exactly what I have to do.

"Give me two hours," I say, suppressing the urge to grin. If Victor hears me sounding cocky, he may wonder why.

THE FINAL GAMBIT

LACY

*D*riving from my apartment building to Sterling Manor, I feel more calm and collected than I have been since this whole thing started. I should be freaking out, but it's funny that the prospect of facing Victor Calloway head-on doesn't fill me with fear, only a dark anticipation, a twisted sense of excitement. I'm also more than a little angry every time I think of all the lives that this man destroyed for what I suspect is a personal vendetta against the government agency who employed him.

I plan to make Victor eat every little snotty remark he threw my way, both at the summit meeting and over the phone a few hours ago.

I'm late for our meeting. Usually I would hate to be late for a meeting as important as this one, but in this moment I really can't bring myself to care. I had to go back to my apartment to shower and change, because I'd be damned if Victor sees me looking anything less than stylish and professional. I'm wearing one of my favorite Chanel business suits and have my hair tied in an elegant twist on top of my head. The suit is a wine-red color, and I know it's one of my best.

A lot of people dismiss clothes as just something you put on your back, and although I can feel just as confident in a t-shirt and jeans as an expensive business suit, sometimes perception really is everything. I've seen the sort of people Victor likes to surround himself with, and I've seen how he dresses as well, how he carries himself. This is going to be a power play, and I have to make sure that I'm not at a disadvantage from the start, that Victor sees me as a worthy opponent from the moment I walk through the door.

The second reason I had to go back to my apartment was to set up a little safety net. I left my laptop there, and there's an automated message that I typed to Evan that will send him all the details about where I've gone and why, what I found out about Calloway, the whole nine yards. If something were to happen to me, at least Evan will know what I know.

The message is set to go off at 10:00, so that gives me an hour and a half to talk to Victor, to try and convince him to give back the client information he stole from me and make him see that the best course of action would be to give himself up. If I can convince him that it's the only way he'll survive this, then maybe I'll have a chance.

Of course, Victor is unpredictable, and I have no idea how this is really going to go down—hence the excitement.

I drive through the wooded area and see the manor in all its lighted glory, sitting atop a hill. The view from there must be breathtaking. The manor is the epitome of style and grace, a mix of opulence and old world charm. It sits like a gem in the middle of perfectly manicured gardens, emerald green in the moonlight. The slanted roof and high, ivy-covered walls rest against the star-strewn sky as a backdrop. Not so much looming as patiently waiting, the only sense of foreboding this masterpiece of architecture and design carries is the monster residing within its walls.

I can see why Victor chose this place to meet. It's certainly impressive, and I know the other reasons why it carries so much importance for Victor.

As I stop in front of Sterling Manor, a man at the door greets me. He's neatly dressed in a suit, and I guess he must be the butler. A manor of this size probably needs a lot of staff to keep it running smoothly.

This tall, distinguished gentleman greets me by name. He has obviously been expecting me, and now informs me that Mister Calloway is waiting for me in the study. He takes my coat and then shows me the way up the stairs. It gives me an opportunity to satisfy my curiosity, and as we walk, I peek inside many rooms that we pass. The whole place is richly decorated with crystal chandeliers, beautiful antique furniture, and art chosen by someone with a good eye for detail and impeccable taste.

We stop in front of a huge dark wooden door. The butler knocks politely, opens the door, and walks inside. "Miss Langford has arrived, sir."

I see Victor Calloway sitting behind a large mahogany desk. It's also an antique, and must be worth a fortune. It's a beautiful piece, as is every other piece of antique furniture in this study, including an enormous bookshelf to the left of the desk that almost covers one entire wall. The window behind Calloway shows the manicured gardens, the wall surrounding the property, some of the woods, and beyond that, far below, a breathtaking view of the Washington city skyline.

Victor glances up from his paperwork and removes his delicate round glasses as he regards the butler. "Thank you, William. You may leave us."

William nods and closes the door behind him, leaving me and Victor in a charged silence. For a moment, we just regard each other.

"I've arranged for this meeting to be completely private. The staff all cleared out, so it's just us chickens, I'm afraid." The words feel deliberate, like he's subtly reminding me that no one's around to help if things go wrong. My heart skips, but I hold his gaze, refusing to let him see the unease creeping through me.

"Would you like to sit down and have a drink with me, Miss Langford?" He gestures to a liquor cabinet at the other end of the room. The thought of drinking anything that this snake of a man gives me fills me with revulsion.

"I would prefer not to."

He grins, then puts on an over-exaggerated woeful expression. "Oh Bartleby, what am I to do with you?"

A grin flits across my face before I can help it. He's of course referencing Herman Melville's story *Bartleby, the Scrivener,* where Bartleby, a previously excellent worker, suddenly responds to every request from his exasperated boss with "I would prefer not to."

I give Calloway a slight nod, acknowledging the reference, and then I sit down and fold my hands together neatly to show him I'm serious. This isn't a social call, after all, and I would prefer to get down to business.

"I must say, I'm impressed by all of this." I gesture to the surroundings, meaning, of course, the entire manor. "Beautiful home. Your family has lived here for some time, I believe? It suits you, and I'd guess is meant to press your importance and standing upon anyone who visits."

Victor doesn't say anything, just smiles coldly. I'm guessing it's a ploy that always works because people don't often see through it, and even less of them have the courage to comment on it even if they do.

"It makes sense, considering what I learned about you these last few days, Mister Calloway. You are an enigma, wrapped up in a mystery. At least, that's how you want to appear. Not so surprising for a former Central Intelligence Agent." I wasn't certain that that was the agency that Victor was employed by until this very moment, when his eyes widen slightly and the color of his face darkens, betraying his surprise and his annoyance at me for knowing what I know.

I pretend not to notice as I continue: "Which brings me to the death of Thomas Albright. I believe you orchestrated his death. I believe it's part of a conspiracy to place certain people in key positions of power, to ultimately bring down the agency, perhaps even the U.S. government as a whole. I have a recording in my possession of you, where you state how Albright should be gotten rid of. I believe the police will find it very interesting in light of his recent death."

This time, Victor gives a derisive smirk. "I commend you, Miss Langford, on being very clever. You've solved quite the puzzle there, haven't you? However, you're putting too much stock in the evidence you think you have. At most, that recording you have will be slightly embarrassing to me if it surfaces, nothing more than a minor inconvenience, I assure you. What I have of yours, on the other hand, will be devastating to you if it's leaked. All your clients suing you for damages to their reputations, losing the business you've worked so hard to build. I'd hate to see that happening to someone like you, who doesn't have the financial means to start over." His tone is dripping with contempt. "Do you really think anyone will believe I had anything to do with Thomas Albright's death?"

As Victor regards me with an intensely speculative expression on his face, the moment is suspended between us. I hear a slight *click,* and then a door to the left behind Calloway opens. I hadn't noticed this door situated right next to the large bookshelf. A silhouette appears on the floor. In the reflection of the windows, I see who it is, and I wonder what he's doing here.

If Victor turns his head to look that way, he will discover Marcus listening in on our conversation. I have no idea how that will play out, so for the time being, I decide to proceed as if I hadn't noticed Marcus's appearance either. It does, however, give me an idea for moving forward with this conversation.

"Congratulations on using Marcus Grayson so effectively to distract me and keep tabs on how I was progressing with the investigation, by the way."

Calloway smiles mockingly, but then waves it away as if it doesn't matter. "It was nothing personal. Given your history with the man, he was the logical choice. He managed to get close for a while, but am I right in suspecting we made a slight faux pas at the summit meeting and you saw our interaction? Marcus said he suspected you saw us converse outside on the terrace that night, and after that, your trust in him was broken. It couldn't be helped, unfortunately. I had some critical information to pass on to Marcus."

I keep quiet, unwilling to say anything about that one way or the other.

Calloway nods, as if my silence is answer enough. "It's a pity. The man jumped at the opportunity to get close to you. I think me paying him was just the excuse he needed." Calloway shrugs. "He does seem rather obsessed with you."

I stand up, as if upset by what Victor is saying. I position myself in front of the slightly open door and glance at Marcus. He gives me a predatory smile, the one he gave me the last time we saw each other. He said then that at some point he's going to see me suffer. Is this it? Is this why he isn't intervening, but just standing there?

I also take a moment to glance at the clock on the highest shelf of the bookcase. There's so much time left. So many minutes to fill before Evan will even get my message. How long before he can raise the alarm bell? Will he even be able to?

I know that I can't depend on help to come. I must finish this thing between Victor and myself on my own terms.

I walk over to the chair in front of Victor's desk, and feel his eyes following me, tracking my every move as I make them. I fold my hands and lean forward, ready to play the last bit of this game, to toss the die and see where it lands.

I start by listing all the moments during Victor's career with the agency where he made mistakes, all the scandals he was linked to, and how in a lot of ways, his own arrogance led to his downfall. Just as I suspected, these reminders of his failings rattles Calloway in a way that accusing him of murder didn't. Even informing him that I have evidence linking him to the murder didn't seem to concern him one bit, but now, as I force him to listen to all the ways I know he failed as an agent, where he was reprimanded, punished, forced out, he becomes white as a sheet, and stands up from behind his desk.

He is so angry he gives me a hate-filled look that would have scorched the skin off my bones if looks could do that. He is nearly shaking, he is so angry. It's clear that what I said struck a nerve.

"You have no idea what you're talking about," he says softly, his voice little more than a whisper.

He gets up from behind his desk and walks over to the liquor cabinet. He pours himself a stiff drink of some sort of amber fluid on the rocks. In his hands, the crystal decanter sparkles in the soft light of the chandelier above. He doesn't offer me one, but takes a sip of his drink before turning to look at me once more.

Pacing up and down, Victor tells me of the injustice of it, being accused of going behind the back of his superior and taking charge of missions because the people at the top of the agency were too afraid to "do what needed to be done."

"The people I killed while working for them were never innocents.

Put that notion away. They were all bad people threatening the very way of life that people like you, who have no idea what's going on in the larger world around you, hold dear. It's because of people like me and the actions we take, the choices we make, that you can sleep so soundly knowing you are safe."

Now I have my hand in my pocket as Calloway makes his long-winded speech. Fingering the little listening device that I swiped from my apartment earlier tonight, I hope it's recording every word that Calloway is uttering. This is exactly what I was hoping for; the kind of stuff that I was waiting for all night, baiting him into admitting.

"I realize that," I say quietly, trying to make my voice as soothing as possible. It's the same tone of voice that I use with clients when they're telling me important things about themselves, things that are difficult to admit to. "It must have been a heavy burden to carry." Victor glances at me, surprised that I seem to have changed tactics.

"Is that why you hold this place so dear? Not because you truly love it, but because you need to remind yourself why you are doing all of it? Is it because this is where your mother committed suicide after you were fired?"

Victor splutters on his drink, and looks at me like I just punched him in the gut. Very few people know the truth of that particular part of the Calloway family history. I have Jamie's brilliance and computer skills to thank for finding it. It wasn't easy, because Victor bribed the medical examiner to sign off on the death certificate that his mother died of natural causes. There was an alternative report, though, that one particular doctor compiled because Agnes Calloway, Victor's mother, was his patient.

This house belonged to Victor's mother. She was the heiress, the one with the old money and status, the person his father married for those things. To Victor's mother, status and standing in the community meant everything. After the death of his father, Victor's elderly mother was all he had left, as he never had any brothers or sisters. The scandal of him being fired from the Central Intelligence Agency wasn't a blow his mother could take. On the face of it, it doesn't make sense, as very few people would have been privy to Victor being an agent in the first place. When he was fired for misconduct after botching too many operations and settling too many personal vendettas, I think with government resources, then Victor was no longer protected by the secrecy of the agency he worked for, but was fair game.

There were also rumors that Agnes Calloway suffered from the early stages of dementia. That, coupled with the perceived scandal of her son being fired, was too much for a woman like her.

Part of me really does have pity for Victor because of his mother's death. That universal empathy with another isn't something I can just switch off. Part of me understands why he is so angry, why he wanted his revenge. I never would have scratched at Victor with this if he had left me any other choice. His personal suffering isn't an excuse, though, for the monstrous things he did.

Now, he looks at me wide-eyed, and the drink falls from his hand onto the floor, ice scattering everywhere, but Victor doesn't even realize.

He walks past me to the bookshelf. He doesn't see Marcus, just pulls on one of the books, and the shelf splits open, revealing a secret doorway behind it.

I stand up from my chair, afraid that Victor is about to escape. "Victor, I really am sorry about your mother's death, but that's no reason to destroy so many people's lives. Victor, listen to me!"

I take the bug out of my pocket to show him that he really has no choice but to give himself up quietly, when he suddenly appears in the secret doorway again. He is grinning manically, holding a gun.

I raise my hands, truly afraid for the first time tonight. The listening device is all but forgotten, clamped in my tight fist. As I step back, I glance over at Marcus, who hasn't moved from his spot in the doorway but seems to be enjoying my predicament, the fear he can see etched on my face as I stare down the impossibly dark barrel of Victor Calloway's gun.

END OF A LONG ROAD

EVAN

$\mathcal{A}$s I ride in the back of the cramped black van with the tinted windows and the word SWAT, it all feels unreal, like all this is happening to someone else. I'm sweating like mad underneath the bulletproof vest that they gave me. It was part of the deal I made with Qual and Helmsley. I had to dig my heels in to be able to come along on the ride in exchange for the information Lacy sent me. What swayed the odds heavily in my favor was when I showed them the live feed from the single listening device Lacy found, dismantled, and took with her.

On it, Qual and Helmsley could clearly hear Lacy talking to Victor Calloway. Until half an hour ago, I had no idea who Victor Calloway was, but Helmsley made a point of pressing upon me what a precarious position Lacy is placing herself in by meeting with Victor alone at Sterling Manor.

At this point, as we're driving on a dark wooded road, the van shaking because of the rough terrain, I can't help but wonder if we're going to be too late to save Lacy. Since I found the bed next to me empty, I've been in a state of panic over where she could be. My search for her led me to the van, and when I found the monitor on instead of switched off like I left it, I realized that Lacy must have been suspicious of it all along. She must have stolen my keys and gone to see what the monitor was. What she found—camera feeds showing different angles of footage all over her apartment—must have pissed her off royally. I regretted right then not telling her about the Federal Bureau's interest in the case and how they had threatened me into helping them monitor her movements. I should have been upfront with Lacy from the start, but then again, she should have been honest with me too. We have a lot to talk about, it seems. I can only pray that we'll have a chance to do that. That there will, in fact, be an "after."

As Sterling Manor comes into view, I feel a nervous lurch in my stomach. The mansion is grand, impressive, and under normal circumstances, I'm sure it would have been beautiful. Now, however, I see it through the eyes of someone who fears for the woman he loves, and I imagine it as an evil place, filled with unimaginable danger.

It takes the tactical team a few minutes to bust through the locked gate, and as we drive up to the front door, I see Lacy's car parked to one side of the enormous driveway. The car is, of course, empty.

We exit the van, and Helmsley catches up with me just before I can follow the SWAT team into the mansion. "Hey, Steele," he says, and grabs me by the front of the vest so I have no choice but to look at him. "You let these guys handle it. You hear? No matter what you find up there. You stay back and let them do their job." He slaps me on the side of the tactical helmet with the plastic visor that I have on.

He lets me go only when I nod, unable to speak. My stomach feels like a mass of slithering snakes moving over each other and twisting around. I follow the SWAT team inside, mindful of letting them move out in front. The visor on my helmet gets foggy with every fast breath I take, but I know not to lift it up. They fan out and search the first few rooms, making sure the ground floor is empty. They do so quietly, sneaking around, not making a sound, and I have to admire the precision and authority with which they move.

Up the stairs then, and the agents eventually gather in front of a heavy wooden door. It is so quiet that a person can hear a pin drop. A single drop of sweat rolls down from my forehead into my eyes, and stings, making it water. There's the sound of voices murmuring on the other side of the door.

Then we hear the sound of a woman's voice calling out in distress. One of the members of the SWAT team puts his hand up and starts counting down from five. Then he opens the door and walks into the room, followed closely by the other agents. As they step in, they fan out, surrounding two figures standing in the middle of the study. I'm peeking around the door, and I see a nightmarish sight.

Lacy is there, holding her hands up. Both her hands are clenched into tight little fists, and I'm so relieved to see that she seems to be unharmed. The man with her, a tall, gray-haired gentleman in a stylish three-piece suit, is sweating, looking wild-eyed, and is holding a gun to Lacy. This must be Victor Calloway. His mouth is hanging open as he stares in wide-eyed fear and amazement at the agents surrounding him, all of them pointing their guns at him and shouting at him to put his weapon down.

Eventually he complies, and is quickly cuffed. The agents escort Victor Calloway out past me, and our eyes meet for a moment. He looks dazed, and I shiver slightly, because there's nothing behind his eyes, nothing at all. Is this really the dangerous man that Qual and Helmsley seemed to revere when they told me about him?

The mansion soon becomes a cacophony of activity as agents in suits come up the stairs to search the place for further evidence even as Victor is taken away. The whole place is suddenly oppressively crowded. I take my helmet off, because the danger is over. The villain is in hand-cuffs, and I want to find Lacy and make sure she's okay.

When I enter the study again, I see her standing there, looking confused. An agent is speaking to her, but she doesn't seem to be listening.

"Lacy!" I call out, and when she turns around and sees me, her whole face lights up with joy.

"Oh my God, Evan!" We crash into each other, and I hug her tightly even as she's standing on her toes to plant kisses on my face. I realize she's crying, and I pull her away from me to look her in the face.

"You did it, Lace. Victor is caught, and you did it!"

I know this moment must be enormous for her. After all the

months of worry and her life being in danger, after all the months of sneaking around, trying to solve this mystery and trying to keep those close to her safe while doing so... she's finally at the other end of it.

"Come on," I say as I take her by the hand. "Let's get out of here so these agents can do their job."

We make our way to a huge living room and sit down on the couch. I'm guessing that we can't leave just yet, as the agents, especially Qual and Helmsley, will want to talk to Lacy and get a statement from her.

At some point, a female agent who introduces herself as Heather Gallagher brings Lacy a blanket and provides us with bottles of water. Lacy drinks thirstily, and I'm glad she's looking much better. The shock of almost getting killed by Victor Calloway seems to have worn off.

That is how Helmsley finds us a few minutes later. He takes Lacy's statement, asking her questions that she answers honestly and intelligently.

"I'm sure Marcus can give you all the details about the conspiracy. Victor told me he hired Marcus to get close to me, to find out what I know, and to derail my investigation."

"Wait, Marcus Grayson was here too?" I ask, confused, because I haven't seen him.

Lacy nods. "Yeah, you arrested him too, didn't you?" We both look over at Helmsley expectantly. Helmsley is shifting uncomfortably.

"You didn't arrest him? But why not? He's part of all of this!" I can understand Lacy's outrage. Marcus Grayson is a snake, whatever else he is. I thought that with Lacy's evidence, the FBI would be all over Marcus.

"There's no evidence that Mister Grayson was here. Anyway, his involvement in this is—"

"A matter of national security. Yeah, you've said." I say this angrily, and Helmsley has the grace to flush at my anger. He shrugs, and it's clear that he's not allowed to tell us more about it.

That's when Qual enters the room with a cellphone in his hand. "Uhm, Miss Langford? I have someone here who wants to speak to you." He hands Lacy the phone, and as she looks down at the screen, I see it's Jamie, Lacy's assistant, who I believe is now one of her friends.

Lacy squeals with delight, and fresh tears roll down her cheeks. "Oh, Jamie! Where did you go? I was so worried about you and the kids!"

I look up to say something to Qual and Helmsley. Maybe "thank you" for giving Lacy the opportunity to speak to Jamie. Or maybe "well played" for so neatly distracting Lacy from any further questions she may have about Marcus. They've left the room, though, and closed the door behind them to give Lacy some privacy to talk to her friend.

"The FBI showed up and whisked us away to witness protection. I'm not allowed to say a word about where we are, and I have no idea where we'll end up. I just wanted to congratulate you for finding the last clue. I had to leave it in a hurry, and I'm glad you found it."

Through her tears, Lacy gives a chuckle. "You draw terrible pigs, Jamie, but I'm so happy you and the kids are okay."

Jamie smiles, and then she says, "There's someone else here who wanted to thank you." A man shifts in front of the camera, and Lacy sucks in her breath as he smiles at her surprise.

"Tony! But how... why... I saw Marcus torturing you! I had a video of it!"

"Yeah, he did, and I still have no idea who he was or why it happened, but I wasn't dead. Neither is my friend Nathan Shepard, or his family. The FBI took us into witness protection and promised that Jamie and the kids would be okay. I had no idea the bastards were going to use my family as bait to try to lure out the guys behind all of this. I thought it had to do with drugs, and a shipment of illegal weapons Nathan and I came across, but now..."

We see Tony being jostled, and I think Jamie must have elbowed him in the ribs to be quiet. I don't blame Tony for being angry, though. Jamie is right too, however. Their little family is at the mercy of the federal government, but at least they will be able to get a new life, all of them together.

Tony nods to his wife in an *okay, I get it* way that makes me smile. I never knew Jamie very well, and I have no idea who this Nathan person is, but I always liked Jamie and her little family. I'm glad all of them are alive and safe. That the nightmare is finally over for them.

"I can't thank you enough for what you did, Lacy. We don't know if we'll ever see you again, but please know you'll have my gratitude, and the gratitude of my family, forever."

When the phone call ends, I hug Lacy tightly. "You really are an exceptional woman, you know that?"

She shakes her head. "I'm very flawed. I nearly pushed away the one person who would literally risk his life to keep me safe."

"We can talk about all of this later. I guess we have to at some point, but Lace... can we just please go home, get some dinner?"

Lacy laughs, looking at her watch. "Another hour or two and we can have breakfast! But where shall we go? Your place is a mess and full of Jamie and the kids' stuff. My place is full of cameras, and I don't know about you, but I don't like the idea of a bunch of agents watching our reunion."

"Mmm, what sort of a reunion did you have in mind?" I wiggle my eyebrows suggestively, and Lacy laughs. It's good to hear the sound of it, carefree in a way she hasn't sounded in way too long.

She stands up and holds her hand out to me. "You'll have to wait and see, mister. I know where we can go. How does spending a few nights at the Intercontinental strike you?"

I look at her, surprised, and whistle. Lacy and I both do well professionally and financially. We're comfortable, but that particular hotel is a bit rich for my pocket. I know it's a bit much for hers, too.

"Don't worry," Lacy says as she hooks her arm into mine and we open the doors of the living room. "I plan on sending the bill for our stay to the offices of the federal bureau. Didn't your agent friend thank me just a while ago and tell me how much they owe me for bringing an end to this conspiracy?"

Now it's my turn to laugh as we walk down to Lacy's car. I open the driver's side door for Lacy, and as she gets in behind the steering wheel, I have the distinct impression that someone is watching us. Someone filled with hate and anger at seeing the two of us together and happy. It's just a feeling, like a goose walking over your grave, as my mother would say. I do know of one particular person who it could be, though. A person who disappeared into thin air in the middle of the confusion while Calloway was being arrested.

I glance around, carefully looking at the faces of the people milling about. I don't see Marcus Grayson anywhere. The fact that he's somehow involved, perhaps in a deeper way that neither Lacy nor I can know, the fact that he seems to be quite untouchable, coupled with Helmsley and Qual's obvious fear of the man, tells me that he may be a person to watch out for in the weeks, days, or months to come.

I saw how Marcus was with Lacy, and now I think what he feels for her is a lot more dangerous and obsessive than I guessed. Sure, he was paid by Calloway to keep an eye on Lacy, to get close to her and to rekindle their past relationship. I believed Lacy when she said that, and it makes sense that Victor would have hired a person like Marcus.

I do think, however, that it was more than an assignment for the elusive, enigmatic Grayson. Is he somewhere close by, watching us, hating Lacy for slipping through his fingers again?

I shake my head. Marcus got away, and it would be crazy of him to stick around just to watch Lacy. He's probably long gone, never to be heard from again.

I close the car door and get in, fastening my seat belt just as Lacy drives down the road toward the gates of Sterling Manor.

THE LAST WORD

MARCUS

I stand silently, listening to the psychological warfare unfolding between Lacy and Victor. I can't help but feel a reluctant admiration for this remarkable woman. She certainly surprised me and turned out to be a worthy adversary after all. I thought it was going to be easy to get her to fall in love with me, to fall into my bed, everything. She's certainly not as easily charmed with me as she used to be.

Not to say that Lacy was ever meek. Oh no, even as a younger woman fresh out of college, when she was just honing her skills, she was a delightfully complicated person. Only back then, she was a lot more innocent, a lot more willing to be led by the nose, especially if it was somewhere that she really wanted to go anyway but was held back by reservations.

I never should have underestimated her. She's become a lot stronger and more self-assured than I was willing to give her credit for.

Now she's facing off with Victor, and it's one of the most beautiful things that I've ever been a witness to.

At one point, Lacy walks over to this side of the room and is in my line of sight. Our eyes meet. The glance only lasts for a few seconds, but it seems quite a bit longer than that. It's an intense moment. Right now, I don't know if I want to fuck her brains out or kill her. Honestly, it's a bit of both.

Nothing went according to plan with Lacy, and her rejection of me in favor of that jackass Evan still rankles. I could have offered her the world. Instead, she chose to make an enemy of me. Well, fine! I have no idea how all this is going to play out between her and Victor.

I'm glad he doesn't see me, and for whatever reason, Lacy doesn't alert him to the fact that I'm here, that I can hear every word spoken between the two of them. She proceeds as if she hadn't seen me, and the conversation turns to Victor's personal failings, events that I already know about from Victor himself and many talks we had about why he wants things to change by destroying and then rebuilding the American government system.

It's typical Victor, and I roll my eyes as I listen to him yammering on. I have yards of respect for Victor; he was my mentor, after all, but I do find it tiring listening to him talk. He does have a tendency to start whining when he feels he is not being listened to. He's always been a singularly focused individual, and that makes him a strong opponent. He's nothing if not self-righteous, believing in the cause he is fighting for. It of course makes him completely arrogant and blind to the fact that he's not really the one running this show, that there may be elements to this operation that he knows nothing about. That he, too, is but a pawn in a much larger game.

Depending on how things will go in the next few minutes, it may be time to cut Victor loose. If he has compromised the mission by exposing himself to this extent, then yes, the time has come to let him go. As they say, though, it's not over until the fat lady sings.

As I listen, wondering how this whole thing is going to be playing out, I hear Lacy make a reference to Victor's mother. That's news to me! I had no idea about the death of Victor's mother, that it was anything but a tragic accident. Is Lacy serious, though? Was all this personal for Victor Calloway after all?

I shake my head sadly. Often with a great teacher, this is the case;

they cannot follow their own pearls of wisdom and often make mistakes they would discourage their pupils from making. The first thing Victor ever told me, the one thing I took to heart, was in this game, nothing you do should be personal, because if you make it personal, then you've already lost.

By the tone of Victor's voice, I can hear that Lacy dealt the death blow in this fight between the two of them. Victor can't and won't recover the ground he lost in this argument. For all intents and purposes, Lacy has won. I smirk, enjoying the discomfort I hear in Victor's voice.

Then I hear something click, and I hear Lacy calling out to Victor. I risk a quick peek around the corner, and see the bookcase is open. It's the panic room that Victor disappeared behind. He had it built a few years ago, convinced that his enemies were going to catch up to him sooner or later. For however infallible he wanted to seem, Victor Calloway was paranoid and filled with fear these last few years.

Lacy goes after Victor, concern clear on her face. Then, in an instant, her hands raise into the air, her movements sharp with fear as she steps back from the doorway created by the bookcase. A moment later, I see why—Victor is holding a gun on her.

For a split second I consider intervening, pulling my own gun and putting an end to Victor, but I don't. Instead, I watch, curious. I've always admired Lacy's ability to fight through impossible situations. And part of me wonders how she'll get out of this one. Part of me wants to see her strength, wants to see her suffer just enough to remind her of the stakes—but not break. Not completely.

If Victor shoots, she'll die... but I almost hope she doesn't. No, not yet.

I can only see Victor in profile, but I can tell he looks demented. I think he's going to do it. I really do.

"You think you're so clever, don't you?" he hisses at Lacy. "With your pretty little face and eyes, your pretty little mouth, and all the twisted things you say to get under a person's skin. You think you are untouchable, don't you? Well, here's news, darling—that's exactly what I thought I was until you found that goddamn file!"

She's shaking her head. "No, Victor. Please, listen! Your only choice now is to give yourself up. Look!" She shows Victor something in her hand. "This bug has been transmitting our entire conversation. I think the police have been watching my apartment. They've heard everything you've said. It's over."

Shit! Is this true? I can't believe I was so stupid! I know exactly who's behind planting those bugs in Lacy's apartment, and it's nothing as mundane as the local police. Didn't I help her get rid of a whole bunch of them? Either I missed one and she found it on her own, or the bureau was a lot more creative and determined than I thought they would be.

As I watch, the door to Victor's study bursts open, and a whole bunch of agents dressed in tactical gear come running inside. They surround Victor and Lacy faster than Victor can react, and they all have their guns pointed at him.

I breathe out—I didn't even realize I was holding my breath—and retreat behind the door again. They didn't notice me, and it's time for me to retreat. My position here can easily be compromised when Lacy starts running her mouth, as I'm sure she will once the shock has worn off and the chaos subsides.

I'm not too worried about what she'll tell the bureau. I know that Qual and Helmsley will only challenge me if they have evidence, and they won't find any here among Victor's things. I made sure that Victor didn't leave any evidence of our dealings.

I make my way downstairs by a back exit through the servant's quarters. I'm glad that Victor sent the staff away and emptied Sterling Manor in preparation of his meeting with Lacy. If he hadn't, I would have had the unfortunate task of eliminating possible witnesses, and dead servants would have supported Lacy's claim that someone else was here.

Soon this place is going to be crawling with feds, and I can't have them catch me on the scene.

As it is, I just make it to the tree line when more cars come riding up through the gate and park out in front of the manor. From my vantage point, I can watch the entire thing unfold. It's not as interesting to see something like this as people might think. There's a lot of milling about and pointless standing around by agents just in case they are needed. Inside is where the action is happening, and I can't be among it right now.

Still, I'm unwilling to leave. I'm rooted in place, mesmerized by the idea of seeing Lacy one last time. Just one last glance... until we meet again.

It's hours before I'm rewarded for my patience. Lacy and Evan come walking out of the double doors of Sterling Manor. My eyes narrow, and I feel a ball of rage churning in my stomach as I watch the two of them. They seem to be flying high on the feeling of victory. The monster has been caught, after all. I saw Victor being escorted to a federal car a while ago, and he was taken into custody.

So yes, I can understand what Lacy and Evan are feeling. I've felt it many times before myself, and there's nothing quite like the feeling of coming face to face with death and coming out on the other side victorious.

Evan, the insufferable shmuck, opens the car door for Lacy. He hesitates then, and looks around as if he can sense me watching them, can sense my disapproval. The idea that he can, that he somehow senses how close I am—close enough to point my gun at his head and pull the trigger, in fact—amuses me.

I won't do that. It will be much more satisfying to get Lacy at some other point in time. Will Evan be sad? Will he perhaps blame himself for her death, for not being able to protect her? Of course he will.

When I see Lacy's car disappearing through the gate at Sterling Manor, I know it's time for me to leave this place as well. I have things to do and people to see, don't I?

ON A RAINY TUESDAY AFTERNOON A FEW WEEKS AFTER THE events at the manor, I'm sitting in my car at a red traffic light. I look up, and there, crossing the street right in front of my idling car, are Evan and Lacy, walking arm in arm together under a big umbrella. They are wrapped up in their coats, carrying bags of takeout.

I stare at them, unable not to. At one point Lacy's gaze falls on my car, right on me, it seems. My heart misses a beat.

The expression on her face doesn't change, and I'm guessing she was just looking around randomly as people do, and it doesn't mean anything. She doesn't actually see me. Not through the sheet of rain that's pouring down from the slate gray Washington skies this afternoon. Such are my feelings for Lacy, as an adversary and as a woman I desire, that I can recognize her in any crowd.

I have the sudden urge to press down on the accelerator, to let my car jump forward and run down both of them in the street. It probably won't kill them, but serious injury isn't completely off the table.

The urge is so strong that my knuckles turn white as I grip the steering wheel more tightly. It takes every ounce of self-restraint not to do what I can so easily imagine doing. The only thing that keeps me from acting on this impulse is the memory of the note I left for Lacy at her apartment a few minutes ago.

In the note, I make a reference to an event that hasn't happened yet. Lacy won't understand it, and knowing the way she is, it's a mystery that will drive her nuts. Even if she shows it to someone afterward, the note will not implicate me in the upcoming events.

When she sees the articles in the news after the event has taken place, then she'll know. She'll remember what the note said, and she'll blame herself for not figuring out the implication of it sooner.

They cross the street safely, and I see Lacy glance up at Evan, smiling adoringly at him. It makes me sick to my stomach.

Just you wait, my dear, I think. *The two of us are not finished dancing yet.*

EPILOGUE: UNFINISHED BUSINESS

LACY

*I*t's with much laughter and joking around that Evan and I enter the apartment with our bags of takeout on this rainy afternoon. He shakes the excess water off the umbrella and hooks it on the coat rack by the front door. I see a bundle of post, a few flyers and one or two bills, lying on the floor, and pick it up before we can trample it with our wet and muddy shoes that we take off and leave in the foyer to dry.

We take the food through to the kitchen. I throw the bundle of mail that was delivered through the mail slot down on the kitchen counter and busy myself dishing up for me and Evan while he pours us each a glass of wine to go with our meal.

After having our late lunch, I make us each a cup of tea, and we sit on the sofa together, chatting. Him moving in with me is the best decision we ever made, and we've never been happier.

After the events that resulted in Victor's arrest, Evan and I had quite a few talks about us and where we want our relationship to go. We decided that moving in together would be the next step in our relationship. I'm not certain about marriage or children yet, and Evan seems to want me even if it means never having them. I feel like this test has made our relationship stronger.

We agreed never to let secrets and uncertainty drive a wedge between us again. I was honest with Evan about my attraction to Marcus. Though short-lived, it was undeniable, and I didn't want to lie to Evan by downplaying it and pretending it was never there.

He was gracious about it, understanding that it was a unique situation. I was scared and felt alone, feeling as if I couldn't confide in the people close to me, unwilling to drag them down with me. Marcus seemed like a life raft to me on stormy seas. It's important that I eventually saw through him, and that I'll never trust him again.

It's scary knowing Marcus is still out there, plotting. Some of Victor Calloway's associates have been arrested, and the truth about Thomas Albright's death was revealed. I'm glad for Albright's family.

I suspect there must be more people behind the conspiracy who haven't been caught, and Marcus Grayson is one of them. How deeply he's connected, who and what he really is, remains a mystery. All that I know is he lied to me from the start.

My life is good at the moment. Evan is happy, more at peace with himself.

He's made a decision about what he wants to do with his life when playing hockey is no longer an option. He's started taking classes at the university focused on obtaining a bachelor's degree in intelligence. With it, Evan wants to become an intelligence analyst. That's one good thing that he managed to take away from his short stint as an undercover agent when he agreed to keep an eye on me. He realized that he would like to have a career with one of the many government agencies that employ intelligence analysts. He's been excited in a way that I haven't seen in a while, talking about what he finds interesting in the classes he takes, including political science, international relations, and criminal justice.

And me? Inspired by Evan and his willingness to start on a whole new career path, to expand his horizons and gain new knowledge, I've enrolled myself in a course at ONLC, a downtown Washington site that exclusively teaches computer courses. It's been hard work juggling it with my business, with seeing clients and meeting my other social obligations, but it's definitely been worth it. Time and again during the events with the file and the conspiracy, I was at a disadvantage because of being technologically impaired. Well, no more. I feel stronger, smarter, more ready for whatever the future will throw our way.

Smiling, I regard Evan as he's chatting away. His excited expression, the way his eyes light up and his smile dimples the corners of his mouth... I feel my love for him like a glowing ember of heat in my heart. Inevitably, that warmth spreads and tingles through the rest of my body.

I lean over and kiss Evan on the neck, working my way up his jawline to his earlobe. I feel his skin flush under my lips, hear him faltering in what he was saying. "Hmmm," he murmurs, "I didn't realize political science turns you on."

I laugh, but don't stop nibbling on his ear.

He turns his head and kisses me, lightly at first, and then with a deepening need that we've rediscovered as our relationship grew and evolved these last few months.

Evan leans over and starts unbuttoning my blouse. His fingers move expertly, unfastening the little pearl buttons. Then he kisses me down the neck, down my chest. He buries his face between my cleavage for a moment, taking in my scent while his hands move down to the lace cups of my bra.

My orgasm washes over me in glorious waves, drowning me in pleasure until I become aware only of my own voice calling his name over and over again.

Afterward, while I'm still drunk with passion, Evan plops down on the bed next to me and holds me tightly, giving me a chance to gather the shattered pieces of myself again.

As we lie there snuggling, I can feel Evan's hardness pressing against me, and a wicked idea crosses my mind. I excuse myself, telling him to wait on the bed for me, and walk to the kitchen, naked and free knowing that after months of secretly being watched through hidden cameras, Evan and I are once more really alone here.

I open the freezer and get the tub of ice cream that we bought a few hours ago. I get a single spoon from the kitchen drawer.

When I return to the bedroom, Evan looks up and regards the ice cream in my hands. "Really? That's what you crave right now?"

I climb onto the bed beside him. "Yup, this is exactly what I want."

He shrugs and rolls onto his side, prepared to humor me. I extract the spoon full of ice cream and lick it suggestively, watching him watch me as I do it. "Hmmm, aren't you going to share?" His voice is gruff and thick with lust. He must be thinking of what else I'm planning to use my tongue for besides eating ice cream.

I put the spoon back into the ice cream, and then push Evan back onto the bed as I climb on top of him. Straddling him, I take the spoon and smear some of the ice cream down his chest. He breaks out in goosebumps and gives a shiver of anticipation, excited by where he knows this game is leading.

After a moment, he takes my head in his hands and lifts it up, looking down into my eyes. "God, I love you, Lace. You know that, don't you?"

Afterward, in the sweet, warm glow of what we feel for each other, we talk about our plans, our hopes and dreams for the future. It's one of those dreamy conversations lovers have when they're both trying to stay awake but are losing the fight bit by bit, and drift off to sleep holding each other, surrendering to the pull of darkness.

~

I STIR AWAKE AT SOME POINT, AND REALIZE WHY: EVAN pulled the blanket off of me in his sleep again. When he's awake, he's the kindest man, the most generous lover one can possibly ask for. When he's asleep, though, he's a dirty blanket thief.

I get up quietly and find a pair of sweatpants and a long sleeve t-shirt in the dark, careful not to wake Evan. Falling asleep so early last night means I'm wide awake now, long before the sun will be up. I might as well get up for a while and do some preparations for meeting a new client later today.

I stop in the kitchen to throw the ice cream away. It's ruined, but it was totally worth it. Smiling ruefully to myself, I switch on the kettle to make myself a cup of tea, and spot the pile of mail that I threw on the counter earlier and promptly forgot about.

I pick it up now and give a wide yawn as I stand over the garbage can, discarding most of the nonsense junk mail we receive. I shake my head as I notice all the flyers to sporting goods stores and men's recreational activities. Before Evan moved in, I never got junk mail like that.

Halfway through the pile, my hand freezes over the letter with the gold trim. There's no postage stamps, and only my name is written on the front of the envelope in neat, clipped handwriting.

I think I know who delivered this letter, pushing it through the mail slot while Evan and I were out buying food yesterday afternoon. The handwriting seems horribly familiar. I tear the envelope open, and with my hands shaking, I read the letter.

At the bottom of the page, it says, "Love, Marcus." Of course. It's from exactly who I thought it was. When did he deliver it? Did he walk right past us while we were walking home? Was he watching us from a distance? It disturbs me to think that he was there, so close, and I had no idea.

The letter seems friendly on the surface, but all throughout, reading between the lines, I can pick up on subtle threats; assurances that he's not done with me yet, that he'll see me again at some point, and that he'll never be very far away.

The worst part of the letter, the part of it that scares me the most, is where Marcus hints at some big event that will take place in the future. I have no idea what form this supposed catastrophe will take, but it's painfully obvious what Marcus's intention was when he wrote this. He wants me to try and solve the mystery, to obsess over it even though it's obvious I won't be able to guess from the limited amount of information he gave me what exactly he's planning to do. Then he wants me to feel personally responsible when it happens, even though I couldn't have done anything to stop it.

He knows me very well. Of course I'm going to try and solve the clues. Of course I will do everything in my power to try and stop him.

For a moment, my knee-jerk reaction is to hide the letter, to try and protect the people close to me from Marcus by keeping this a secret. Luckily, I've learned how stupid that is. It's a relief not having to carry this burden on my own anymore. Besides, Evan and I promised each other that there will be no more secrets between us.

Evan finds me a few hours later, looking like a vision with only a pair of boxers on so I can appreciate his perfectly toned upper body, and he's carrying two cups of coffee. His hair is twirled in cowlicks from sleep. I hand him the letter and watch his face as he carefully reads it while I sip at my coffee.

Evan finishes reading the letter, and then looks up at me. "Well, we knew he wasn't done with you yet, that he'd be back. I'm actually relieved, because it means we don't have to wait for him to resurface anymore." He comes over and gives me a hug. "He'll have to go through me to get to you, Lace. I promise, I won't let him touch you."

He pulls away then and kisses me on the forehead. "Until then, there will always be pancakes for breakfast. What do you say?"

I grin, and then finally laugh. Evan has a way of reminding me not to take myself too seriously. And he's right, of course. Obsessing over what Marcus is planning, letting my life slip through my fingers while I wait for him to show his hand—that's letting him win, and I'll be damned if I let him ruin my life.

I follow Evan to the kitchen. He makes the best pancakes I've ever tasted. I grin secretly, wondering if I can recreate the same trick as last night with maple syrup instead of ice cream.

THANK YOU

Dear Reader,

Thank you for joining me on this thrilling journey through *Lethal Liaison: The Lacy Langford Chronicles*. I hope Lacy's story brought you moments of excitement, intrigue, and a little heart-pounding suspense along the way.

If you enjoyed the book, I'd be incredibly grateful if you could take a moment to leave a review. Your feedback not only means the world to me but also helps other readers discover Lacy's adventures. You can share your thoughts here:
Leave a Review on Amazon

Your support fuels my passion for storytelling, and I can't wait to bring you the next chapter in Lacy's journey. For updates on upcoming releases, exclusive content, and more, don't forget to visit **Joey-Jaymes.com** and sign up for the latest news.

Thank you for reading, reviewing, and being part of Lacy's world. Your enthusiasm means everything!

With love,
Joey Jaymes

Printed in Great Britain
by Amazon